DIVINE REALMS

To Brenda—
Love ya—
Thanks for coming ½
being my friend of
42+ years!
Love Susan.

DIVINE REALMS

Canadian Science Fiction and Fantasy

edited by
Susan MacGregor

RaveN
STONE

published by Ravenstone
an imprint of Turnstone Press
607 – 100 Arthur Street, Artspace Building
Winnipeg, Manitoba, R3B 1H3 Canada
www.TurnstonePress.com

Turnstone Press gratefully acknowledges the assistance of the
Canada Council for the Arts, the Manitoba Arts Council and
the Government of Canada through the Book Publishing
Industry Development Program for our publishing activities.

Le Conseil des Arts | The Canada Council
DU CANADA | FOR THE ARTS
DEPUIS 1957 | SINCE 1957

"In the Beginning, There Was Memory" by Ven Begamudré appeared in
Laterna Magika and is used by permission of Oolichan Books and previously
appeared in *ON SPEC*, Spring 1996. "Flesh and Blood" by Brent Buckner
appeared in *ON SPEC*, Fall 1991. "The Power of Faith" by Jason Kapalka
appeared in *ON SPEC*, Fall 1993. "On the Edge of Eternity" by Steve Stanton
is an excerpt from *In the Den of the Dragon*, published by Skysong Science
Fiction, 1996. "Best Damn Cheesecake in the Universe" by Diane Walton
appeared in *ON SPEC*, Fall 1991. "Not in Front of the Virgin" by Mary
Woodbury appeared in *Prairie Fire's* Special Speculative Fiction issue.

Original cover artwork by Matthew Sloly
Design: Manuela Dias
Author photograph: Derryl Murphy

This book was printed and bound in Canada by
Printcrafters for Turnstone Press.

Canadian Cataloguing in Publication Data
Divine realms: Canadian science fiction and fantasy
ISBN 0-88801-227-6
1. Fantastic fiction, Canadian (English).*
2. Short stories, Canadian (English).*
I. MacGregor, Susan, 1953–
PS8323.S3 D58 1998   C813'.087608054   C98-920164-3
PR9197.35.S33 D58 1998

CONTENTS

ACKNOWLEDGMENTS

ANTHOLOGIES LIKE *DIVINE REALMS* do not happen as a singular effort, and I'd like to thank the following people who helped me and the collection along our way: Derryl Murphy for squeezing in my call for manuscripts after the *SF Canada* newsletter deadline and for his photography expertise; Claude-Michel Prévost for being the first to send me his manuscript; Jena Snyder for her continuing support, offers of help and friendship; Sandra Riedel, Louise Marley, Keith Scott, and Ven Begamudré for their support when I needed it (fine people that they are, they probably weren't aware that they gave it); Bruce Kemp for his thoughtful critique; Peter Watts for writing me something "original"; Erik J. Spigel for his humor and for unwittingly providing me with Brent Buckner's address; Steve Stanton and Donna Farley for their faith and generosity; Jean-Louis Trudel with his last-minute help with semantics; Manuela Dias and Patrick Gunter at Turnstone Press for being a pleasure to work with (every writer should be so lucky as to work with publishers like this); and last but not least, my husband Mike MacGregor, for his love, support, and computer know-how, and my kids Brennan, Dylan, and Erin for putting up with their mother when she had deadlines to meet and computer time to spend. Finally, I also want to thank the One who started me on this path, for encouraging me to do it. It's been a worthwhile and terrific experience with unseen and unexpected ramifications that far outreach the confines of a single, simple book.

Thank you all.

—Susan MacGregor, April 1998

INTRODUCTION

THE INSPIRATION TO COMPILE *Divine Realms* came from two sources. Originally, I'd been toying with the idea of creating a collection of my own short stories that explored faith, God, and the universe in a speculative vein. But as I began work on "Drying Out in Purgatory," I reflected that it might be better to offer more than one viewpoint, more than one slant on reality other than my limited voice. After all, my own faith borrowed from a number of others; shouldn't the anthology as well? Convinced that this was the way to go and curious to find who else was out there, I put out the call for submissions.

Much to my surprise, I received "Omer and the Zobop" by Claude-Michel Prévost a few days later. I was pleased to find that there were others who were working in the same sub-genre, particularly since speculative fiction does not often lend itself to spiritual or religious themes. As I read Claude-Michel's story, I found myself thinking, Yowza! A voodoo and Christian story? Fireflies and Catholic priests? Not what I expected, but very potent work. I couldn't wait to see what else the mail might bring.

A few others promised me work prior to my call for submissions—Erik Spigel for one. His story "God Is Dead," where the physicist Tesla kills God in a dream, is included here. Other stories and poems came filtering in, as well as cards and e-mail offering me much-welcomed support. Jena Snyder, my friend and co-editor for *ON SPEC* magazine, took time from her work on her novel to write me a piece, risking that it might not be what I had in mind for the collection. It was, and "Little Bones," a story about a dowser who finds bodies instead of water, is the result.

As more manuscripts arrived, I began to think that all people needed was the excuse to write along these lines, an opportunity to answer the question *what do I really think about it all?* Certainly, this was what I had in mind when I put out the call for manuscripts. I wanted to generate a dialogue regarding spirituality, both on internal and external levels. I wanted to provide a forum for personal belief. Several times, I was also faced with the quandary *what do I do about a manuscript that is brilliantly written, but with which I disagree?* The answer? Include it. See what happens.

Before you is a collection of stories that run the gamut of spiritual beliefs (or disbeliefs). A mix of literary styles from Peter Watts' "The Second Coming of Jasmine Fitzgerald," based on Tipler's *The Physics of Immortality*, to Louise Marley's "Body and Blood," which considers the manifestation of stigmata in a cloistered, acolyte nun. Here you'll find the Alpha in Ven Begamudré's "In the Beginning, There Was Memory," and the Omega in Allan Lowson's "The Thousand Words." Other works explore the future, the past, and the in-between. An unusual and eclectic collection, I think.

As for the second source of inspiration to compile this anthology, all I can say is I felt encouraged to do it. It was a matter of faith, of being connected to something greater than myself. I know what I think. I'll leave it to the reader to decide from whom or where my encouragement came.

As the Buddhist saying goes, there are many paths that lead to the peak of the mountain. Some of these pieces point out well-trodden paths, others bushwhack their way to the top. What they have in common is that all of them are signposts, every writer, a guide.

It's been a pleasure compiling this anthology. I hope you find truth, humor, and honesty within its pages.

DIVINE REALMS

THE POWER OF FAITH

Jason Kapalka

Up until the affair with St. Gudrune's jawbone, Pirando and I were honest thieves. Pride, Pirando always said, was the one vice a thief could not afford; a proud thief, he told me, was no better than an archbishop and nearly as bad as a public official. It was a subtle sort of robbery we practiced, true, but we always knew it for robbery, and our hearts were humbled by the knowledge. But now, now it seems that humility may be lost to our souls forever.

We were sellers of relics. The bones of the saints seem to litter Europe like scattered kindling, and a less perceptive man than Pirando might have imagined the market to be long since glutted. After all, one can scarcely pass a roadside chapel that does not lay claim to the arm or thigh bone of one of the Roman calendar's innumerable saints, and even Pirando will admit that the golden age of the relic-merchant passed some three centuries ago, in the wake of the Crusades.

"In those times," he recalled, as though he had been there himself, "a wooden bit of the True Cross might fetch two hundred florins. Two hundred florins!—and if you had gathered together all the lumber thus sold you might have erected a Norwegian cathedral. Ten thousand neck caskets of the Virgin Mary's tears were sold at a hundred florins apiece. Ah, her tears, her most copious and golden tears!" Here, he became so caught up he sometimes had to blink back moisture from his own eyes, which were nearly useless by reason of the eerie white film that covered them.

"And clippings from Peter's toenails might be priced from thirty to forty florins, depending on their size and quality. Sacks of clippings! Peter's toes must have been great in number, and their nails prodigious indeed." And here he would punctuate his speech with a dreary sigh.

"But you and I, we must content ourselves with the bone-bits of minor saints. These are harsh times we live in, you and I, harsh times." Pirando was old and, consequently, much given to windy diatribes of this nature.

Still, his wisdom was undeniable; though his milky eyes were almost blind and he required me to read for him, his inner vision grew ever more acute as the years passed. Often while we were sorting through the detritus of some ancient crypt in search of an attractive bone, Pirando would speak on the most fundamental tenets of our calling. "It is unnecessary for us to prove that a relic is authentic," he told me. "It is only necessary for us to show that it may be genuine. The power of faith is very great, and will accomplish the rest." How terrible those words seem now!

You see, in this dark new age of reason, relics are almost daily discredited by the men of science, and not even the most faithful will continue to pay homage to the ankle bone of a mule, though up until last week it had been venerated as the holy remnant of St. Augustine. The priests of such newly unendowed churches must bear the shame as their congregations flock elsewhere, and yes, the loss of the tithe-revenues must weigh heavily on them as well. For example, before the men of science came with their yellowing books on anatomy, their clay flasks of alchemical concoctions, many pilgrims used to travel a hundred miles to make donations before the teeth of St. Kea, in hopes of the miraculous cure of mouth disorders. No longer; the teeth proved to be the ossified molars from a mere tax-collector's mouth.

Naturally, it behooves such churches to seek out replacements for their discredited relics. Where should they turn? Having been defeated by science once, they are unlikely to snatch up the first petrified bone-hunk that comes their way lest it be proven to have originated with a rogue hanged but ten years ago. No, they must be very circumspect, very cautious, and it is at this stage, generally, that Pirando and I appear to offer our assistance.

The affair in Brussels that led to our downfall seemed no different in its inception. The Monsignor of a great church there had employed us once before, when the toe bone of St. Pancras which graced his parish was examined and consequently identified as false; indeed, the men of science claimed that not only had the bone not belonged to St. Pancras, but that it was not even a human remnant, having instead originated with some species of long-extinct lizard. Though they were thought somewhat disreputable, these "scientists" exerted considerable influence over the common folk through their demeanor and rhetoric: the display of a few dusty volumes of Aristotle and some smoking chemicals was enough to persuade the groundlings that they were confronted with unimaginable erudition, though as Pirando and I knew, the methods of this new philosophy of "science" were often as dubious as any of the Church's antiquated dictums. In any case, Monsignor's parishioners grew doubtful of the toe bone, then openly scornful, and alas, few were capable of the acrobatic theology he offered as justification for the bone's authenticity. Instead, they simply took themselves to a neighboring church, which, for all its obvious shortcomings, maintained a fragment of the thigh bone of the martyred Pope Callistus which was apparently genuine, or at least not demonstrably fake.

Gaining an audience with the Monsignor at this point was not difficult. After basic introductions had been made, Pirando tilted his milky eyes upward and speculated idly.

"It is an idle speculation I make here, Monsignor—"

"Yes, yes, go on."

"Hmm. Let us imagine that in some unforeseeable fashion I should come upon, oh, let us say, the collarbone of St. Adam."

The Monsignor, a pudgy thick-necked man of elderly mien, scowled. "You might well be deluded in believing it to be so."

"Let us further imagine that the scientific and alchemical methods of the day, such as lime-casting, dousing in acidic solutions, 'pore-coaxing' with a lens of glass, and the like—though, of course, I profess no great knowledge of such techniques—should prove the veracity of my claim, or at least produce no actively negative evidence. What then?"

"One might imagine a small stipend being paid over to the recoverer of such a relic," the Monsignor said grudgingly. He and Pirando imagined gradually growing sums of money together, until at last a satisfactory, though, of course, hypothetical, figure was reached.

After the relic was produced, the Monsignor called in local scholars and scientists to examine it; as we promised, they were unable to determine more than the bone's general age and told the Monsignor that it was genuine, in perhaps less than enthusiastic terms, more to the effect that they had no concrete proof to the contrary. Pirando and I consequently retired for a few months to a remote area of Spain, where we rented a villa and had all our various physical and emotional needs attended to by enthusiastic young locals.

We hadn't thought to have another occasion to visit the Brussels Monsignor, but as we were engaged in the pursuit of a perhaps corruptible team of historical excavators—along with this new fad of "science" had come yearnings for things like "history" with all its concomitant artifacts and bones—we heard news of strange developments back in Brussels. Apparently, St. Adam's collarbone had begun to stir the parishioners into disturbing states of thought: Adam, it seemed, had been a bishop in a northern province who raised taxes with insensate recklessness, and who perished when his own parishioners broke into his house, beat him, burnt him alive, and subsequently buried his body beneath a heap of rocks. The general feeling among the Brussels folk was that Adam's sanctification had been perhaps too hastily conferred, and in any event, the general discussions about taxation that his collarbone provoked did not please the Monsignor to any great degree. Immediately, Pirando began to consider him as a possible customer for the relic we were even then hunting down, as we had dealt with him before and consequently knew him to be trustworthy (as priests go), and his treasury to be large.

We found a delivery-house man who was, for a time, in charge of the shipment of historical specimens we were pursuing.

He grunted in an unencouraging fashion in response to our introductions. Pirando, however, knew how to make even the most thick-witted and ill-mannered lout into a cooperative ally, all within the space of a few seconds.

"My good fellow!" he shouted heartily. "What are you doing here, late at night, watching over worthless bones and dust? Don't you know the beer keg in the tavern has burst? It's free drink for all!"

I belched and hiccoughed and shouted merrily to reinforce Pirando's theme. Eventually, the man was persuaded that it would be all right for him to nip off for a few drinks, so long as we stayed to watch over the warehouse in his stead. His lack of concern was scarcely surprising, since few but Pirando would have known the true value of the ancient debris packaged within one of the crates housed there. We watched briefly, to make good on our promise, then departed with our prize.

Amongst the valueless pots and plates were catalogued the calcified remains of several persons. Through his vast erudition, and some lucky conjectures on information gathered over the years, Pirando suspected that the remnants of the saint Gudrune were to be found there, unknown to the delivery-house man and even to the historians who had dug up the assorted bones.

Now, Gudrune was a bland saint indeed, notable for only two characteristics: the extraordinarily violent manner of his demise—he was tortured, stoned, and beheaded by barbarians—and his singular dental features. This second point was what allowed us to finally identify the martyr, or rather what was left of his corpus after the rigors visited on it by the barbarians, the passage of centuries, and various rough transits: for the only part of him to survive was his huge and unpleasant jawbone.

"Gudrune was said to have," Pirando quoted from memory as I pondered the relic, "tremendously large and crooked teeth, along with a marked overbite." In examining the jaw, I agreed that the record was accurate in this regard, if somewhat euphemistic: the saint possessed a jaw like a crocodile's.

We packed the jawbone with the rest of the dusty debris and set out for Brussels. Though Gudrune was minor in importance and lacking in interesting features, he was nonetheless a verifiable saint, and one that under no circumstances would provoke a philosophical debate on tax practices.

With this in mind, we were amazed when the Monsignor's subordinate ordered us out of Brussels after taking but a single glance at the jawbone. "Can you not at least let us show the relic to the Monsignor himself?" Pirando asked.

"No," the priest replied, somewhat haughtily in my opinion, "and for this reason: this jaw you claim as St. Gudrune's displays tremendously crooked teeth and a marked overbite, and on the whole presents a most uncomely vision. A saint embodies the aspects of man closest to God, and his relics cannot but fill the viewer with zeal and inspiration. All that ugly remnant inspires is nausea: thus, to claim it as the jawbone of a saint is a palpable falsehood. Now, be gone from my sight, lest I call the city guard."

We left disheartened. "Perhaps some other parish will not be so fastidious," I said to cheer Pirando, but he simply looked at me, or in my general direction, with his white-filmed eyes and sighed.

The old, I have noticed, and Pirando in particular, are given to much sighing, but in this case, the judgement implied by the sigh was correct. Not a single church would offer money for our hideous relic, genuine or not.

By this time our funds were running alarmingly low. In desperation, Pirando took up another of the skulls we had received in the misdirected shipment. He pried off the jawbone and said, "We shall sell this one instead."

"But we've already showed the bone to every prelate in the district!" I protested.

"That is true. We will tell them an error was made and that we should have realized immediately that no saint's jawbone would be malformed." Pirando mused briefly. "We will tell them that you, being young and a fool, accidentally mixed up the correct jaw with a flawed specimen. And I, with my blindness, noticed the mistake only now."

I disapproved of certain phrasings in this idea, but admitted I had no better solution. And certainly, the new jawbone was very handsome, with strong straight teeth and a pleasing profile. Pirando said it probably belonged to a butcher who had lived next door to Gudrune; but if there had been any justice in the world, the saint would have possessed this butcher's fine mouth in place of his own dragonlike maw.

"Still, historically, they will know this bone cannot belong to Gudrune," I complained. "His dental deformity is well documented."

"That cannot be helped," Pirando said. "We must trust in the power of faith."

We took the false bone back to Brussels and this time gained an audience with the Monsignor. He examined the relic reverently. "Truly, this is the jawbone of a saint!" he exclaimed.

Pirando briefly introduced some theoretical conceits concerning the transference of funds. Monsignor did not quibble: "Any price is fair, if only the parishioners will stop yawping about taxes and Adam's sainthood and learning unholy things such as philosophy! Tell the servants to take that accursed collarbone away."

Prior to paying us, he brought in the scientific men of the district once again. They were gray, weary-looking men, by now very tired of this task, and after pondering the bone with a large glass lens, dusting it with lime, dipping it into a mild vinegar solution and checking their folios, they quickly decided that the jaw's age was roughly congruent with Gudrune's known lifespan, and issued a terse statement to the effect that our specimen was just as likely to belong to that worthy as was any other three-hundred-year-old bone. Convinced beyond a doubt, the Monsignor gladly paid our fee and rushed off to install his new relic.

We ourselves were in no small hurry to vacate the region. In a profession such as ours, it is important to know both the newest scientific techniques and the oldest lore of history and the Church, but the knowledge of secluded regions in distant countries becomes truly crucial when our skill in the former areas fails us: and in this case, we had good reason to believe that the deception would be uncovered sooner rather than later. Thus, we retired to a laconic Italian village where we might rest and distribute some of the Brussels tithe-money to the peasantry.

All was peaceful for a time, which was as we had planned. Our money was well respected in this distant corner of the world, and we lacked for little in the way of comforts and distractions. Several months later, however, we noticed there were an unusual number of travelers passing through the village on their way north.

Curious about this phenomenon, Pirando spoke to our innkeeper.

"The pilgrims?" he grunted. "They all seem bound for some ungodly northern country. Belgium or such. But they're not so odd as that other group that's been lurkin' 'bout town the last few days."

I inquired of whom he spoke.

"A bunch of hefty fellows being led around by a priest, they all armed like they was to a war. Say they're from where? Broosles or such. Keep asking around for a half-blind oldster and a gawky stupid-looking stripling. I tell you, I don't know what to make of it."

"The ways of foreigners are indeed strange," Pirando agreed, "but would you mind tallying our bill for the rooms? My apprentice and I are late for an important meeting far to the south of here and must leave on the instant. In addition, a large gratuity will be rendered to you for your taciturn, untalkative nature."

Unfortunately, we were met at the edge of the village by just such a group as the landlord described. "I believe I have seen those you are looking for," Pirando told them. "They left by the north road just this morning; if you are swift, you may yet catch them."

"Hmm. You two seem very familiar," said the priest who was leading the men. Though Pirando's blindness no doubt kept him from noticing, I saw immediately that it was the Monsignor's assistant who had ejected us from Brussels the first time.

"Please sir," I pleaded, "we meant no harm."

"Harm?" he asked. "What do you mean? The Monsignor has sent for you to come to Brussels. It is a wondrous strange thing, is it not?"

"Indeed," Pirando mused, squinting and peering and abruptly coming to a fuller cognizance of our situation. "I thought these burly men were to fall upon us and beat us till we were dead."

The Monsignor's subordinate laughed in an odd fashion. "No, no! They are to escort you and make certain no harm comes to you on the way back!" And so we departed for Brussels with our new escorts.

At first, I was certain we were merely being preserved for a more formal execution there, but after a few days along the road it became clear that this was not the case.

"You see Alexander there?" The priest indicated a very largely built man. "Alexander's nose had dropped off from leprosy, and now he is cured." Alexander nodded in assent, and in truth, I would swear that the man did indeed now have a fine, large nose.

Alexander knelt before Pirando and kissed his hand, then repeated this procedure with me.

"I gather something momentous has occurred in Brussels," Pirando cautiously posited.

"Indeed!" The Monsignor's servant spread his arms expansively and declared: "It is a miracle." When the silence had grown heavy with our lack of response, he continued.

"A month ago, one of the supplicants at the church, a man who suffered from spasms of the intestines, leapt up after having made the customary genuflection before Gudrune's holy jaw and proclaimed that he had been completely cured!"

"Truly," Pirando said thickly, "this is a great miracle."

"No, no, there is more! While we were pleased, in honesty, events such as this one are not unknown, and their veracity not uniformly verifiable." The priest shook his head sadly.

"But then a month ago," he continued eagerly, "in the middle of Monsignor's service, a crippled beggar maddened by the ague rushed forward before any could restrain him and broke the glass of the relic's casement. He seized the jaw and kissed it—and before the eyes of everyone present was visibly cured of all deformities, his stump of an arm abruptly restored to a fresh pink hand! Needless to say, the commotion was extraordinary! Fortunately, Gudrune's jaw was recovered and order restored."

I glanced at Pirando. His whitish eyes looked very thoughtful. We accepted the rest of the priest's story in silence.

"Soon after," he said, "the sick and diseased were coming from all over Brussels to queue for the honor of touching this holiest of holy relics. And as they touched it, all their ills were cured, be they ague or leprosy or toothache. I myself," he proclaimed proudly, "was cured of a chronic numbness of the foot."

We waited, but this was apparently the end of the priest's tale. He stood beaming at us in silence.

"And so," Pirando at last asked cautiously, "what is to become of us?"

The priest grinned and embraced him. "Why, you are to be honored as befits the discoverers of this most holy jawbone, of course! You will receive the gratitude of the whole Church and all of Brussels!" Though the priest did not embrace me, he did offer his assurances that the aforementioned honors would be accorded me as well, and with this I was forced to content myself.

Our arrival in Brussels was indeed glorious as we had been promised. First, we were washed and groomed and fitted with expensive new clothes and other finery, rings, perfumes, belts, and the like. We were then passed down along the avenues of the city and cheered by the crowds lining the streets. The civic officials greeted us and gave us a large number of importantly worded plaques and certificates, whose import, if not entirely clear to me, was almost certainly positive. After the parade, we were taken to the old church that housed the purportedly miraculous jawbone, and were there met on the steps by an assembly of high figures from Rome. A procession of archbishops moved past, hands extended to allow us to kneel and kiss their rings. Several stopped to engage Pirando in hushed, excited conversations; and though none spoke directly to me ("By reason of your extreme youth and foolish-looking appearance," an attendant kindly explained), they did murmur Latin benedictions over my bowed head.

Overwhelmed by this dizzying rush of events, we scarcely noticed when we were whisked into the church by our old friend the Monsignor. "I never thought," he whispered as he pulled us aside, "that is, I had my private doubts, especially after the collarbone. But oh, I was wrong! Anything you wish is yours; merely ask." He stared at us earnestly.

Pirando said, "I should like to see the jawbone."

"Hum?"

"Of St. Gudrune," I clarified with a nervous glance at Pirando. "The jawbone of St. Gudrune."

"Oh, yes! Of course! Come this way!"

We were led through the cavernous interior of the church.

Perched on the altar, guarded by a set of men with swords, was the jaw which Pirando had pried off Gudrune's neighbor, the butcher. I personally could detect no palpable aura of holiness, but the Monsignor bowed his head and began to speak in hushed tones as we approached.

"Almost incredible, isn't it?" he whispered.

"Yes," Pirando nodded, "indeed."

"You may prostrate yourself before the relic if you wish. I was myself cured of a lingering case of brain-sickness after touching Gudrune's holy, most holy jaw." The Monsignor looked up into the arched shadows of the church. "Oh, it is a great miracle!"

Pirando shrugged, then turned away to give attention to the jawbone, which I could already see had become smooth and polished, presumably from the countless touches of Gudrune's supplicants; Pirando doubtless was considering the pecuniary opportunities that would present themselves when this bone had been worn down to dust.

The Monsignor lowered his gaze from the ceiling and seemed pensive for a moment. "It is curious," he said at last, "that the books describe St. Gudrune as having tremendously ugly teeth and a marked overbite. How could so great an error have been made? Surely, no saint as great as Gudrune would have crooked teeth!"

I nodded wisely, but could think of no suitable response. Pirando was still bent over the relic and said nothing. "What do you think?" I prompted.

He turned to us. The milky film had completely disappeared, and his eyes were brilliantly blue. "I think," he said slowly, "that the power of faith is very great."

And so, after a week of appropriately pious feasting and rioting in Brussels, we repaired to the country mansion thoughtfully provided us by the archdiocese. There, when we were not responding to the requests that came from all across Europe urging us to continue our trade in holy relics, or entertaining the various office-holders and clergy who now sought our advice, it seemed, on every tiny matter of policy, we conferred on the doom that fate had brought upon us.

"Now we are as pompous and foolish as them," Pirando groaned. "What future is there for a vain thief?" I could only shrug.

With nothing else to do, we returned to our trade though we were no longer secure in our humble beliefs, and supplied the dainty wrist bones of the Virgin Mary to another church in Brussels, and to another seven or eight churches across Europe. The men of science like to shriek of this obvious counterfeiting, but no one listens to them anymore, and it seems likely that the public infatuation with "science" is ending. We have already heard reports of people experiencing religious ecstasies and of hardened criminals devoting their lives to the priesthood after touching the wrist bone installed in a certain French cathedral. We have not yet endeavored to make a journey to ascertain whether or not these rumors are true; Pirando is already certain that they are.

"They wish me to hold public office," he says. "And perhaps in the future, I'll be an archbishop as well. Perhaps when I die, I will be sainted!" He chuckles uneasily, but his blue eyes are very clear, and his jaw, I think, is very handsome, and I can say nothing to reassure him on this point. He wanders about the mansion in a daze, drinking in the colors and shapes with his newly restored sight, and sometimes, he reaches to touch his eyes as if to confirm that they are actually there. There is little I can do to comfort him, for more and more these days I, too, find myself reaching for some sort of assurance that this new-found fortune of mine is real and not merely a bizarre prank played on me by my own senses—or a worse possibility: that I am sane, and it is all still a joke but one perpetrated on us by some unknown, and, perhaps, unknowable, agency.

"What folly! What madness! How can it keep on like this?" Pirando laughs hysterically, deranged by the infinitely quixotic machinations of heaven. "How can it continue?"

I must answer him slowly and reluctantly. "The power of faith is very great," I always reply.

Jason Kapalka: At its core, this story is less about religion than faith, I think, and how the two are not necessarily the same thing. Religion in the story (and arguably reality) is essentially silly . . . a sham run by hucksters and frauds for the edification of idiots. Yet despite all the rationalist arguments to the contrary, I find myself unable to completely dispel the notion of some "higher power," as do, I suppose, many self-proclaimed agnostics and atheists. Which leaves one with a disturbing thought: If God, whatever He/She/It/They may be, is a jester, He may be the only one who gets the joke. . . .

BEST DAMN CHEESECAKE IN THE UNIVERSE

Diane L. Walton

I SAW THE SIGN OVER THE DOOR FIRST. It was small, but loud and effective. "Best Damn Cheesecake in the Universe," it proclaimed in a blaze of pink neon. Just under the sign, in far smaller letters, was another sign. It said simply, "Melissa: Prop." I'd go a long way to get good cheesecake, which is why I'll never, ever be a size ten. Seeing a claim like this, I naturally rose to the challenge.

It was odd that I hadn't encountered Melissa's place before. She occupied a small niche in the basement of an office building across the street from mine—just off the LRT station tunnel. She may have been there for years, for all I knew. There were certainly never any newspaper reviews of her place, as there were for the many trendy downtown eateries who were desperate for a share of the clientele.

I happened upon it late one lunch hour as I hurried back to work. I drive to work and never use the subway, but The Bay was convenient for some quick lunch-hour shopping. There was a way to get from my building's basement parkade across to the underground station. It's well lit and the drug dealers are usually not up before noon, so it's a reasonably safe walk, even for an unprotected woman. After five years in the big city, my mother was still asking if I was "taking precautions." I would nod and, with a clear conscience, smile at her. Mother firmly believed that a woman, by the very act of walking alone in dark places, was

15

wearing a "Hey, guys, come and rape me" sign on her back.

It was the neon sign over the door of the shop that caught my eye. Not much I could do with only five minutes left of the lunch hour, but I made a mental note of the place and vowed to return. That grandiose claim was not to be taken lightly.

When I got back to the office, I asked around to see if any of my fellow gluttons had ever been to Melissa's. Nobody had heard of it. Norma asked me if I was dead certain that I even saw a restaurant there. She seemed to remember that there'd been a fine-art reproduction shop that had gone out of business several years before, but she wasn't absolutely certain that anyone had taken over the space.

"Looked pretty occupied today," I replied, "and I haven't hallucinated a restaurant for, gee, I don't know, months, maybe. I'll let you know what it's like."

As soon as work finished, I found myself heading across the street in the direction of the LRT station. Cheesecake before supper? My mother would shake her head in dismay. You have to eat better meals, Meredith, more vegetables. How do you expect to keep your health? No wonder you catch so many colds.

I could have kicked myself for not checking to see what their hours of operation were. "Open 11 to 3, Daily," the small sign inside the door read. I should have known. A place in this sort of location would do the bulk of its business during the working day. Nobody in their right mind (other than a real cheesecake fanatic) would want to go there at this time of day, I reasoned, and it probably wouldn't attract much of a dinner crowd. As a matter of fact, beyond the coffee machine and the sign advertising cheesecake, I didn't see any hard evidence that they actually served anything else there. Maybe that was all they needed to serve. Business must be good. But had there been any customers at noon when I went by? I couldn't be certain.

Next day, as soon as my last client left just before noon, I was on my way. I couldn't convince anyone to go to lunch with me, but that was fine. I didn't mind being the one who would make the glorious discovery and then generously spread the news to my fellow slaves. We took our cheesecake very seriously in my office.

This time when I approached the front door of the restaurant, I did notice that it was empty of customers. I feared that I may have missed a sign that was going to tell me "Closed For Renovations," or even worse, but the door opened easily at my touch, and I went in. A bell tinkled shrilly as the door swung shut.

It was a tiny place. Barely enough room for the three small round tables, covered with those ubiquitous red and white checked tablecloths. In the far corner I noticed an antique cash register, without the fancy computerized keyboard they all seem to have these days. It had one of those pop-up displays where the totals of your purchase appear on little white cards. I remember that it read "NO SALE" in black upper-case letters. I don't think it has ever said anything else.

Beneath it was a refrigerated glass display case. Inside this, I hazarded a guess, were the best damn cheesecakes in the universe. I was prepared to make the caloric sacrifice to find out if this was truth. While perusing the place, I realized that I, too, was being observed. A small, redheaded woman stood behind the display case. She was wearing a pale green waitress uniform, with white eyelet lace trim and a white apron. Her cheeks were bright with rouge, and there was a heavy coat of metallic blue shadow on each eyelid. Her hair was tightly curled close to her head, as if she'd just come from getting a new perm. Perhaps it hadn't begun to relax, as the hairdressers always promise that it will. My perms never relaxed, and always went frizzy, so I gave up on them a long time ago.

She was smiling broadly at me as though I were a long-lost relative. Maybe she didn't get that many customers after all.

Her first words were a surprise to me. "So you found the place, did you? So many don't. How can I help you?"

I found this a little odd. Why else would I be there except for what they advertised as their specialty? "I hope you can help me to some of your famous cheesecake," I replied. "Are you Melissa?"

"You bet, honey," she answered. "And you must be . . ." I was astonished to watch as she consulted a large book that lay on the top of the counter. "Yes, there you are! You are Meredith Clearwater, attorney at law, daughter of Ethel and Franklyn Clearwater of Grande Prairie. I should have known that."

Now I was really confused. "What do you mean, you 'should have known that?' How could you possibly have my name in a reservation book? I only told a couple of people at work that I was coming here. Is there a hidden camera here, or what?"

She laughed. "This is no reservation book, honey. Not the way you think of it, anyhow. People don't come here because they want to. They come here because they need to. Sit down, and I'll bring you some coffee."

I needed more than coffee. "Yes, I know," she added, as though reading my thoughts were part of the service here, "but the cheesecake requires a bit more finesse. We have to match you up with the cheesecake that is perfect for you, or it just won't work."

"What won't work?" This was driving me batty.

"Why, the promise on the sign, of course." She looked at me carefully. "You came here for the best damn cheesecake in the universe. But it might not be here yet. The universe is a pretty big place, you know."

I sat obediently at the table she pointed to, and shortly thereafter was sipping a steaming cup of pretty good Kona coffee while I tried to take stock of my situation. Here I was, on my lunch hour, waiting while this woman told me (in spite of the fact I could see a display case absolutely loaded with cheesecakes) that mine might not have arrived yet! I was more than willing to sample the vast assortment I could see there. A B-52 cheesecake was that moment high on my list of priorities. Perhaps fresh peach, if they could get them from somewhere like Chile at this time of year. Hell, they all looked good enough for me. Then I stopped to consider. Maybe they were just there for display. Maybe they were all Styrofoam, like wedding cakes. I'll never forget my disappointment at learning that those marvelous, multi-tiered cakes were just for looks, except the part the bride and groom would slice for photographs. Maybe that's what always turned me off the idea of marriage.

But this thought did nothing to make my stomach feel better. I had skipped morning coffee break to make room for this, and here was this woman telling me that I'd have to wait longer.

"Maybe days," she added, casually. No wonder business was slow! Perhaps this place was little more than a convenient tax write-off for some corporate bigwig. My stomach growled in protest.

"Would you please tell me why this is so important?" I asked in desperation. "And just what is in that big book, anyhow? Do you have the names of all the people who work downtown or something? Even so, how on earth could you have known about me and my parents, unless someone from my office called you?"

She went to the counter and lifted the book. It was a large black volume, not much different from the family Bible we'd inherited from my grandmother a few years back. On the cover were some letters in gold, gothic script. "Cheesecake Lovers of the Universe," it read.

"They come from all over," she said conversationally. "The trick is, we don't just give you any old cheesecake. Of course they're all good! We give you THE cheesecake. Once you have had it, you never really need another one."

"That's a very depressing thought," I responded, feeling the slightest bit nervous. "I can't imagine never wanting another cheesecake again."

"Now don't get me wrong, honey," the woman replied seriously. "I didn't say you'd never want another cheesecake. I said you'd never need another cheesecake. There's a big difference."

I mulled over that one briefly and supposed that she was right. How often in the past had my mother said things like "Now dear, you know you don't NEED those new shoes; you just WANT them." Or else, "Sweetheart, I think you really NEED a haircut." Or else, "Meredith, I think you NEED to go out with young men more often. Even if you don't like the ones you go out with. After all, you never know. While you're out, you might meet someone."

"This is very nice coffee," I said after a few moments. "But I'm starving here. Can you tell me when my cheesecake is going to be ready?"

"I don't know. The book hasn't told me yet."

That was as much as I could take. I gulped the rest of my coffee, left a loonie on the table, and fled the shop before Melissa had a chance to utter another demented word. Before going back to work, I grabbed a salmon salad sandwich in the Food Fair at Scotia Place. When I got to work, I hid in my own office behind a closed door. I didn't want anybody to know that I had gone out for cheesecake and ended up talking with a nut bar.

Which is precisely why I found myself, three days later, walking through that same door under that same pink neon sign and seating myself at that same table. Melissa did not seem surprised.

"Not much longer," she said. "Maybe today, even." I didn't even ask how or if she really knew.

There was another customer there, too. A sad-looking old Oriental man sat hunched over his coffee, reading a thick paperback. It was covered by a handmade cloth book jacket, so I couldn't see the title. I'm always snoopy about what other people choose to read in public. On airplanes, I often find my gaze straying across the aisle, to the laps of total strangers, mostly male. It can get embarrassing sometimes.

Melissa brought my coffee and gestured toward the old fellow, saying with a whisper, "Sad case, that one. He's been coming here for nearly twenty years. Ever since his wife passed away, poor soul. I keep hoping that his cheesecake will come, but it never does."

"Do you mean to tell me that in all this time he's never had ANY cheesecake?" I asked in a horrified stage whisper. That would be like dying of thirst in the desert while an A&W root beer stand stood right in front of you. "Couldn't he have one of those other cakes while he's waiting?" I think I wanted her to tell me they were all fake, and have done with it. I still didn't know exactly what this "wait" would be for, but I sure didn't want to see myself in twenty years hunched over this checkered tablecloth with my coffee and a book. And no cheesecake.

"It wouldn't be the same" was all she said. And then a little while later, she came by my table, shaking her head sadly. "Try again next week, honey."

That cheesecake became an obsession with me. I didn't give up dessert entirely while I waited for it, however. Do I look that stupid? Over the weeks that passed, I ate out as often as I ever had and sampled the best cheesecakes that Edmonton had to offer. But it wasn't the same, somehow. I always had the feeling that I was missing out on something elusive that only Melissa's cheesecake could give me. So at least one lunch hour a week, you could find me there, drinking coffee and reading a paperback novel.

Occasionally I would nod and smile to Mr. Wu, the old Chinese gentleman, and he would nod and smile back. We never spoke. What would I have said to him? "Hello, Mr. Wu, how's the cheesecake?" We knew we were both in the same bizarre situation. Melissa would bring us our coffee and shake her head and say something comforting like "Maybe next week, honey," and then go back to cleaning the counter, or whatever else she did to pass the time. And at the end of the lunch hour, I would leave the coffee money and a small tip on the table, close up my book, and return to my office, stopping to pick up a sandwich along the way. Mr. Wu may have stayed until closing time each day that he was there. I didn't ask what he did the rest of the time.

When I walked in one particular day, I knew that something was different. Melissa's black book was open wide on the table in front of Mr. Wu, and she was showing him something. "It says today for sure, Mr. Wu. Gee, I'm gonna miss you."

I wasn't at all sure that I should be there to witness something this intensely personal. "Should I leave?"

"No, honey. Stay! This is something that really ought to be shared. Mr. Wu would be so disappointed if he thought he'd driven you away. Wouldn't you be, Mr. Wu?" The old man nodded slowly, his eyes never leaving the pages of the large book. I wished I knew what it said. I wondered what my page would say when my time came.

Somehow, I was expecting a fanfare or drum roll as Melissa proudly carried the plate with Mr. Wu's cheesecake to his table. I remember that it wasn't a slice of cake, as it would be had she taken it from one of the larger ones in the display case (which may or may not have been fake). It was a small, but complete, round cheesecake, made exclusively for Mr. Wu. Of course.

She placed it before him and stepped back in respect as he lifted the fork. He carefully plunged his fork into the cheesecake (was it lemon?) and brought the first piece to his mouth. I felt myself holding my breath as I watched him chew slowly. A smile began to grow on his lips as he savored every morsel of that first mouthful. I watched, mesmerized, as Mr. Wu continued to eat what I knew had to be the best damn cheesecake he'd ever had in his entire life. I felt like I was sharing some sort of religious experience. It was weird, but I felt at peace, just sitting there with my coffee forgotten, watching Mr. Wu eat that cheesecake.

After polishing off the last morsel from the plate, he sat awhile sipping his coffee and smiling. I felt a tinge of jealousy and then remembered what Melissa had told me about his twenty-year-long wait for this very moment. He'd paid his dues for certain. Then Mr. Wu carefully wiped his hands and mouth with the cloth napkin that Melissa always provided, stood, bowed slightly to Melissa and to me, left a hundred-dollar bill on the table, and slowly walked out of the coffee shop without another glance back. On his way out, he bowed to the pink neon sign.

Melissa waited until he was out of sight before she sighed, "I'll miss the old guy." Then she busied herself with clearing the dishes from the table and wiping up any crumbs. She picked up the bill he'd left, grinned at me, and pocketed it. "Pretty nice of him to do that. We don't charge for the cheesecake when it comes."

I watched her with curiosity as she took his plate and fork and reverently carried them to a small door in the wall, near the back of the restaurant. She pulled on a wooden knob, and a sort of chute opened. She tipped the plate and fork over the lip of the chute and watched them slide down to somewhere. We were already in the basement of the building. There must, I thought, be a sub-basement. Then she closed the little door.

"Interesting way to get the stuff to the dishwasher," I remarked.

"Oh no, honey. We don't wash any of the cheesecake plates and cutlery. That would be disrespectful. We dispose of them by returning them to their original elements. It's the only way. I would never expect the next customer to use a plate that some-one else had used."

I let this one slip past me without commenting. The concept of returning a china plate and stainless-steel fork to "original elements" was just too odd for me, even in this place. "Can't Mr. Wu use that same plate and fork the next time he comes?" I asked.

Melissa just looked at me for a moment. Then she said quietly, "You don't know, do you? He won't be back here. Ever. He doesn't need to anymore, you see."

"That's just it, I don't understand!" I answered. "Doesn't any-body ever come back after they've eaten their cheesecake?"

I could tell she was trying to be patient with me. "Like I said. Once you've had the best damn cheesecake in the universe, you won't need to come back." And she turned and walked through the little door behind the display case that held all those wonderful-looking cheesecakes. I sat for a long while, until my coffee grew cold and it was time to get back to the office. I left my loonie on the table, as usual.

That was several years ago. I've been going to Melissa's every week on one of my lunch hours. I don't work at the firm down-town anymore, so it's a bit awkward to get there, but I do. I haven't seen any other customers in all that time since my lunch hours with Mr. Wu. Perhaps they go on different days or during different hours. Perhaps there aren't many others like me and Mr. Wu. Melissa says that it is pretty rare that two customers are there together, and that I should feel honored to have seen Mr. Wu get his cheesecake. Some days, however, I have arrived just in time to see Melissa reverently pouring the used plate and fork down that little chute in the back. I bite my lip and hold back tears over someone else's good fortune and my envy.

Every week she greets me with my coffee and a hopeful smile. "Any day now, honey. I'm sure of it."

Every week I read my book, sip my coffee, leave my loonie on the table, and pick up a sandwich on my way back to the office. I'm a senior partner now, so getting back on time isn't as critical as it used to be. I always wait until the last possible minute. Besides, some of my most creative thinking and decision making have been done during those lunch hours. Cheesecake or no cheesecake, those hours have been good for me—sort of mini retreats in the middle of a busy week.

My mom passed away last spring. Dad has been seeing a widow who goes to the same church as he does, and it's been good for him. I think Mom told him before she went that he should remarry quickly so he wouldn't be lonely. She always did try to take care of us. I don't know what she would say about my visits to Melissa's. I always kept those to myself and never told her. I miss her advice, though. I think that even when I ignored it, I was still using it, and she knew that.

I don't really know why I do this. I can't imagine waiting as patiently for anything else in the whole universe.

But I will always remember that smile on Mr. Wu's face. That smile, I think, is as good as it gets. I heard a song by the Indigo Girls that talked about being "closer to fine." I like the sound of that. I think my life is pretty close to fine. And my cheesecake will be coming to me soon. Any day now.

I'm sure of it.

Diane L. Walton: My inspiration for "Cheesecake" was Spider Robinson's Callahan's Saloon series of stories, more or less. I had toyed with the idea of writing a Canadian version of those tales, always set in the same location with some standard characters and lots of different situations. So the location presented itself . . . a cheesecake shop. I always have food on my mind, I guess. But then as I started writing it and created the character of Meredith, I got more into the spiritual quest presented by such a story. Not being a religious person, I thought long and hard about the strength of faith that people have in something intangible—Mr. Wu's faith in the cheesecake that never comes. But in the story, I knew that he'd get his reward for sure, and this would give Meredith the incentive to continue her visits to the shop. I also knew that the story would be open-ended. It was originally meant to be quite tongue-in-cheek, but as I wrote it, I came to realize that it was the strength of faith in anything which helps us to get through our lives. Call it religion, call it cheesecake, call it the Brotherhood of Mankind. Whatever.

BODY AND BLOOD

Louise Marley

COMING INTO THE SHADOWED APSE from the summer heat, the girl dipped her fingertips into the silver basin by the door and crossed herself. She looked startled by the coolness of the holy water drying on her forehead, as if she did not realize what she had done, and she wiped her fingers quickly on the cotton of her summer shift.

In the nave of the church several people knelt in the pews or in the saints' niches where votive candles flickered in tiny glass cups. The girl passed the tiny chapel where the Blessed Sacrament rested in its gilt case. She started to genuflect, but then, with one hand already on her knee, she straightened and walked on through the sanctuary until she reached the bars of the visiting room that flanked it. The afternoon sun shone on the marble of the altar, and the plaster walls of the little church glowed in the filtered light from the stained-glass windows.

The extern sister had been waiting; she waved a greeting before disappearing through the plain wooden door at the far end of the visiting room. The girl sat down in the hard-backed chair by the speaking grille, smoothing her shift with her hands. She watched the door and waited.

Another girl, wearing the habit of a novice, came through the door and walked slowly across the visiting room. Except for the brown and white of her habit, she looked exactly like her visitor. "Felicity!" she said softly.

"Come on, Pep, call me Flicka," her visitor answered. She pushed a little package through the bars. "Here, I brought you some goodies from home."

"Thank you," the young nun said, taking the package. She sat on a chair that matched the one on the other side of the bars, the draperies of her habit sighing as they settled around her. She smiled, her skin crinkling slightly against the white wimple that bound her forehead. "How are you?" she asked.

"I'm fine. You?"

"Wonderful."

"Pep, I came to tell you something," Flicka began, but Sister Perpetua was speaking.

"Have you been to Mass, Felicity?"

Flicka suddenly grinned. "Come on, Pep, you're doing enough of that for both of us!"

The nun's eyes were a soft brown, milder than her twin's, and they turned away now to gaze at the wooden crucifix that hung over the altar. "I can't do it for you, Felicity," she murmured. "You need to do it yourself." Her eyes glazed as her sister watched, widening and shining strangely as they fixed on some imaginary point. A pencil on the shelf between them began to roll.

Flicka caught it as it fell. "Oh, Pep! Are you still at it?"

Perpetua's eyes cleared, and she turned back to her sister. "It still happens, if that's what you mean," she said calmly. "I don't do it exactly."

"But, Pep . . . don't they mind?"

Sister Perpetua stroked the simple pectoral cross that hung from her neck. "I don't think they notice me much at all, or any more than the other novices, anyway." She put her hand out through the grille. "I'm a lot better, Flicka," she said. "Nothing has happened for a long time. Really."

"That's good." Flicka stroked her hand.

"You should go to Mass and take Holy Communion, though," Sister Perpetua repeated. "You need the Eucharist, Felicity."

"That's always been your department," Flicka answered. "You and Mom."

"You know what the best thing about the convent is?" Perpetua went on, as if she had not heard her sister's answer. "It's the Eucharist. It's the exposition of the Blessed Sacrament. We kneel right over there—" She pointed her finger to the row of kneelers behind her in the visiting room. Her heavy sleeve fell in graceful curves from her arm. "We can see it perfectly from there. Even novices can pray before the Blessed Sacrament for as long as they want, hours even." Her face shone, and a gentle light flickered behind her eyes.

Flicka moved uncomfortably and drew away her hand. "I hoped maybe you wouldn't be so obsessed with the sacraments now, Pep. I mean, now that you have them all the time."

"It's not obsession," her sister said simply. "It's devotion. It's the body and blood of the Lord, Felicity, just as it says in the Mass. For you, too," she said, looking into her sister's face. "'This is my body, given up for you. This is my blood, shed for you.'"

"But not really," Flicka said.

"Felicity!"

Flicka sighed. "Let's not have this argument again," she said.

For a moment there was silence between them, as stiff as the iron bars of the grille. Then Perpetua said, "I'll pray for you."

Flicka smiled at her. "Okay," she said. "Listen, now, I have good news." She waited for her sister's full attention. "Pep— Timothy and I are expecting." She stood and smoothed the cotton dress to show her gently swelling abdomen. "Look at me!" she said. "Five months! Isn't it great?"

Perpetua said nothing. Her eyes closed, and she paled and swayed in her chair. Her mouth moved, but no sound came out.

Flicka rubbed her bare arms as if feeling a sudden chill. "Pep?"

Perpetua's eyes opened slowly. "But you mean . . . you've been . . . you've had . . ."

"Pep, I've been married a whole year!"

Perpetua pressed her hands to her own stomach. "But you can't! We can't . . . we have to be chaste, we have to be clean. . . ." She stood up abruptly, knocking her chair to the floor. The package from home fell beneath it, and the worshippers in the nave, disturbed by the noise, turned to look. The extern sister immediately opened the door and hurried toward them.

Flicka reached out to take hold of one of the bars. Urgently, she whispered, "Pep, you're the one who's chaste. You're clean, and so am I, perfectly clean! Pep!"

But Perpetua had drawn away, her hands buried under the folds of the habit. Her head turned back and forth, back and forth, and words spilled from her mouth in an unstoppable stream. "Pray, Felicity . . . pray to be washed clean. Pray before the Blessed Sacrament. . . ."

The extern sister shook her head gently at Flicka and put her arm around the novice. "Come along, Sister Perpetua," she murmured. "Come along, now. You don't want to upset your sister, do you, when you won't see her for another three months? Say goodbye, now. Come along." She drew Perpetua, mumbling, imploring, toward the door.

Flicka stood still, gripping the bars of the grille. She leaned her forehead against the cold iron and shut her eyes. The door into the cloister closed, softly but firmly, and she was left alone on the outside.

Sister Elizabeth Mary, Sister of the Devotion of Santa Fina, reflected that the plainchant, also known as Gregorian chant or plainsong, had changed very little over the centuries. Some of the melodies catalogued by the first Pope Gregory had survived more than fifteen hundred years, celebrating the ancient words of the Mass and the Divine Office. Their patterns, she thought, were as abiding as the faith they supported.

She knelt in the choir and tried to concentrate on the Office, but her voice trembled. Other voices faltered, too, spoiling the phrases. Only Mother Superior kept on without stumbling, her voice reedy but steady as she chanted. She sang with complete devotion, just as she had done every day of her life for forty-five years.

The clamor outside had shattered the sacred silence of the cloister. Lauds, the early morning service, had been almost drowned out by it. The racket was a constant reminder to the community.

Elizabeth Mary glanced to her left, where the novices knelt in the lower stalls of the choir. The white veils distinguishing them from the professed nuns glowed in the candlelight of the chapel, but they were not bowed in concentration as they should have been. The novices had given up the prayer completely. Two were gripping each other's hands and leaning together, a complete breach of ritual, and one looked back over her shoulder as if the noise were an intruder that might take corporeal form at any moment. Elizabeth Mary's heart beat fast for them, the heart of a mother whose children are frightened.

In many ways they were her children. She was mistress of novices, and she had them in her care.

Sister Elizabeth Mary had prayed all day for charity, but anger still disrupted her devotions. Those awful people had tried to take communion! They had forced themselves in among the faithful who came to daily Mass at Santa Fina, and then they had come again this morning, laughing and elbowing each other. When the priest refused them a second time they rioted, and the media arrived shortly after. Now cameras and noisy reporters besieged the church and the convent, and the nuns struggled to maintain their routine through a tumult that should never have happened.

The Divine Office dragged to its end at last, and the sisters rose from their knees, shaking out the folds of their long brown habits. Mother Superior broke the habitual silence that followed choir.

"Dear sisters," she said, "pray for our Sister Perpetua, and for all of us. The bishop is here now, and we'll be glad of his guidance. Please, in the meantime, do your best to go on about your duties. Remember—" The noise outside seemed to surge as she drew breath, and she hurried to finish. "Remember—work is prayer." They crossed themselves, and then the line of nuns and novices, twenty-three in all, filed in silence out of the chapel, their hands clasped beneath the plackets of their habits, their coifed heads bowed.

Mother Superior stopped Elizabeth Mary at the door. "Could you come to my office, Sister?" she asked. Her voice sounded exactly as it did on any normal day, dry and calm.

"Shall I call Sister Perpetua?" Elizabeth Mary asked.

"No. We'll talk with the bishop alone."

Together the two nuns went out through the shadows, blinking away the brilliance of the summer sun that filled the courtyard. The compound of the convent was not large, and they had only a short way to walk around the end of the vegetable garden and back into the coolness of the tiled hall.

Mother Superior's office was tiny, and crowded with bookshelves and a large desk. On every wall hung religious pictures collected by Mother Superior or her predecessors, and small icons rested in the narrow spaces beside the books. Sister Catherine, the extern, waited by the window. Her veil and headpiece were much less concealing than those of the cloistered nuns, and her reddened eyes and pale, weary face filled Elizabeth Mary with sympathy.

"Is Bishop Damato here, Sister?" asked Mother Superior.

The extern nodded. "He's in the church now." She was nervously pleating and repleating the folds of her modified habit. It was the extern sister's duty to be liaison between those in the cloister and those without, and today her job was very difficult indeed.

"Sister Perpetua's family called, Mother," Catherine said nervously. "Her mother and her twin sister. Her mother is afraid . . ." Her voice broke and she stopped. Mother Superior raised her eyebrows, creasing her forehead against the stiff head-piece of her coif.

"I know exactly what they're afraid of," Elizabeth Mary said bitterly. "They're afraid we'll send Sister Perpetua home."

Again the extern nodded, her short veil trembling. Mother Superior frowned. "We'll see what the bishop says," she murmured, "before we make any decisions. It may be that sending her home is our only course."

Elizabeth Mary said nothing as she followed her superior from the office, but her heart rebelled, and she prayed quickly for the grace of obedience. She didn't know how she would bear it if Sister Perpetua was sent away from the convent . . . because she didn't know how Sister Perpetua would bear it.

Even a bishop of the diocese was not allowed through the doors and into the cloister of the Convent of Santa Fina. Only the extern sister, and the doctor and dentist who treated the nuns once each year, were allowed inside. Groceries and sundries delivered or donated to the sisters were handed in through the "turn," the revolving cabinet that connected the foyer and the kitchen. Any other contact with the Sisters of the Devotion of Santa Fina took place in the visiting room that flanked the nave of the church, separated from it by bars as stiff and forbidding as those in any jail. Elizabeth knew that people thought the bars were to keep the nuns in; but the sisterhood thought of them as their protection, their spiritual security, a wall to keep the world out. The Sisters of Santa Fina chose to isolate themselves from the distractions of secular life, to immerse themselves in the sacred. They took pride in having more postulants to their conservative, contemplative order than were attracted to the active orders. It was a confirmation to them, a sign of grace.

Sister Catherine escorted Mother Superior and Sister Elizabeth Mary across the hall and into the visiting room. It was cool in the church, the sun shaded to dimness by the colored windows. Through the bars Elizabeth saw that the nave was empty. That meant the sacristan had locked the outer doors, but she could hear the talking and shouting outside just the same. She prayed briefly to their patroness for protection.

"Hello, Mother Superior, Sisters," the bishop said. He came forward from one of the saints' niches to the speaking grille and sat down. The nuns sat too, and looked through the bars at the bishop in his black suit and clerical collar.

"Hello, Bishop," they murmured.

"Is it true?" he asked.

Mother Superior was very calm as she answered. "It is, I'm afraid."

"Did you have a hint of this sort of . . . hm, activity, when you accepted her?"

The older nun turned to Elizabeth Mary. "Perhaps you could explain, Sister."

Elizabeth clasped her pectoral cross and searched for the words that would both explain and save Sister Perpetua. Outside the clamor went on, an oddly pointless noise like that of a television left buzzing in the common room when no one was there.

"When Perpetua came to us as a postulant . . . ," she began.

"When was that, Sister?"

"It was five years ago. She was sixteen," Elizabeth said. "She had her family's wholehearted support . . . well, perhaps excepting her twin sister. Flicka." She paused, hoping for inspiration, but had to go on with only facts to help her. "They did warn us."

"About what?" The bishop looked matter-of-fact, but Elizabeth Mary's mouth was dry. She held her cross tightly.

"Perpetua had trouble in school and at home. Odd things happened around her, and upset her family, especially her father. . . ."

"Things?" the bishop urged. Elizabeth Mary felt his impatience and tried to speak more quickly. Within the cloister, they almost never had to hurry. And it seemed so important to get this right.

"Yes, things like . . . well, she broke things, and got in trouble at school." It was lame, and almost not quite true. "When she was thirteen, it got more serious."

Elizabeth shook her head. It was such an improbable situation. Even to her, it sounded like a medieval story. She should be reading it from some dusty illuminated manuscript, not telling it to a modern bishop in this urban convent. She sighed and went on.

"Sister Perpetua bleeds. Her hands, and her feet. It happens during moments of intense prayer, or other stress . . . she bleeds."

The bishop looked more curious than shocked. "You took a postulant with stigmata?"

"Well, her mother calls them stigmata, but her father accuses her of scratching herself." Elizabeth Mary was on firm ground here because this was clear truth. "Flicka, her twin, says it's 'no big deal.'" The quote made them all smile. "It's not a dramatic amount of blood, really. And it hasn't happened in a long time."

"But, still, Sister . . ."

Elizabeth Mary released her breath. "Sister Perpetua has a vocation, Bishop. A real one. I'm sure of it. She is utterly devoted to prayer, and especially to the adoration of the Blessed Sacrament. She can't help the other things, at least not yet. One reason she came to us so young was that her family didn't know what to do with her. Except Flicka. Felicity, actually, but she goes by Flicka."

"They're named Perpetua and Felicity? Twins?" This exaggerated Catholicism seemed to grieve the bishop.

"It's a very devout family, Bishop. I believe the mother actually was a novice of the Sisters of the Blessed Sacrament at one time, although she didn't take final vows. In fact, I'm afraid she left under rather drastic circumstances, although Sister Perpetua hasn't said . . . In any case, what happened with Perpetua was too much, even for her."

Mother Superior put in, "We've had no real trouble, you know, until lately. The . . . phenomena, if you will . . . seemed to ease once she came into the convent, and became quite sporadic. She's rather a simple girl, actually, quiet, hard-working. She's been very happy here."

Elizabeth added, "I've been mistress of novices for twelve years, Bishop, and I've never known a postulant or a novice more eager. It was just . . ." She hesitated.

"Yes, Sister?"

"Well . . . something set her off, that's all. She was doing all right, and then . . . then she wasn't." Elizabeth held her cross to her breast.

"Does she know what's happening? About all of these people outside?"

"No," Elizabeth Mary said, and she prayed quickly to the Blessed Mother for the bishop to understand. "It gets worse when she's upset," she added.

"And now it's more than stigmata."

Elizabeth Mary was silent. It was not a question. She would have to examine her conscience later, and probably confess sins of omission. She was afraid that if Mother Superior and the bishop knew everything, she would be censured, and Sister Perpetua with her. Perpetua was so fragile, so easily disturbed despite all their efforts to help her channel her devotions. Sister Elizabeth Mary bowed her head and said nothing more.

By suppertime, quiet had returned to the convent grounds. The sisters gathered in the refectory and seated themselves according to seniority, the brown veils above and the white below. They ate their customary supper of thick soup and fresh bread baked by their own hands, and listened in silence as the assistant superior read aloud to them. The novices still looked strained and afraid. Elizabeth Mary smiled gently at them and thought she would try to speak with them during recreation, when their silence could end. Thank the Blessed Santa Fina that the Rule no longer forbade that! Her order had made some important concessions after the Second Vatican Council, and Sister Elizabeth Mary was grateful for them. She was just as grateful that when other orders were giving up the habit and the cloister, the Sisters of Santa Fina had been steadfast in those traditions. She loved the discipline, the ritual ... the peace.

When recreation was over, and the novices somewhat soothed by being able to talk freely, Elizabeth Mary was given dispensation by Mother Superior to receive a visitor. The permission was necessary, as the cloistered nuns received visitors only once a month, and her brother had come to see her just three weeks ago, bringing her precious niece with him. She had stroked the little girl's soft head through the bars. The novices, of course, were allowed visitors only once a quarter.

Elizabeth Mary went into the visiting room with Sister Catherine. The church was still empty. Only Flicka, Perpetua's twin sister, had been admitted by the extern, and now sat on the other side of the speaking grille looking distressed. There were drops of water drying on the young woman's forehead.

Elizabeth Mary knew that Flicka had sworn to leave the church forever when Perpetua entered the convent. But the customs of religion can be very comforting, and Elizabeth Mary gave silent thanks for the grace of faith.

"Hello, Flicka," she said, smiling.

"Hello, Sister. Is Pep all right?"

Elizabeth Mary looked fondly at the girl's curly hair and dark brown eyes. Flicka looked so like Perpetua that it was astonishing, even though her personality was utterly different in almost every essential. And of course, Flicka was visibly pregnant under the summer dress she wore.

"Yes, Sister Perpetua is well," she answered. "She hardly seems aware of all the upset around us."

"Can I see her?"

"Well, probably not tonight. And we have to ask Mother Superior, in any case. It is not the week for novices to receive visitors."

The girl frowned and clenched her fist as if she would strike out against the strict Rule that dominated her sister's life. But then she opened her hand and passed it over her eyes.

"You look tired, Flicka," Elizabeth said quietly. "Are you taking care of yourself? You need lots of rest when you're expecting."

"Oh, I'm okay. My family is a wreck, though . . . Mom, and James. He came home from the university. Mom's been on her knees all day, praying. That's what she always does! Dad's just furious, stomping around like he's going to tear the house down."

"And your husband?"

At this question, Flicka's face softened, and she glowed from within, as if her inner self were lighted by the same votive candles that glimmered in the church behind her.

"Timothy's fine," Flicka said. "He just can't wait for the baby. I can't either, but now I'm so worried about Pep."

"Sister Perpetua is very lucky to have you."

The girl leaned forward. "Sister, I want you to know," she said in a low and intense tone. "I want you to know that if you kick her out, she can come to us. To me and Timothy."

Elizabeth Mary drew a sharp breath. She had the abrupt sense of an abyss opening around her, a perilous darkness, and she clung to her pectoral cross. The image of Perpetua at home with the pregnant Flicka was terrifying, fearsome, but she couldn't think why. She had never felt such a sensation in her life. She made a great effort to control it, and murmured, "I hope very much that will not be necessary," when she could speak.

"But you're thinking of it?" There was a heartbreaking flash of hope in Flicka's face.

"Not I, Flicka," Elizabeth said firmly. "Certainly not I. I think this is where Sister Perpetua belongs."

"What about your Mother Superior, then?"

Elizabeth had to drop her eyes to her lap, and she caressed the wooden cross in her fingers. "I don't know," she said. "We must wait and see. And pray," she added, looking up again into Flicka's face.

Flicka shook her head and the brown curls bounced. "Not me, Sister. I gave that up when Pep came here. She prays enough for both of us." She rolled her eyes. "And so does my mother, believe me. She spends half her life on her knees. It drives my dad crazy."

"Well, then . . . I will pray for you, Flicka."

The girl hesitated, and Elizabeth Mary feared she might be angry again. But she smiled, and looked very much like her cloistered twin at that moment. "I do appreciate the thought, Sister. Thank you." She passed her hand slowly over her swelling abdomen, and Elizabeth Mary observed the beautiful gesture, as old and as reverent a sign as those of religion.

There was a moment of silence, both within and without the church, and Elizabeth Mary accepted it as a sign of grace.

Flicka broke it. "You know, Sister," she said softly, "things were a little strange when we were kids."

Elizabeth Mary nodded and waited. She was used to the whispered confidences of young women.

"It was as if they divided us," Flicka went on, half to herself. This was like confession for her, Elizabeth Mary thought, the baring of her soul. "Dad resented the Church a lot because Mom was so religious. He liked me to be active, fun . . . and Mom made Pep into the religious one."

"The grace of faith is in no human's power," Elizabeth Mary murmured.

"Well, maybe," Flicka said, "but it seemed like if I played the tomboy and Pep played the nun . . . it kept Mom and Dad from fighting. The worst part is that I liked it that way, and I let Pep bear the heaviest load. I shouldn't have done that." Her eyes were full of pain. "I grew out of it, Sister. I thought Pep would, too, but I guess now she can't."

Sister Elizabeth Mary stretched out her brown-habited arm through the grille and gave Felicity her hand. "You mustn't worry about your sister's vocation," she said. "It seems to me to be very real, and she has been very happy here in our community."

Flicka nodded. "I know she's been happy, Sister . . . until now. I caused this, didn't I?"

Elizabeth Mary hardly knew how to answer. Flicka pressed her, "She doesn't like me being pregnant, but why not? This is bad, I know, as bad as when we got kicked out of St. Anne's. But we were thirteen then, and we're twenty-one now, grown up. I just don't understand."

Elizabeth Mary shook her head. "I only know that you mustn't blame yourself," she said.

Flicka sighed and stood up with difficulty, her hand on the back of the chair.

"Thanks for seeing me, Sister," she said.

"Try to rest tonight," Elizabeth Mary said, just as if Flicka were one of her novices. She rose from her chair, and the extern sister came forward to usher Flicka out of the church. Elizabeth Mary watched her go. Like Perpetua, she looked small and vulnerable.

As Sister Elizabeth Mary made her way back into the cloister, her habit rustled on the floor, but there was no other sound. The Silence had begun, when each of the professed sisters, the novices, and the postulants made their evening prayers alone in their cubicles, and then lay down on their solitary cots to contemplate the miracles of Santa Fina. Elizabeth stopped in the nuns' private chapel for one stolen moment of prayer before the Blessed Mother, not forgetting her promise to Flicka, and then went wearily down the corridor to make sure her novices were safely abed. It had been a long and difficult day, and tomorrow promised to be the same. Elizabeth was grateful for the refreshing silence of the night and prayed fervently to Santa Fina for renewed strength to come to her in the morning.

"Come in, Sister," said Mother Superior. Elizabeth went into the little office to find Sister Perpetua seated across from Mother Superior. The novice's head was bowed under her white veil, her hands clasped before her. Elizabeth Mary put her hand on

Perpetua's shoulder, and the girl stirred as if waking from some strange dream.

"Sister Elizabeth Mary," she said eagerly. "May I go back to chapel with the novices now?" She held up her hands, palms outward, to show they were clean and unmarked.

Elizabeth looked to her superior for guidance. There was a little silence as Mother Superior turned to the novice, and through it Elizabeth heard once again the racket on the borders of the convent, and she wondered what it must look like out there.

It was hard to imagine. She had not seen the outside of their building in eighteen years. She had hardly paid attention to it when she had arrived as a nervous, hopeful postulant herself, because it had been the inside she was so eager to see. She supposed the urban setting had changed during her years in the cloister, possibly more shops, newer houses, a busier street around their modest compound of church, convent, and gardens. She tried to imagine the scene outside, the little parking lot crowded with vehicles, perhaps one or two police cars. She hoped some of the police who came were Catholic and would understand about her community. She was aware that some people found it strange to deal with religious.

Mother Superior answered Perpetua, "I think not today, Sister. The other novices are confused and upset. In fact, all your sisters are disturbed."

"But why, Mother Superior?" the girl asked, and Elizabeth Mary saw again that she was truly bewildered. "I didn't mean to do it. Besides, isn't it what we ask for at each Mass?" She turned in hurt and fear to her mistress of novices, and Elizabeth wished she could comfort her. How could she answer such a question? The brown eyes that were so clear and determined in Flicka were soft and suffering in Perpetua, and the curls were hidden by her white veil.

"Sister Elizabeth Mary, can I not at least have Holy Communion? I'll do my penance, whatever you say." Tears welled over the girl's cheeks, and two pens and a paper clip slid from Mother Superior's desk to the floor. "They wouldn't let me go to Mass this morning," she said. She caught her breath in a sob.

Elizabeth Mary bent to retrieve the pens, and her eyes met Mother Superior's as she straightened. Please, Blessed Mother, don't let them send her away, she prayed.

Mother Superior was grim and resigned as she regarded the novice's wet face.

"The bishop feels perhaps you should go home for a time, Sister Perpetua," Mother Superior said.

Perpetua's eyes went wide with shock.

"Oh, no!" she cried. Behind her a small Russian icon, a picture of the Mother and Child, fell from the bookcase with a tinny clatter. Mother Superior turned swiftly on Elizabeth Mary.

"Is it always like this?" she snapped.

Elizabeth Mary strove for calm. "She is easily upset," she said. "If I may talk with her . . ."

The older woman sighed and bent her head for a moment. "I'm sorry, Sister," she said in a quieter tone. "Of course, she is your charge, and you may counsel her whenever you wish. Forgive me." She pressed a blue-veined hand to her forehead as if to relieve the pressure of the coif. "You will understand, Sister Elizabeth Mary," she said in a tired voice, "that I have to worry about all our sisters, not only one novice. And I have a responsibility to the mother house as well."

"Of course, Mother," Elizabeth murmured. "Sister Perpetua, let's go up to your room and we'll talk, and pray together. And try not to worry," she said, but fresh tears already poured down Perpetua's crumpled face. As they rose to leave the office, a little glass angel sent to Mother Superior by a nephew she had never seen skittered from its niche and smashed upon the floor. Elizabeth looked back from the hall and saw the old nun staring at the pieces as if they had come straight from Satan.

The next day, the media subsided in their attempts to wring information from the convent. The sisters chanted the Divine Office in the early morning without distraction and then began their round of daily chores in peaceful and prayerful silence. Sister Mary Elizabeth was called once again to the visiting room.

The nave of the church was still empty, closed to all outsiders. The bishop waited on the other side of the speaking grille, and with him were Flicka and a younger boy who looked much like her. When everyone was seated, the bishop introduced him.

"This is James, Sister Perpetua's brother."

"Hello, James," Elizabeth said. "I'm glad to meet you."

"Hello, Sister."

Flicka spoke. "My father wouldn't come, and he wouldn't let Mom come either. He says he's done with the whole business. He says . . ." She dropped her head a little and then raised it with determination. Elizabeth admired her spirit. "He says she's yours now, and you have to deal with her."

Elizabeth felt a little swell of satisfaction rise beneath the folds of her habit, and she quickly asked forgiveness. But surely Bishop Damato would never send away a novice who had no home to go to!

"We need to make some decisions about Sister Perpetua," the bishop said in a businesslike manner.

James and Flicka looked at each other, and Flicka spoke. "I've already said she can come to us," she told the bishop. "Timothy says it's okay."

"Timothy is Felicity's husband," Elizabeth Mary explained. "But surely, Bishop . . . ?"

The bishop settled wearily back in his chair. "Sister, I had to call every Catholic executive in the city to get the reporters pulled away from the convent. If this should happen again, how can I protect the order?"

"But how can we protect Sister Perpetua?" Elizabeth insisted gently.

"I can," Flicka said stoutly. "I always have."

"Have you, Felicity?"

"Flicka, please," the girl said, and once again she passed her hand over the rising curve of her stomach.

"You couldn't keep her from getting kicked out of two schools," James said. It was not said cruelly, but matter-of-factly.

"Is that what happened?" asked Bishop Damato.

James nodded. "Flicka tried to watch over her, but whenever Pep gets upset"—he grinned with the boyish humor of an eighteen-year-old—"stuff happens!"

Flicka turned to Elizabeth. "It was never serious . . . well, hardly ever."

"What kind of . . . stuff . . . do you mean, James?" the bishop asked.

Flicka put in, "Oh, you know, Father. Poltergeist sorts of things. Things fell off shelves, sometimes things broke around Pep. If people were just nice to her, there was no problem."

"What about that lunch thing, though?" James asked his sister. "That's more than poltergeist stuff."

Flicka looked down in her lap, and the stroking gesture stopped abruptly.

"What happened, James?" asked the bishop again.

The boy leaned forward to be able to see the bishop past his sister. "There was a kid bothering Pep, calling her names, really nasty things. Um . . ."

He hesitated, and the bishop nodded encouragingly. "Sexual things, you know? In junior high at St. Anne's, everybody made sex jokes. Pep was really religious, even then, and she hated that kind of thing. And this guy just wouldn't quit, till that one day when his lunch . . . sort of . . ." He shrugged. "It was on the table in the cafeteria, and it just decayed. All at once. Sandwich, fruit, everything. Turned to garbage."

Flicka said indignantly, "And they expelled Pep! And did nothing to that boy!"

"And after that?"

Flicka looked resigned. "We transferred to the public school. We were thirteen. . . ."

Thirteen, Elizabeth Mary thought. Puberty, adolescence. Such a difficult time for a young, developing girl with a devout mother and an angry father.

Flicka went on speaking. "Things were worse there, really. It was hard for me to keep an eye on Pep all the time, and Dad was furious with her, kept yelling at her at home, and then Mom would cry and get on her knees again. And then more little things would happen, especially at . . ." She was embarrassed, too, and looked down as she finished, ". . . at certain times of the month."

Elizabeth Mary also looked down in shame. She had not told Mother Superior, or the bishop, but even here at Santa Fina, Sister Perpetua's "little things" had usually happened at the times of her menses.

"Finally, the public school asked us to leave, too," Flicka finished.

"Asked Pep, you mean," said James. His sister lifted her shoulders as if to say, It's all the same. James added, "But it was never like this." Elizabeth Mary saw Flicka glance sharply at him.

"What is it, Flicka?" she asked, but the girl only shook her head.

The bishop pressed his fingers together in a tight steeple. "Nothing like this has been happening since she came to Santa Fina?"

"No," Elizabeth Mary said. "At least nothing important, and not for some time. Not until . . ." She broke off. Her eyes turned involuntarily to the swell of Flicka's abdomen.

"Not until now," the bishop finished for her, not noticing the diversion of her glance. "Well, if she can't stay here, and she can't go home, what is she to do?"

"But she can stay here," Elizabeth Mary began. "If she makes her Holy Communion privately . . ."

"She can come with me," Flicka said.

Elizabeth Mary held her breath, feeling the chasm opening once again around the image of Perpetua at home with her twin. She fought against the red darkness, gripping her cross, and she prayed for wisdom for the bishop, for charity, for help.

"I think perhaps that's the best suggestion," Bishop Damato was saying to Flicka. Elizabeth Mary swayed in her chair, suddenly faint. The chasm became a dark gulf, a sea of blood, and she teetered helplessly on its edge. Only her will kept her sitting upright, kept her from falling. It seemed many moments before she was aware of the room around her again, and then it was like coming awake from a dreadful dream. By that time, Sister Catherine had gone to tell Mother Superior to speak to Perpetua, and the bishop and James and Flicka were talking to each other in the church. Sister Elizabeth Mary made hurried goodbyes and walked as fast as any nun would dare to the image of the Blessed Virgin in the chapel, falling on her knees and praying long and fervently for the safety of Perpetua and Felicity . . . and Felicity's unborn baby.

Two weeks passed in the cloister in apparent calm and routine, but not since her novitiate had Sister Elizabeth Mary been so concerned about what was happening outside the walls of Santa Fina. She went about her duties as if in perfect acceptance of the bishop's ruling, and only she knew how much time she spent in prayer for Perpetua and her family. During recreation the other novices asked about Sister Perpetua with fearful eyes, and Elizabeth Mary had to simply say that it had been decided Perpetua would be better off at home. She worded her explanation carefully so as not to lie to her novices; she would surely have to confess a sin of omission if she implied that she agreed with the decision.

She was overseeing the weeding of the garden by her novices when Mother Superior's secretary came looking for her. The

August sun blazed into the walled compound, and the sisters' habits were tucked up around them, their sleeves rolled and their veils pinned back. As calmly as she could, Sister Elizabeth Mary let down the skirt of her habit and pushed her sleeves down to her wrists, but her hands were shaking. Sister Therese, the secretary, was frankly in a panic, and the novices stood open-mouthed as she gave her message.

"It's Sister Perpetua," she said in a loud whisper that the novices could hardly have missed. "Her sister and her brother... they want you to come, Sister, and Mother is going to send you! Out of the convent!" This last was whispered in shock. "Sister Catherine will go with you... will you?"

Elizabeth Mary nodded, and turned to her charges. "Sisters, please finish this job, will you?" They were speechless around her, and she smiled as reassuringly as she could. "And you could pray for Sister Perpetua, and for me."

There was little time to prepare. It felt to Elizabeth Mary as if she were being dragged bodily from the haven of the convent, even though she actually had some moments to talk with Mother Superior, to receive some instructions, and to gather a hand-kerchief, sunglasses, and her missal. But there was no time for reflection or to gather her strength for the shock of going outside.

The sun made the white pavement brutally hot under her leather sandals as she moved down the steps of the church to the waiting van. Although she bowed her head as the Rule required, to shut out the world with the drape of her veil, Elizabeth could not help looking around her. It had been so long since she had seen any of it, and to her dazzled eyes it was an alien landscape. Ivy grew green and shiny against the outer walls of the compound. She had never known that. The parking lot of the church was bigger than she remembered, and the cars were smaller and sleeker, surprising her even though she occasionally saw some on television. There were still homes around the convent, modest one- and two-story houses with lawns and trees and more cars.

The ride in the van was as exhilarating as a rocket trip to Elizabeth Mary, and she was amazed at Sister Catherine's ability to drive in the rush of freeway traffic. She also saw the need for the extern's modified habit; the full coif and veil would have obstructed her vision. By the time they found the address of Flicka and Timothy's apartment, Elizabeth Mary felt over-stimulated and exhausted at the same time. When they climbed the stairs of the apartment house, she bowed her head again, and this time really did shut out the world in order to gather her strength.

It was James, Perpetua's brother, who let the sisters into the tiny apartment. Their home was essentially one large room, with a kitchen to one side, and a door in the rear that looked as if it must lead to a bedroom. Perpetua, in jeans and a T-shirt borrowed from Flicka, sat on a straight chair by the kitchen table, as still as one of the icons of the church. Her hair, which would soon have been cut short when she made her final vows, drooped in disarray, and her eyes were glazed and distant. Elizabeth Mary saw that she held her missal in her fingers, and that it was stained and reddened as if the leather cover had rusted. Her feet were bare and dried blood marked them and the floor beneath them. Flicka lay nearby on a tattered couch, pale and exhausted, the swell of her abdomen looking too large for her slender body.

"Please help us, Sister," James whispered. Flicka only looked up at them from eyes that were both frightened and sad, and Elizabeth Mary went to her and bent down.

"What's happening, Flicka? Are you all right?" But it was as she had feared. Beneath the girl were several towels, tucked between her body and the back of the couch, and they were liberally stained with blood.

"She won't call the doctor," James said, still whispering. "She's afraid they'll put her in the hospital, and she says she can't leave Perpetua."

"You don't need to whisper," Flicka said harshly. "Pep won't hear you."

Elizabeth looked back at Perpetua and saw that, indeed, her eyes looked on some faraway place, far beyond their own world.

"How long has she been this way?" she asked.

James answered. "Since last night. Since . . . well, see, Pep was really begging for Holy Communion, and we thought . . . it seemed so mean. She's always been the most devout one in the whole family, even more than Mom, and we knew that the church sent communion out to shut-ins, so we called them. They sent a Eucharistic minister. But when she gave Pep the wafer . . ." James faltered.

Flicka spoke up firmly. "There was blood, Sister. On Pep's lips. At least that's what it looked like."

Elizabeth Mary sucked in her breath sharply.

Sister Catherine gasped, "From the wafer?"

James managed a weak smile. "The Eucharistic minister almost fainted. I grabbed a napkin and wiped it away, and we sort of pretended it was something else, but of course they've heard all those rumors." He grew serious again, his youthful face drawn into lines of worry. "But Pep's been sitting like that ever since. All night. She started to bleed sometime in the night, and then . . . so did Flicka, only a lot worse. I've never seen anything so awful," he ended weakly.

Flicka held up her hand. "It's nothing," she said. "It's happened before with Pep. I can take care of her." But her words were choked off by a little grunt of pain, and she pressed her hands to her stomach.

Elizabeth Mary went to her and pulled away her skirt. Fresh blood soaked the towels beneath her. She tried to rearrange them. "What's happened before, Flicka?"

Flicka's eyes closed. Softly, she said, "We used to argue a lot about the sacrament, about . . . about the transubstantiation." She pressed her shaking hand to her lips. "I always said there was no such thing, it was just symbolic, but Pep . . . to Pep it was real, really the body and the blood. It was—"

Elizabeth Mary knelt beside her. She said, "You must go to the hospital."

49

"No, listen . . . ," Flicka said. "The transubstantiation . . . the changing of the wafer and the wine. I shouldn't have argued with her, I should have let it be!"

"Now, Flicka, that's an old, old argument. Why shouldn't you have discussed it with your sister?"

Flicka opened her eyes and she gripped Elizabeth's hand. "I'm so sorry, Sister, but this happened before, years ago. I don't know why the priest didn't know, but Pep . . . she changed the wine, right before I drank it. I should have told you . . . I shouldn't have argued with her. . . ." Her voice trailed away and her face blanched white.

"James, call an ambulance," Elizabeth Mary said firmly.

Flicka shook her head, but there was no resisting Sister Elizabeth Mary, mistress of novices.

"James," she said again, "make the call now. And call Timothy . . . where is he?"

"He freaked," James said bluntly. "He's not Catholic, you know, and he already thought the communion thing was a little weird. Then he saw that blood. . . . That's what happened at Santa Fina, wasn't it, Sister? Pep had blood on her mouth?"

Elizabeth looked at James and the suffering Flicka and shook her head. "It wasn't just that, James," she said in a low tone. The memory still chilled her heart under the heavy folds of her habit.

"At Santa Fina," she said slowly, "the sisters were having Mass in the visiting room of the church, and quite a few visitors were in the church itself. After Perpetua drank from the - chalice . . ." She shuddered, remembering the uproar, the violation. It had been a nightmare, and it had shaken the community to its very foundations.

"There was blood in the cup," she whispered. "The sacristan swore he put wine in it, of course, but it was blood then, or something very like it, and some of the other novices drank from it. They became hysterical." She didn't say that one of the novices had vomited in a corner, or that one of the elderly sisters, seeing the blood on their lips, had fainted dead away and fallen to the floor with her habit rucked up around her. She said only, "The people in the church saw what happened, and that's how the rumors got started."

James turned as white as his sister, and he sat down weakly at the end of the couch by Flicka's bare feet. "So it was true," he said. "I heard it at school. ... There's this group that loves vampire stories; they pretend they are vampires, for God's sake ... but I didn't really believe it." He looked at Flicka, whose eyes were tightly shut. "Sister ... do you think it's really ... really the blood of ... ?"

He couldn't even finish the thought, could not bring himself to speak it aloud.

Elizabeth Mary sighed. "That's a question I'm not qualified to answer."

"Why do you think these things keep happening in our family?" James cried out.

Elizabeth Mary frowned, looking up at him. "What do you mean, James?"

"I mean Mom, too. . . . . She left the convent in disgrace because she was pregnant!" His voice grew shrill and broke like an adolescent's. "Can you imagine? A pregnant novice? They threw her out, and Dad had to marry her, and she never forgave him!"

"They never forgave each other," Flicka stated.

Elizabeth Mary nodded, briskly now. "I'm quite sure your mother was not the first pregnant novice in the world! Now, you must call the ambulance, James, quickly. Sister Catherine and I will take care of Perpetua. And don't worry," she added, with a confidence that was completely feigned.

James went to the phone and dialed, and Elizabeth Mary and Catherine approached Perpetua where she sat pale and unmoving. "Sister Perpetua," Elizabeth called gently. "It's Sister Elizabeth Mary, and Sister Catherine. We need you to come with us now. Can you come with us?" She touched Perpetua's shoulder, and the girl pulled away, ever so slightly. Elizabeth Mary gripped her shoulder and shook her gently, and Perpetua drew a shuddering breath and closed her eyes.

"His blood was shed for me," she muttered. "His body was given up . . ." Her eyes flew open. "I have to go back," she said in a harsh tone. She reached up her blood-stained hand to touch Elizabeth Mary's habit and the wooden cross that swung outward. Perpetua grasped the cross and held on as if for her life. "Will you take me back now? Back to the convent? I have to pray," she said. Tears started from her eyes.

Elizabeth Mary felt the darkness threatening to engulf her again in its bloody shadows. She could hardly pray herself, for strength, for wisdom. "Why, Perpetua?" she heard herself ask. "Why do you have to pray?"

The girl's eyes fastened on her face. "We're supposed to pray," she said, and she sobbed as she quoted, " 'Let it become for us the body and the blood . . .' " She paused, and then, after a moment, " 'For they have shed the blood of saints and prophets, and thou hast given them blood to drink; for they are worthy. . . .' I'm not worthy . . . everyone knows that; I have to pray to be worthy." She spoke faster and faster and her voice dropped until it was almost inaudible. Elizabeth Mary breathed deeply and put her hand firmly over Perpetua's, feeling the crumbs of dried blood against her own palm.

"All right, Sister," she said. Sister Catherine helped her lift Perpetua to her feet.

"Will you take me back?" Perpetua breathed. "I have to go back to the convent. I have to pray to be worthy." The ambulance siren sounded from below, louder and louder as it grew closer to the apartment building. Flicka cried out with pain and James hurried downstairs to meet the ambulance.

Perpetua was whispering frantically now, so fast Elizabeth Mary could hardly understand her. "You have to pray, too, Sister, pray for me. I'm 'the woman drunken with the blood of the saints, and with the blood of the martyrs of Jesus.' I'm sorry, I'm so sorry, but I can't help it. It's the body, and the blood, that will make me clean. His blood, shed for me. His body, His blood. . . ."

The spate of words subsided into a moan as Elizabeth Mary

pulled her to her feet. James opened the door and two uniformed men with a stretcher crowded into the apartment, bending quickly over Flicka.

Elizabeth Mary, with an inner promise to confess later, answered Perpetua.

"Yes, Sister. I'll take you back. We'll pray together. We'll go home."

Elizabeth Mary moved slowly as she prepared to leave the cloister for the last time. She had already taken leave of her novices, who would have a new mistress from the mother house the very next day, and of the sisters with whom she had shared everything for eighteen years. She made a final visit to the much-beloved chapel, bowing her head before the statue of the Blessed Mother which had heard her countless prayers. She walked through the garden, browning now in the early autumn sun, remembering how it had renewed her spirit as it was reborn each spring. Finally she took her small possessions from the little cell where she had lain every night contemplating the mysteries of her faith.

It was very strange to put off her long brown habit in exchange for a shorter one like Sister Catherine's. Her hair, short and growing gray, looked stubby and awkward, and she wished the veil were longer. She felt half-dressed, exposed, but of course it would not do to wear the full habit of a cloistered sister when she was to live and work in the world. She felt she was moving in a dream, a trance like those that dominated Perpetua's life, but she welcomed its numbness. She was afraid if she woke she would not have the strength to do what must be done.

Mother Superior embraced her, and they prayed together for a few moments. When Elizabeth Mary stepped out of the church, she kept her head up. The short veil shut out nothing. Sister Catherine and Perpetua were already waiting in the van.

Elizabeth Mary looked back only once at the modest church and the convent walls which had enclosed and embraced her during her contemplative life. Then she turned her gaze onto the world.

She climbed into the front seat beside Sister Catherine. Her meager possessions, and those of Perpetua, were already loaded in the back. Elizabeth Mary looked out at the traffic and the shops and the billboard signs that advertised things she had had no need of for years.

"Are you all right?" Sister Catherine asked her in a low tone.

Elizabeth Mary looked back at Perpetua, who sat with her head bowed, her loose brown curls falling forward to veil her face. The girl had said not a word since the news of her sister's miscarriage had come three weeks before.

"I will be, with God's help," Elizabeth Mary answered honestly. "Just now I feel like my life is over."

Sister Catherine reached out to touch her hand. "It's not so bad, you know," she said. "Being an active sister has its compensations."

Elizabeth Mary only nodded. She felt frozen, immobilized by sorrow. This was her duty, her own small martyrdom, and she only hoped she would come to understand it one day.

Suddenly Perpetua spoke from behind them. "Sister Elizabeth Mary? Where are we going? Am I going to see Flicka?"

"No, Perpetua," Elizabeth Mary said quietly, and she marveled at the calm reassurance in her own voice. "We're going to our new apartment, you and I together. Our new home."

Flicka had sustained so many losses. Her baby was gone, her young husband fled, her family torn apart. Possibly, Elizabeth Mary thought, she would visit them eventually. Meanwhile there was no one else to care for Perpetua, the lost novice. There was no one but Elizabeth Mary.

Perpetua spoke again. "Aren't we going back, then?" Elizabeth Mary turned and saw that the girl's eyes were clear, her gaze direct. She looked as if she had just awoken.

"No, we're not," Elizabeth Mary answered her.

"You mean, not ever?" Perpetua pushed back her hair and looked out the windows of the van. "Not ever going back to Santa Fina?"

Elizabeth Mary's throat closed with the grief of it, and she could only shake her head. Perpetua put out her hand to touch her shoulder.

"It's my fault, isn't it, Sister?"

Elizabeth Mary put her hand over Perpetua's. "I think it's time to stop worrying about faults," she said faintly. "We must make a new life for ourselves." Her voice grew stronger. "We will be a community, just us."

"I'm sorry," Perpetua said sadly. "I'm so sorry, Sister. I hope you will forgive me."

Elizabeth Mary managed a smile. "Forgiveness is the greatest grace of all."

Perpetua shook her head, and tears welled. She began to speak, but then her face came suddenly alight. "Flicka!" she cried.

"What?"

The door on the other side of the van opened, and Elizabeth Mary saw Flicka's smiling face there, her brown curls and bright brown eyes so like her twin's.

"Hello, Sisters," she said. She had a heavy suitcase with her, and she heaved it up into the van and then climbed in herself.

"Flicka! Are you coming with us?" Perpetua asked, her face brilliant with hope.

"If you'll have me. . . ." Flicka looked at Elizabeth Mary. "Sister? I'm a good cook, and I can run errands for you, whatever you need."

"Flicka, you are grace itself," Elizabeth Mary said fervently. "We will be forever grateful for your company."

Sister Catherine was grinning enormously beneath her short coif. "Surprise!" she said softly.

"Oh, yes," said Sister Elizabeth Mary. "Oh, yes." She bowed

her head for a moment, overcome with emotion. Thank you, Blessed Mother, she prayed over and over. Thank you, Santa Fina.

After a moment she lifted her head and looked back at her two charges, her new community. "I think we can go home now," she said.

Louise Marley: "Body and Blood" is a story about the power of faith. It fascinates me to know that in the late twentieth century, the religious orders attracting the most postulants are the strict ones, the cloistered convents, the monasteries where poverty and silence are the rules. As a Catholic convert myself, I find myself intrigued by the women whose faith calls them to a life shut away from the rest of the world. I am most impressed, when I have the opportunity to speak with them (or sing with them, as sometimes happens), with their sincerity, their peace, and their joy in a life many of us would find utterly alien. My story is about sacrifice and love, obsession and the search for peace, and especially about the incredible mystical power of conviction.

Not in Front of the Virgin

Mary Woodbury

STRANGE SHAPES APPEARED in Wally Jarman's room in late January. His wife Vera was away in Phoenix helping her sister move, so she missed most of the excitement, even though it had really been her that initiated the whole thing by saying "Fix the back bedroom while I'm gone, Wally."

He peeled off the Star Trek wallpaper, replastered the holes from Danny's darts and posters, sanded and washed the whole room until both he and the room were sweaty.

Wally talked out loud to keep himself company.

"So, you're getting a room of your own, after all these years of bunking with others—should be a new adventure—your brother snored, your Navy buddies smelled bad, your first wife Madge tossed and turned like a whirling dervish, and big Vera, well..." Wally blushed, thinking of all the times they had made love over the years, riding, riding, "...that was before you developed your little problem."

Wally pried the lid off the Sears one-coat latex, stirred it and started painting. The roller made it easy.

"The sex therapist on *Donahue* said good sex can last a lifetime. If you don't use it you'll lose it.

"No sense in getting mad, old man. Just because you're not cock of the walk." He startled whistling, "*Ah, sweet mystery of life, at last I've found you. At last I know the secret of it all.* Sure, sure, the secret is there is no secret."

Wally painted the outside north wall, the dark one with no windows; he painted that last because it seemed a little damp.

"Poorly insulated. They don't make walls solid like they used to. Remember when you were a young lather, Wally. The other guys envied you—you had fast hands. You could tie the metal lath so fast, boss didn't like you, it didn't look good having one guy faster than the others. 'Slow down, Wally, you don't want to out-shine the rest.' Not like Walt Disney, he admired your work, stood staring up at you making that complicated ceiling in Disneyland." Wally blushed remembering the great man, tanned, white sweater, creased pants. "He didn't know your name was Wally, too, or that you'd wanted to be an artist.

"Your brother said you never reached your real potential. So did Madge the magnificent. You've been a real disappointment."

Wally stowed the tarps, the cleaned brush and roller in his caretaker's closet. He banged the door shut, listening to its echo down the empty corridors of the apartment complex. He shivered.

Next, Wally hauled furniture, stored in the basement, that he and Vera had collected for his room—a brown tweed hide-a-bed, and a maple chest of drawers they had found at a garage sale. The small color TV with remote control was a gift from one of the condo owners at Pine Meadows where he was night security.

He lit a Camel, turned on the TV, adjusting the picture carefully. Colors sharp and clear. Good color, like good sex, takes effort, he guessed.

Wally sat there, on the nearly new couch, a plate of cheese and bread, a glass of Royal Crown cola, the new remote control on the TV table, close to hand.

"Kinda magic the way this little box can control the whole screen." Wally shook his head. "I don't understand how they do it without wires, do you?" Lifting his eyes as if to talk to the room, or the other self he sometimes felt around the corners of his life, a self he glimpsed out of his left eye. That's when he spotted the dark shapes on the far wall.

"You're going to have to give that wall another coat, Wally. You sanded it, too." He smoothed prickly hairs on the back of his neck with his rough hand.

"Forget the damn shadows, Wally. Go to work." He sprung to his feet, nearly knocking over the TV table. He straightened everything and carried the dishes to the sink. He brought his uniforms from the double closet in the big bedroom and hung them in the freshly painted closet in his new room—the tan school-bus driver, the gray security guard, the green caretaker's overalls, and his navy blue blazer with the Navy crest for weddings and funerals.

"What a closetful of disguises. No one has ever seen the real Wally Jarman—he's incognito." He laid the school-bus-driver outfit on the couch before throwing his dirty paint pants and shirt into the clothes hamper and turning on the shower.

"If Vera could only see you now." Wally scrubbed the paint flecks off his stubbly face. Standing there, letting the hot water sluice him off, Wally got a hard-on. He grinned and started whistling "*Ah sweet mystery . . .*" again.

"Not like when you were touring Europe after the war, the dashing young sailor in bell-bottom trousers. Hey, Wally, what a guy! Chasing girls, chasing dreams, glad as hell to be alive, glad as hell the guns had stopped thundering over your head."

The water turned cold. Wally's skin shriveled, goosebumped. He wrapped a bath sheet around him. Trouble with being alone, you think too much. He pulled on his uniform.

"So, you toured cathedrals and art galleries while the guys laughed, you even sketched the David, copied Leonardo's roughs, visited Bernini's fountains in Rome, and best of all, you spent one whole afternoon in front of the Pieta in St. Peter's Basilica in the Vatican—dreaming of being an artist, feverish, scared of what . . ." Wally buttoned his jacket all the way to the top, pressed down the lapels, caressing the safe shiny fabric with scarred journeyman's hands. Maybe he should phone Vera, tell her to come home. Talking to yourself could mean trouble.

Mila from 202 hailed him from her balcony. "Hey, Wally. I want to see you."

Wally revved the motor of his used Lincoln Continental and sped away.

The bus smelled of stale oranges, rubber boots and kidsweat.

"He tore my picture, Mr. Jarman," a little blonde whimpered beside him.

"You aren't supposed to be out of your seat," Wally yelled.

The kid kept crying.

"It fell on the floor," a red-faced kid in a torn leather jacket sneered.

"He stepped on my horsie."

"It looked like a sick dog to me."

"Okay, you two, stop the fighting." The light turned red. "Here, let me see." He turned in his seat. There was a bootprint on the horse's mane and its tail was ripped off.

"That's a good horse; maybe you can fix it. I used to be an artist." Wally clamped his mouth shut and glared at the bully. "Pick on someone your own size," he shouted. The whole bus hushed for ten seconds in surprise. Wally gripped the wheel tightly, focused on the road ahead till his eyes hurt. He held his back stiff until the last kid stepped off the bus.

The first thing Wally did when he got home was flip on the over-head light, hit the remote control so the TV blared, and peer at the wall. His throat dried, the palms of his hands sweated, his fingers twitched. The dark shadows, foggy like distant mountains earlier, had taken on definition, become the outline of two figures, one a seated woman with a shawl, the other a man stretched awkwardly across her lap.

Wally backed into the kitchen, grabbed a Royal Crown cola and lit a Camel. His eyes didn't blink or swivel, they remained focused on the wall, a painting of a marble statue emerging as real and familiar as a roadside cairn.

"If this is some kind of message"—Wally looked through the ceiling to where he had always positioned God—"I don't get it. It's like something out of *Unsolved Mysteries*. Though how those folk ever come forward with their stories I don't know. Must be done by actors. Real folks would get scared."

He gulped—could feel both sides of his head, behind his ears, tingling, could feel a shiver gathering and running down his spine. He recognized the picture. The Pieta, just like the one in St. Peter's, here in his bedroom, on his wall, reminding him of . . . Wally lifted his right hand, scarred by metal lath, stained by nicotine, one black nail from a forgotten accident, the back splattered with freckles, thick veins and knobby knuckles. He traced the outline of the woman's head, the line of her cloak. For an instant blood flowed in the opposite direction, up his arm like hot wind blowing a rushing river upstream. His fingers scalded. He dropped his hand to his side quickly, rubbing it fiercely on his trousers. His whole body quivered.

The next morning the doorbell woke him with its angry peal. Wally unfolded painfully. He'd fallen asleep staring at his bedroom wall, at his own private Pieta. The buzzer rang again.

"Wait! I'm pulling on my pants."

Mila from 202 stood in the doorway. "You've been avoiding me, Wally." Her hands were on her hips. One of her false eyelashes was squewgy. Wally's hand trembled, aching to straighten it.

"Sorry, Mila. Been busy." Wally stepped into the cool corridor, blocking the doorway.

"My faucet's leaking and you're the guy with the tool to fix it." She waggled her head and giggled.

"I'll be up."

"When's Vera coming home?"

"Don't know."

"Who's taking care of you? Swore I've heard you talking to someone in there." She turned and headed up the stairs, her compact cheeks tumbling together under the red polyester slacks. Wally wet his lips.

He shut the door, locked it and went to shave.

"You're a poor old sod, you are," he laughed into the mirror. "Used to have a body like a daytime soap-opera star, now you look older than a grandpa, and you've a bone. It would be funny, if it weren't so sad. I wish Vera were here."

Upstairs, he tightened the bolts and left Mila's body alone.

"Would you like to stay for coffee, a little lunch? You probably aren't eating right." Mila patted his arm as he backed out the door.

Wally escaped to his apartment where he switched on the TV, flipping channels until he came to a *M*A*S*H* rerun, the episode where Frank Burns falls into the newly dug latrine. He laughed at Frank until tears rolled down his face. Didn't the jerk know how ridiculous, how absurd he looked? Wally sighed, mopped his face with the last of the neatly ironed and folded handkerchiefs Vera had left him.

The doorbell rang. It was Mila. "I made some blueberry muffins." She stuck out her skinny arm with a plateful.

"Thanks." Wally moved to close the door.

"Can you eat them all?" She fixed her eyelash. "I don't bite—often."

"Place's a mess. I'm paintin'."

"Vera hoped you would. Keep your hands busy, eh?"

Wally plunked two cups of coffee down, sat opposite her, leaned his chair back against the kitchen wall.

"Aren't you going to show me?" Mila nodded in the direction of the back room.

Damn! What to do? "Someone might tell Vera you were here." His chair bounced down onto the tile floor.

"Like poor crippled Mrs. Hope in #204. I just want to admire your handiwork." Mila's eyes blinked in innocent schoolgirl fashion.

God, woman, leave me alone. "I have to give it another coat."

Mila strode through the apartment, sashayed into his room.

"What are you ashamed of, Wally?"

Maybe the Pieta had faded, maybe he was the only one who could see it.

"What's with the muriel?"

"The what?" Walter joined her standing in front of the Pieta.

"My sister has a muriel of trees, but it's in color. You got gypped; it's all shades of black and gray." Mila reached out and touched the wall. "This ain't no muriel, Wally, you done this by yourself. You've painted a goddamn religious picture on your bedroom wall."

Wally stood with his mouth open, his hands waving help-lessly in the air. Mila was poking through the closet. "Wally, where are your artist's supplies?"

Please, God. Take her away, give me back last night when I was sitting alone, smoking and staring and being alone with it.

The woman stood too close to him, invading the inches near his skin. "What's the story, Wally?"

Wally backed away, closer to his wall, closer to the Pieta. "Lay off, Mila. I haven't painted anything in years. I don't have any supplies. When Vera comes home, we'll figure out what to do about this, okay?" Wally steered Mila through the door, down the hall and out.

"I need my plate." She rushed past him to pick it up off the kitchen table. "I don't think you should hide your light under a bushel, Wally."

Wally closed the door, heard the lock click. She was still talking.

"If you didn't paint it, how did it get there? *Unsolved Mysteries* would pay plenty, wouldn't they?"

Wally wrapped the last two muffins in several layers of plastic wrap and hid them in the breadbox. He'd eat them later when he was alone, when his whole insides weren't in turmoil.

As he wheeled back into the parking lot later that day, with fixings for a good meal of chili con carne and salad sitting beside him on the seat, the skin on the back of his neck prickled again. The CFRN-TV van was in the visitor's parking spot. The parish priest's car was parked in the lane. Mila waved from her balcony, some guy in a fancy red blazer standing beside her, smiling down at him like some kinda angel, or a discount furniture salesclerk.

"There's Wally Jarman, the caretaker," she pointed out. "This is Ted. Sister Bridget is here from the parish. Old Mrs. Hope has had her arthritis cured. . . ." Mila babbled on.

Wally's stomach churned.

A cameraman rolled film. Ted asked, "Could you tell us where you took your art training?"

"Look, I didn't touch the g.d. wall." Wally pushed past the guy.

"Are you saying this painting just appeared on the wall? That's what the ladies claim." Ted shoved a microphone in Wally's face.

Wally glared up at Mila. Mrs. Hope, standing beside Mila, smiled and waved her cane. "It's a miracle!"

Wally pushed the reporter aside and opened his apartment door. He leaned against it, catching his breath, listening to the people's gabbing on the other side. He locked the door. The phone rang.

"Wally?" It was Vera. "What's this about a religious painting on our wall? Mila called."

The sound of her voice filled Wally with warmth and something akin to courage. He cradled the phone in both hands as if it were a precious gift.

"Wally?"

"Come on home, eh," he said. I miss you. I miss you. I need you. "I'll make chili on toast for breakfast," he said into the phone.

The crowd at the door was clamoring. Wally let them in.

He watched as they took footage of his wall. He answered questions politely, with a funny calm growing in his gut.

Mrs. Hope ate blueberry muffins and drank tea. "I had been feeling emanations from Mr. Jarman's apartment for some time. When Mila told me about the Virgin on the wall, I knew. It's a miracle!"

"What do you say, Wally?" Sister Bridget sat taking notes. She and Vera always organized the Spring and Fall Bazaar and Rummage Sale.

Wally lifted his hands, opened them, and stared at Bridget and the cluster of media people, Mila, and Mrs. Hope.

"It's a mystery to me." He moved to the kitchen cupboard, took down a can and measured coffee into the filter carefully, counting tablespoons. "Don't ask too much," he whispered, and began whistling through his teeth.

"*Ah, sweet mystery of life . . .*"

They ran a two-minute segment on the ten o'clock news. The guy in the red blazer interviewed Mila and Mrs. Hope, showed the wall and Wally frowning, his hands pushing away the camera. "Mr. Jarman was reluctant to talk. Hopefully, tomorrow, CFRN can bring you more details. After the case of the tree stump with the Virgin on it in Sudbury, and the false claims from Kelowna of blood dripping from the wall, the latest phenomenon will be of interest to both the media and religious authorities. In other news . . ."

Wally rubbed his hands together, wiped them on his trousers, walked over to his Pieta. He stood sighing in front of it.

The phone rang. His son Danny called to say he and Elaine would be over tomorrow to see their famous father and his mystery painting.

"Don't bust your ass." Wally smirked into the receiver.

His boss from Pine Meadows called. "Are you coming in Monday or have you decided to be a religious nut?"

The *Sun* reporter knocked at eleven p.m. wanting pictures, popping flashes. Wally put a firm hand on the young jerk's arm. "Can I buy one of those photos?"

"Hey, mister, you've got the real thing."

"The real thing, eh?" Wally laughed. "The real thing is in Rome, in the Vatican, behind protective glass, because some idiot wanted to destroy it."

After the kid left Wally pulled the plug on the phone and turned off the lights, stretched out in front of the TV and the Pieta, letting the smoke from his cigarette make a fog between him and the image on the wall. The Pieta shimmered like a reflection in a deep pool. He lay watching until the cigarette scorched his fingers.

The radio alarm woke him. Wally pulled on his jeans and went for Vera. The big woman clambered off the bus and filled his arm, felt the bone in his jeans press into her warm flesh. "What's all this, Wally?" They got in the car.

Wally sighed and reached across to pat his wide woman's thigh. Heat from the trip, or heat from the robin's-egg-blue pant leg, aroused him. The edge of his sadness crumpled.

The traffic stalled in front of the building. Cars circled the block slowly. People on foot patrolled the sidewalks, peering in windows. Vera and Wally slipped in the delivery entrance. They giggled like two school kids escaping detention.

Vera snagged one look at the Pieta and went for a shower. Wally put on the chili to warm and opened two TV tables, set them up in his back room.

Vera joined him, wearing a flowered silk housecoat she had found in a garage sale on the ritzy side of town.

"How'd it get started?" She ate quickly. Her warm body, steaming from the shower, moved against him. Wally slipped his hand through the open throat of the housecoat past the silk roses to a large breast.

"Hungry?" Her eyes sparkled. "Hope springs eternal."

"That's not all that springs."

Vera finished the last bite of chili. "Pretty hot stuff," she said. Wally pushed her down onto the couch playfully.

"Not here, Wally," Vera said. "Not in front of the Virgin." She waved her hand at the Pieta on the wall. "It makes me uncomfortable."

He led her into their old bedroom, tossed her open suitcase on the floor.

"You old rogue," she laughed. "I saw the same *Donahue* show you did." Leaning over the side of the bed she reached in her suitcase and brought out a tube of KY gel. "Remember to go slow."

"That's my new motto. Take it easy. Don't worry, Vera, I know who I am."

It took two attempts, but they both reached a climax. Rockets exploding couldn't have caused any more furor. They sat up in bed, sweaty, sheets pulled over their nakedness. Wally lit a cigarette.

"What are we going to do?"

"I'm a private person." Vera drew the sheet up to her throat. "Neither one of us is real social."

"Danny would want us to charge. Make big bucks."

The doorbell buzzed. The phone rang. "It's going to start again," Wally grunted.

"Send them away for a couple of hours. Tell them your wife needs sleep, the Virgin needs a rest . . . something." She opened the storage closet and started rummaging around.

"Have Jesus' hands started bleeding yet?" Mrs. Hope's voice would crack eggs, it sounded so pious. Wally grinned, humming his favorite tune.

"Did you study art long?" the reporter was asking. "According to your first wife, you had talent but feared success. Is that right?"

"Father O'Neill wants you to talk to the Committee on Folk Religion when you are ready." Bridget's voice was quiet.

"Where's Vera? Didn't she come home?" Mila pushed her way through the crowd. "Have you made a statement, Wally?" The woman with her layers of makeup covering her sagging face walked right up to Wally and stared into his pale blue eyes, looked down at his workman's hands. "Are you trying to cover something up?"

"Dad, when do we get to see the Pieta?" Danny poked his wife Elaine. Wally wiped his sticky, sweating palms down his coveralls.

"You'll have to go to Rome, I guess. Like I did. I'm no bloody Michelangelo."

Vera came out of the back room, washing her hands on a wet rag.

"What about the wall, Mom?" Danny shouted.

"Aren't you going to kiss your mother hello? I've been away." Vera ignored the crowd and crossed to her son. The others stood as the mother and son embraced. Wally and Elaine, feeling sheepish, joined in the family hug.

Mila mumbled greetings. Bridget offered her hand. The reporter and the cameraman stood awkwardly. Mrs. Hope beamed from her couch corner. "We're waiting to see the Virgin."

Wally and Vera glanced at each other. He nodded to her.

"Well, it faded overnight, made the wall look a mess. So we wallpapered this morning." She folded her arms firmly in front of her, planted her sturdy feet wide.

Mila and the reporter stormed past her.

"Where'd you get the wallpaper, Vera? It's nine o'clock in the morning," Bridget asked.

"At the parish rummage sale last year, Sister. Knew it would come in handy." Vera wandered into the back room.

It was good wallpaper, expensive, white nubby embossed with brown leaves and tan ferns. "Only took three double rolls." Vera smiled. "Makes a nice rec room, don't you think?" She crossed the floor and closed the door to the master bedroom so folks wouldn't see the cast-off clothing, the rumpled sheets.

Wally shepherded the spectators out. Complaints echoed down the corridor. "It's not fair," whined Mila. "If it had been me . . ."

"But it wasn't, was it?" sighed Mrs. Hope.

"Why, Dad?" Danny sipped coffee in the kitchen, the family sitting around the table smoking, listening to the clock tick on the stove.

"If you don't know, you don't know your old dad very well." Wally nursed a mug in his scarred hands, his eyes fixed on the back bedroom door.

"It's still under there?" Danny persisted.

Vera passed around Hostess cupcakes with pink icing.

"Let's just say it's a mystery, eh?" Beside him Vera's warm thigh touched Wally's jean-clad leg. God, you dumb kids, when are you going to have enough sense to go home and leave us alone? He lit another Camel and waited.

Mary Woodbury: I have always been entranced by the reports in newspapers about pictures of the Madonna and Child or Jesus appearing on barn walls, in trees, etc. I have a collection of clippings. The different ways people relate to these folk visions is fascinating. What is it in human nature that sees things, builds a shrine, pays court, buys souvenirs, goes for cures? It is outside of the realm of organized religion, and yet there are hundreds of incidents of such "spiritual happenings."

I consider myself on a spiritual journey. However, I come from a society and family that consider such stuff as fiction and fancy to be cured by food or sleep. I decided to explore a "visitation" from the point of view of a skeptical, aging, working man. Discovering what his response would be to an unnatural phenomenon made the writing of this piece great fun. Is it speculative fiction or realistic fiction in a speculative mode?

On the Edge of Eternity

Steve Stanton

A SHARP STAB OF PAIN. A cramp behind the knee. Harlin grimaced as the knots began to form in his legs, tiny little tremors like insects under his skin. He twisted in his restraining suit and drummed his fingers on the control keyboard at his side. Overtime again, and no one to blame but himself.

He'd almost had his rock cradled when a stray had come on the radar—almost home green with the goods. Navicomp had indicated a collision course, so he'd had to break. No sense risking his neck for one lousy space rock. Chalk another one up to the fractional probability, the impossible coincidence of random mechanics. The stray had just grazed his target, knocking it into a new corkscrew trajectory. Harlin had chased it anyway, had synched and snagged it with some fancy maneuvering and a good deal more luck than he was accustomed to. Now he had to pay the price.

The biomeds considered it a psychophysical irregularity—the official title was free-fall stress syndrome, the result of fatigue and the waning hypersensitivity drugs—but the asteroid miners on the belt knew it simply as space cramps and accepted it as another of many occupational hazards. Harlin had seen some bad cases down on the docks—convulsing spider miners with contorted faces, blood crusting on their lips. But he had nothing to worry about, he reminded himself again. He was only a couple of hours over the limit, his rock was secure, his screen was green. Just a quick flight to Base and he could log in his shift. A good burn bath awaited him, and an ultrasonic massage to clear the Hyperstim out of his system, then a chance to relax in his bunk and watch the assay results on his overhead monitor. Good magnetics on this one. Some spots glittered like polished platinum when the sun hit them right. Cobalt, chromium, titanium—any one of these treasures would make the difference.

If he could just stretch out a bit, maybe brush away the sweaty brown curls on his forehead. If he could just scratch that infernal itch behind his left knee. Overtime again, with cramps on the way. Trapped in a bullet. A stripped-down, computerized tin can.

More like a coffin, Harlin mused.

Harlin flipped on his com unit and winced as the Base chatter flooded his tiny crypt.

"Spider Seven to Strategic Metals Control," he signaled.

The reply was immediate. "Harlin, you vac-head, where in space are you? I've had you on Overdue since I got up this morning."

"Okay, Control, don't panic. I'm right here on your radar screen. I should be visual in a minute or two. That you, Eddi?"

"I was just getting ready to shoot you down for a stray, you cowboy. You know you're supposed to keep com open. I'll have to log a memo now. My guns are already mobilized. I told you last time."

"C'mon, Eddi. I'm way outside the sphere. You know the background noise drives me crazy. I can't concentrate with the com on. Give me a private beam, and I'll keep you company all day."

"Don't make me quote regs, Spider Seven. Just don't cut it so close on your approach."

"Sorry," Harlin muttered wearily.

Eddi's voice came softer now, with a note of concern: "You sound a bit shaky. You sick?"

"Not bad. A bit tight. No memo this time?"

A sigh. "No memo, Harlin. You holding?"

"Yeah, just under max—good magnetics."

"That makes the cramps worthwhile, eh?"

"I hope so."

"Have you checked your chrono lately?"

"No."

"Does it help?"

"Not really."

Harlin's left leg began to tremble in its close-fitting plasti-foam sheath. He tried pressing upward and bending the knee a fraction, which seemed to ease some discomfort. His other leg had gone completely numb.

"You're clear on the Main, Spider Seven. I have visual confirmation now. You're glistening like a palladium pendant. Some guys have all the luck." Eddi laughed, a nasal guffaw that sounded like static over the com. The sparkle could be ice, he knew, but Eddi had been on Control long enough to know how to treat a shaky miner on his way in. Besides, it could be platinum or its more valuable cousin rhodium. Everybody on the shift got a bonus when a lucky rock came in.

Harlin Riley stood in the doorway to the lounge and concentrated for a moment on the press of the floor against his feet, the slight tension in his muscular legs. Eighty-five percent earth-g here on the outermost level of the huge spinning wheel. The comforts of home. He lifted up his right foot and felt the ground pull it back down. He planted both feet firmly. As sturdy as a rock. Immovable.

The community lounge swarmed with spacers—biomeds in white linen, comtechs in gray polyester, spider miners in sky-blue jumpsuits. Scattered naval personnel in characteristic black uniforms milled among the regular crowd, off-duty crew from a docked Space Navy freighter.

"Hey, Prophet!" a voice called out above the chattering drone.

Harlin winced at the name—a private irritation between him and fellow spider miner Jim Nichols.

"Hey, Prophet! Over here." Nichols waved a meaty arm in the air, his blond hair wild above his high Nordic forehead. Another colleague, Eric Apa, sat with him, along with two unfamiliar young men in sky blue. They must be fresh recruits, Harlin decided, and as he got closer, he noticed that they both sported bright green hair. He hoped it wasn't contagious.

Eric made the introductions, calling Harlin "an old pro." Eight years in space, thirty-six from the womb, now suddenly old.

Harlin shook the proffered hands, thumbs-up spacer shake.

"Was that Ken Lamoosoo?" he asked as he sat down.

"Lamosieu," the young man repeated with a vaguely French accent. He had brown eyes, brown skin, possibly some African blood, but the green hair tended to obscure racial characteristics.

"What's with the lemon-lime hair?" Harlin addressed the other recruit—white skin, gray eyes. "New fashion?"

"Sure, everyone on Luna has green hair these days," Fred Carter replied. "Buy you a draft?"

"Just a citrus, thanks." Harlin signaled his order to the bartender and tried to imagine seven hundred thousand people with green hair. A search for cultural identity, he supposed. Response to anomie. It made sense in a way. Colonists on Luna could never have the same goals and aspirations as Earthmen, their lives too removed from the wife-and-kids-in-the-suburbs routine of middle-class luxury. So if they weren't Earthmen, who were they? Moonmen? Lunatics?

"What brings you two out to the belt?" Harlin asked with a smile as Fred signed for his drink. "Fame and fortune?"

"Just fortune," replied Ken Lamosieu. "The money sounded good."

"Good money, all right," Eric broke in, "but wait'll you see the bill for that beer you're drinking."

The five miners laughed heartily, though the joke was well worn and cut too close to the heart. There was nothing more expensive than imported mass in the belt, and the trappings of civilization came with exorbitant price tags. Rumor had it that Eric was in fact under some pressure financially and in dire need of a lucky rock, though he had bankrolled a long list of relatives Earthside over the years. With short black hair and finely chiseled Italian jaw, he looked as though he had just stepped off a shaving commercial on the holo.

"Speaking of money," he continued, "I hear you plucked a nice rock last shift, Harlin."

"Prelim looks good." Harlin grinned. "An iron for sure. Trace counts for cobalt and manganese."

"Sure took your time coming in," big Jim Nichols observed in a sluggish drawl. Nichols had brought in a "dirtball" last shift—almost pure silica and utterly worthless—and had been drinking steadily all afternoon as a result. "Have some trouble?"

Harlin nodded grimly. "A stray clipped my rock just as I was set to cradle. Blew my synch completely."

"What?" Ken exclaimed. "You had a collision mid-maneuver and still brought your rock in? I don't believe it."

Harlin shrugged muscular shoulders. "I was out over a full cycle. I just started from scratch on the new trajectory."

"Great space! I didn't have that one on my simulation runs."

"Well, it looked like a decent chase. My credits were down. You know how the Company gets when production lags."

"No one would have blamed you if you let it go," Eric pointed out.

"Green truth," Ken stated flatly. "I'm coming in every half cycle, rock or not."

Harlin nodded. He'd heard that line before, straight out of the Station regs. He'd even said it himself once, long ago. He began to feel old. What was he doing out here, anyway?

"Yeah, well." He shrugged. "It looked like a decent chase."

"So why are you called Prophet?" Fred Carter asked as he set his half-empty mug on the table.

Jim Nichols picked up his own mug and smiled into it. "Yeah, tell them about your sprite, Prophet," he prodded, then turned to the recruits with a patently innocent air. "Harlin's got one of those little alien ghosties in his brain," he told them. "Like a pet, you know. Only we don't know yet who's the pet and who's the master." He laughed, the conquering Viking.

The recruits stared at Harlin wide-eyed. Eric Apa looked uncomfortably at his hands and rubbed a scab on his thumb.

"Red flash," Fred drawled, shaking his head.

"No, really," Jim maintained. "I carried one myself once, believe it or not. My mother had it planted when I was a kid. 'Course I had it removed as soon as I realized the truth. Not the Prophet, though. He's going right to the wall with his. What do you think? You got room in your head for a baby parasite?"

"C'mon, lay off, Jim," Eric muttered.

"Green?" asked Fred.

"It's not like he says," Harlin replied.

"You callin' me a liar, Prophet?"

"So does it talk to you or something?" Ken asked. "What does it say?"

"It doesn't say anything. It's just there, watching."

"Red flash, man," Jim interjected. "What about the Manual?"

"Well, yeah," Harlin admitted, "there's been some communication, but not to me personally."

"Those sprites are gonna take over, I tell ya. They're sending out spies to plan their attack."

"Bloody red," Harlin countered. "The sprites don't need our universe. They live in a different dimension. Outside of space and time."

Fred whistled. "Heavy tech."

"I think I'd prefer a computer implant," Ken offered. "At least then you know what you're getting."

"Yeah," Eric jumped in defensively, "it's no worse than an

implant. Jim just likes to ride him. We've been out in the belt too long. Space happy, you know." He lifted up a full beer stein. "Space happy?"

The miners raised their glasses.

"Space happy," they repeated, and tipped up four golden brews and one citrus punch.

"Have you ever stopped to examine his point of view, Harlin? You know, looked at yourself from the outside?" Eric leaned back in his chair and propped his feet up on Harlin's narrow cot.

"He thinks with his head, not his heart," Harlin answered, reclining, staring at the blank monitor above him.

"Is that so bad? To reason with the mind?"

"Not everything is amenable to reason."

"Perhaps not, but you can't live your life in a dream, without foundation."

"A sprite is no dream, Eric."

"I didn't say that. I know they're real. But I've never understood what they are."

Harlin raised empty palms up. "Neither have I."

"That's just it. You're running on blind faith here. Doesn't it scare you sometimes?"

"I know what I'm doing. You've seen my scraps from the Manual."

"Four or five pages from a book that may not even exist? You call that assurance? You're willing to bet your life on that?"

"Well, what are you betting your life on?"

Eric sighed, shook his head. "Okay, you've got something. I'll admit that. And it's intriguing, I'll admit that too. But great space, Harlin, it could be dangerous. There's something living in your brain, for heaven's sake, and you don't even know what it is. Did you ever see the old storybook holo where the aliens' instruction manual turns out to be a cookbook?"

"Look, you and Jim can talk about it all you want. And make jokes in front of the femmes and the recruits in the lounge. But I'm going to find out the truth. It's important to me. More important than all the chromium in the belt, more important than all those Earthside grounders living in that chemical stew, more important even than my own life, if it comes to that. Just stay clear if it bothers you. That's why I came out here in the first place—to get away."

Eric held up his hands as if to ward off the words. "Okay, slow down. I'm your friend, right? Wasn't I on your side in the lounge? I admire your stand. Sometimes I wish I had the guts to do it myself."

"Why don't you then? What's holding you back?" Harlin swung his legs off his bunk and sat up. "If there's truth in the universe, don't you want to know about it? Be part of it? We're never going to get out of this solar system sub-light. We're never going to discover all the answers without the sprites to help us. They can go anywhere. I think they might already exist every-where at once. Don't you see how puny we are without them? They can offer us everything, the galaxy, immortality. How can you pass it up?"

Eric rose to his feet. "That's your trouble, Harlin. You're too pushy. You think that just because you make a risky decision everyone else should follow your example. The sprites are using people like you to evangelize the human race. They're tampering with your mind." He held out a warning finger. "You almost had me convinced once, till Jim explained the sprites' methods. I'm not going to be part of some alien plan of conquest."

"Red flash, Eric."

"Maybe it's not true. Maybe what you say is green. But I'm not going to jump into a nightmare without a decent reason. Show me some proof, Harlin. Show me some good old-fashioned rational evidence."

"The sprites aren't going to do miracles for you like a dog performing tricks."

"Then they don't need me bad enough." Eric started toward the door.

"They don't need you at all, Eric. You need them."

"I'm doing fine on my own, thanks," he said as he stepped into the hallway.

Harlin hung his head and scratched at a tangle of brown curls behind his ear. Maybe he wasn't doing the right thing. Certainly he had nothing to show for his years as a sprite carrier. One by one he'd driven away family and friends. Step by step he'd retreated into space—first Luna, then on to Eros, finally to Base Station just inside of Jupiter. He had no place left to run now, and not a friend left in the universe. Just a few pages of hand-copied loose-leaf and an invisible hitchhiker in his head. And vague promise of something more.

Harlin stretched out his last spider leg and drilled in his anchor. His screen flashed green. Rock secure. A smaller rock, about ninety meters in diameter, but a good iron. A few strays drifted nearby on the radar, but none close enough to disrupt his maneuvers. Harlin smiled as he angled his boosters anti-spinward. Money in the bank. He had a long trip back to Base but would get in under time with any luck. If only he could stretch out these aching muscles.

He plotted his course as he killed rotation. It had been a good chase but he was way out of standard hunting ground. A lot of garbage in the area. A tricky route home. He punched it in and redirected his boosters. He flipped on the com.

Silence.

He checked the frequency and punched the signal amp.

Nothing.

A visceral clamp seemed to tighten in his abdomen. He turned slowly, dreamily, as though removed from his body and watching from a distance, to scan his long-range radar.

Nothing but strays and belt debris. Base Station was nowhere to be found.

He gasped for air as a wave of dizziness washed through him. He steadied his reeling mind. Think, he ordered himself. Could they possibly have blasted out of orbit without notice? Some emergency? Impossible. Too much mass. At best the crew could have evacuated in the lifeboats. At worst . . .

He keyed in a signal to open his porthole shutter. He stared out at eternal night and searched for any signs of life.

So cold out there. So quiet.

Eric, Eddi, Jim Nichols—all dead. Quick frozen like vac-pak dinners. All the pretty tech girls, the nurses, the mechanics.

So cold out there. So quiet.

Harlin checked his air reserves and reset the mix for conservation. Two cycles at the most. He switched his radio to emergency band and quickly dialed down the volume as the signal stretched.

"Eeeeeeeeeeyaawwk—from Pallas Central and can receive you with minimum time lag. Please signal if you are able. This is an automated survival search for any craft in the vicinity of Strategic Metals Base Station. We are broadcasting from Pallas Central and can receive you with minimal time lag. Please signal if you are able. Over."

During the pause Harlin thumbed his transmitter and twice repeated, "Spider Seven to Pallas Central."

The reply came a few seconds later, a woman's voice in place of the automated baritone: "This is Pallas Central. We are receiving a strong signal from you. Please repeat your call numbers."

"I'm not sure I have call numbers. They're probably in the computer somewhere. My name is Harlin Riley, if that's any help. Who's this?"

"My name is Armstrong, Florence, Mister Riley. It's a real pleasure to hear your voice."

"Call me Harlin, Armstrong Florence, and tell me what happened to my Base Station."

"I really can't say, Harlin. I've heard everything from a core meltdown to little green men. We may never know what caused the explosion. Can you tell us anything?"

"No, I seem to have missed the whole thing. I was working outside the perimeter. . . ." Harlin lapsed into silence as it occurred to him that he could expect no miraculous rescue from this woman. Pallas was at least four or five days away at full thrust. He was going to die in this tin can after all.

"We've got a good fix on you now, Harlin. How many survivors do you have in your lifeboat?"

Harlin sighed. "I haven't got a lifeboat, Pallas Central. Just a spider with two days' air."

Silence stretched out around Harlin as Florence Armstrong spoke frantically with her supervisor on an in-house line. The facts were inescapable: space was too big and atomic propulsion too slow. And Florence Armstrong suddenly found herself in the executioner's shoes. Press this button and the current will pass through the victim's body. Speak these words.

When she finally came back on the air a few minutes later, her meek and broken voice confirmed Harlin's worst suspicions.

"Harlin, this is Pallas Central again. We—uh—haven't been able to contact any other craft in your vicinity at the present time."

She's going to cry, Harlin thought to himself. She's going to break down.

"I understand," he said evenly. This was all going on tape, he reminded himself. This was his last contact with fellow humans, his last message to a civilization that had rejected him. He could think of nothing to say.

"I'm so sorry," Florence breathed into her microphone, feeling the ache of death in her throat, the emptiness of space eternal around her. A colleague's hand gripped her shoulder from behind to help support her burden, and she reached up to clutch his fingers spasmodically.

Harlin winced at the sound of her plaintive whisper, his own melancholy overshadowed by the acute embarrassment he felt for the poor woman. Torture enough for both of them, he decided, and switched off his com for the final time.

Cold and quiet he drifted, and a vast universe swallowed him like a dust mote, like a puff of sacrificial smoke in the wind, a brief scent of salt on the inland breeze.

"Just you and me now," Harlin said aloud. "Just you and me and the naked truth."

He knew from the Manual that the holy sprites never died, that they were not bound by timespace nor constrained by speed of light or antimatter reactions. He had memorized what scraps of the Manual he had chanced upon in his travels, hand-copied doctrines passed by mnemonics and smuggled from place to place. He had heard the promise of eternal life.

What he did not know and could not fathom was what exactly survived the death of his body, what exactly the sprite carried with him from the corpse. A mind, a soul, memories, purpose? Would Harlin remain an individual, a conscious entity, or merely a vague recollection in the nethermost reaches of the sprite's consciousness? How closely was he intertwined with the eternal aspect of the symbiosis? Would death be the end or the beginning of Harlin Riley?

All the posturings and prayers had come to an end, the accouterments of life stripped away. Nothing left now but a naked, cold, hard kernel. A seed perhaps. Harlin closed his eyes and waited for the cramps to begin.

Steve Stanton: "On the Edge of Eternity" is an excerpt from my SF novel In the Den of the Dragon. *The novel itself is an attempt to express the working of the Holy Spirit in a Christian's life, the "holy synchronicity" of events within the Body of Christ. The events detailed in this short prelude present the question of whether a man's faith is rewarded, in this life or in the next.*

The idea of being trapped in a "computerized tin can" arose from a personal experience. At the time of writing, I was employed as an overhead crane operator in a factory making mining equipment, working up near the ceiling and communicating with co-workers through hand signals and other nonverbal cues. For eight to ten hours a day over a period of many years, I was confined to a four-by-four-foot steel cage, surrounded by high-voltage controllers and humming fuse panels, continuously bathed in an invigorating aura of pulsating electromagnetic radiation that, no doubt, accounts for my deeply disturbed imagination to this day.

Thanksgiving Day at the Temple

Donna Farley

I GIVE THANKS! I AM DYING, my dear Tbithi, but, happily, I am in a temple here in the homeplace of the strangers.

There are many wonderful things here, although something troubles me about this temple. Of course I do not expect it to be exactly like ours . . . but never mind that for now.

Doctor Edmonds, the priest who attends me, gave me a thing called a recorder, like a palm-sized ax head, with marks on the side. I press one of these marks, and the recorder takes my words and keeps them inside itself, until I push another mark, and then my own voice speaks to me, repeating each word as perfectly as a Storyteller of the High Rank. I give thanks!

They tell me I will never go home to our own temple in the bright mountains of Kalbara now. Their traveling-ship has a strange magic, for though we traveled only a few sleeps, yet they tell me many winterturns have already passed in Kalbara. They were very perplexed when they found me in their ship, for by then we were traveling to their homeplace—past the stars, they told me—and they could not take me back.

Soon after this I began my journey down the death-trail, with burning hot skin and soreness in all my joints. When the ship arrived here in their homeplace, they brought me at once to this temple. Despite all this, I have managed to learn their language a little.

Tbithi, my beautiful *sziilla*-bird, though you will never hear these words, I will pretend I am telling you this by firelight between the moonrisings, the two of us perched together on the posts on the hill. As we look out over the newly harvested fields with joy, I say that I am cold, and you laugh and wrap your glider membrane around my shoulders and rub your furry thigh against my side. I would like to make more children with you. But you give my ear a playful bite and tell me to go on with the tale of my adventure.

Though some unknown thing makes me feel uneasy in this temple, I am not sorry I went into the strange people's ship. I was very afraid, but a priest must not curl up to hibernate like a furry *miliuk* in Longwinter. Long ago, Great Kavvathi our ancestor . . .

I pressed the little mark on the recorder, because I did not want to save the sound of my fearful coughing. But I want to keep saving words, for who knows? Maybe they are the gift of the gods to these people.

Our great ancestor Kavvathi went courageously to the place where the lightning struck, and so the gods gave us the gift of fire. His famous daughter Chayilliya braved the anger of her tribe to plow and seed the first field, and so the gods gave us the gift of the first harvest. So I could not refuse, either, to seek a gift from the gods, could I?

The white-coated priests here tell me I am on the death-trail because the life-spirits in my body do not have the right weapons to battle their homeplace death-spirits. Perhaps that explains my uneasiness here. And yet their rituals of life-battle are not altogether different from ours. Several times now they have taken of my blood, using a little instrument with a needle, sharper than your sister's bone sewing-needles, and shiny. The red wonderful blood flows up into a little clear tube. I give thanks!

I cannot perch—a heaviness afflicts my glider membranes,

and I must lie on a pallet. Doctor Edmonds says this heaviness is the reason his people are big and heavy and do not have glider membranes like our people.

Think of that. It must be like dying all the time, not to be able to soar between the cliffs. . . .

I grew too tired yesterday to say more, so I pressed the mark on the recorder. Last night I told Doctor Edmonds I was dying more and more, and he became angry. I have never seen a priest angry at a dying man before. He is short, for these people, and the fur of his head is a fiery color. "You will live, do you hear me?" he shouted.

I said I hoped so, but first I must die a little more. There was too much to learn to start living again already.

I asked Doctor Edmonds how many times he had walked down the death paths. He seemed most surprised at my question. He said he had been fortunate and had never been near death.

"Never?" I asked, horrified. "But a priest must have traveled toward death many times, on little trails that double back on themselves and bring him back to life almost at once, or on wide paths that carry him swiftly almost all the way to the gate of death itself. How else can he find wisdom to bring back to his people?"

Tbithi, I think he was trying not to laugh at me. He said that his people have learned so much that they live a long time. "I will not die till I'm much, much older, I hope," he said.

Tbithi. These people believe that when they are just a little bit sick, that that is not dying. And to have priests who know nothing of death!

I told him, "I was trying to learn if the gods had a gift for me in your ship. There is a saying in Kalbara," I said, "'Curious as a priest.'"

This made him laugh, and I was happy, because I could laugh

at that too. But then I asked him about his gods, and I wish I had not, for now I don't know what his laugh meant.

He said, "Doctors do not believe in gods!"

Then I realized how I had been misunderstanding. I had thought their word "doctor" meant priest, but it does not. It means one who does healing work, if you can imagine, Tbithi, life and death without the gods. If you can imagine dying without a ritual.

"The sky ship, the little tubes for taking blood, the recorder—what can these be but gifts from the gods?" I said.

"*We* make them," he said.

I did not know what to say, Tbithi. I make my own arrows, and your sister makes clothes with her sewing needle, and your brother makes teaching stories, but would we dream of not thanking the gods for these things, just because we have made them? We did not make the stones I use to make the arrowheads, or the *kliththa* fibers your sister weaves to make cloth.

Doctor Edmonds could see how unhappy I was, and I think it made him unhappy too. "Look, I don't know anything about religion," he said. "I've got a friend—maybe he can make sense of all this for you."

I feel a little stronger today. And I have met one of their priests now. His name is Father Steele.

He is thin and dark, and walks stooped and looking over his shoulder, as if he were afraid of the other people in the temple. Perhaps there is a reason for that: he does not wear a white coat like the other people in the temple, but is dressed all in black, as if his work is the very opposite of the healers' work. But Doctor Edmonds had asked him to come, he said, out of friendship for me.

He told me that three days from today would be the day of a great festival amongst their people. You will not believe it,

Tbithi—they call it Thanksgiving. I thought I had misunderstood again, but after much questioning I knew that, yes, it was a festival of rejoicing and thanking the gods for the harvest.

I began to sing one of our thanksgiving songs then. Father Steele listened quietly, and when it was done, he gave a wistful sigh.

"I will hear your people's songs of Thanksgiving too, in this temple, then?" I asked

But he said no, not here. This was not a place of worship. Worship was only permitted in a few special buildings and on certain lands called reservations, where the people who believe in worship are allowed to live.

Just as I was mistaken about doctors, so I was about hospitals. Tbithi, I am dying, and the place I am dying in is not a temple....

After a while I asked, "And if I do not return from my death-walk, will they bury me in the womb of the earth beneath this . . . this hospital?"

He looked troubled. "The dead are burned here," he said. "It is the law."

I wept, Tbithi. The dead, the most venerable, treated like garbage.

"But I do not know what they will do with you." He looked around, as if he feared others might be listening and disapproving of what he told me. "I think . . . they will wish to keep your body, to study, and learn more of your people."

After a long time I said to him, "Father Steele, I must leave here and find a temple, if I can."

Father Steele said, "They will not let you go."

It is the day of Thanksgiving now. I have turned back from the death-trail, Tbithi. I now cough only a little, though the great heaviness is still with me. But I can eat, and perch again, if only briefly. Doctor Edmonds says my body has adapted, and my life-spirits have won the battle. Now, he says, I am living enough to go with some people who want to learn our language and all about Kalbara.

But I asked, are these people who say they want to learn true priests, and not only half-priests like all the white-coated people in Hospital?

He looked as if he wished to avoid my eyes, but at last he told me, "No, they are not priests, they are warriors." He spoke the word meaning "warriors" as if it were something unpleasant to him.

I said I wanted to go to a temple. He came back later that day and said my request had been refused. Refused! Tbithi, what sort of people can refuse any man, especially a priest, the right to go to a temple?

They brought the evening meal, the meat of a large bird they slay just for this feast. Even in this place, where they do not worship, they eat as if they *had* worshipped.

But I started to wonder who had slain the bird, and what they did with its blood. And I would not eat it.

I must go to a temple, Tbithi. Even if it brings war on our people, I must go. And I know every one of our people would clap their glider membranes together in approval.

Once before I did such a thing as I now plan, when I was held captive by the Downriver people in my youth. My claws and teeth are sharp still. And if I do not succeed, it is certain one of these strangers will walk the death-trail along with me.

I give thanks! I am dying again, Tbithi. But this time, I am in a real temple.

My claws did their work. One of the warriors came to talk to me; I pretended friendliness, then when he turned to leave I jumped on his shoulders, putting my claws to his throat. "Take me to a temple, or you will fall headlong down the swiftest of death-trails," I said.

He was a very big man, with hard muscles, and he did not frighten easily, but he felt the sharp prick of my claws and knew I could do as I said. He carried me out of the room on his back, and cautioned all the others who came running to stay their distance.

Doctor Edmonds was there, his eyes round with shock to see me threatening the warrior. He cried out for someone to call Father Steele. Then he talked kindly to me, asking me to let go of the warrior, but I would not listen. After what seemed a long time, Father Steele came and also tried to persuade me to take my claws away from the warrior's throat.

"You dare call yourself a priest!" I said to him. "You who let warriors and death-fearing healers tell you what to do!"

He looked very ashamed at my words.

"Let me go, and we can talk," said the warrior.

"In a temple, we will talk," I said.

The warrior cursed loudly. Then he said, "All right—Father Steele, let's go to, uh, the boardroom?"

I saw a surprising change in Father Steele then. He stood up straighter than he had before, and his eyes burned bright. "He isn't stupid, Colonel. If he wants a temple, nothing else will do."

My left claws dug deeper into the warrior's shoulder, and my right claws itched to slash his throat. Colonel swallowed fearfully. "Edmonds, I'm putting you on report. You had no business bringing this religious fanatic on base to contaminate the subject's mind!"

Doctor Edmonds went very pale, but Father Steele smiled. "Actually, it's our little subject who's contaminated the rest of us. And may I remind you that religion is still perfectly legal."

"In its place!" said Colonel.

Father Steele spoke coldly. "On the reservations, yes, where it won't disturb secular minds with thoughts about eternity."

"There are licensed city churches too. I don't know what the hell more you fanatics want," said the warrior.

I thought the two of them might have fought then, but I said, "I want to go now."

Colonel, the warrior, growled. But at last he agreed. They took me in a *car*, a sort of enclosed land ship. I saw little as we traveled, keeping my attention on Colonel and my claws at his throat.

At last we came to the temple. As we were entering its grounds, the warrior said, "Steele, you bastard—this is a religious reservation!"

"Yes," said Father Steele. There was a laugh in his voice.

"Car, turn around!" cried Colonel, for the magic machine obeys his voice.

But I pricked him with my claws and said "No!" and he had to make the car keep going.

"He cannot make you leave here now," Father Steele told me, and at last I became hopeful again.

"We'll see about that," Colonel grumbled.

Father Steele shrugged. "Here come the sisters," he said, as the car came to a stop in front of the building. "They've seen him now. The world will hear about him and his wish to go to a temple. You know how people have been talking lately. If you try to do him any harm, or to intimidate the nuns, you just might have a religious backlash on your hands."

We got out of the car, myself still clinging to the warrior's back, and I was frightened at first by the noisy flying machines that hovered overhead. But Father Steele told me to pay them no attention, and I held tight until the blue-robed acolytes called sisters brought us inside to the worship hall.

There I let go of the warrior, for as soon as I came into the hall, I felt safe. Little flames burned in small containers all around, and a great shining altar stood on a raised place at the far end. I fell on my face and gave thanks.

Even in the holy place Colonel did not give thanks, but shouted and cursed at Father Steele.

I rose from my prostration. "Colonel, I am happy now. I will stay here. If the people of the temple here allow it, you can come and ask me any questions you wish about Kalbara."

Colonel's mouth fell open, but he did not give thanks. He only shut his mouth again and went away grumbling.

My sickness has returned, Tbithi, and so I am dying. It is not so bad to know that you must be dead already, since so many winterturns have passed in Kalbara, for then I know you will wait at the end of the death-trail for me. I am sorry the sisters and Father Steele have no healing knowledge, though, for that makes them only half-priests too. But that is not their fault.

"Our rulers forbid believers to learn what they need to become doctors," Father Steele told me. "It was not always that way, before the Separation laws and the reservations. One day, we pray, it will change again."

"On that day you will give thanks," I said.

That made him laugh. "Yes. But even now we have many things to give thanks for, and I am glad you have reminded us of that, my friend."

And the singing of the sisters is very beautiful; they carry me into the worship hall at least once a day to listen. They have taught me their chief prayer, "Our Father," and they promise I will have their death rituals.

Best of all is the window. I can see through it from my bed and watch the trees and clouds. And the graveyard. It is a little different from ours in Kalbara. The stones are shaped in special ways and stood upright on each grave, and the name of each person is marked in magic symbols. These are very old, for as I learned before, the rulers no longer permit burial of the dead, even on the religious reservations.

"I think the colonel and his people will still try to take away your body," said Father Steele.

This is why the temple people have decided not to let the

warriors come here to question me. Instead one of the sisters talks with me, and she sends her recorder with our talk about Kalbara to the warriors.

"When you die, we will not let them know until we have secretly buried your body where they cannot find it," they promised me.

One of the sisters told me they believe a time will come when all the dead will rise up, like green grain springing from the earth. How beautiful! This, I told her, would be the best gift I could take home to Kalbara, if only I could go.

"Some day they will have it," the sister said, very firmly and with a shining smile on her face.

That will be a real Thanksgiving Day, Tbithi.

Donna Farley: "Thanksgiving Day at the Temple" had its genesis as described in this piece I sold to Scavenger's Newsletter *in 1991: "I was thinking about my mother-in-law who is now so ill she might not be able to die at home. Doctors and hospitals have completely taken over the management of birth and death in our society. Wouldn't a visitor from another planet be sure to think that doctors are priests and hospitals are temples?"*

Eastern Orthodoxy has a holistic view of life, whereas contemporary Canadian society is terribly fragmented. Much lip service is given to tolerance and multiculturalism, yet traditional Christianity is increasingly vilified and squeezed out. To me, the idea of religious reservations in our future seems all too chillingly plausible.

STONES

Ursula Pflug

FROM A NOTEBOOK, TEN YEARS AGO, a scrap of a story: "Tomorrow I will go up to the land. I will bring Fletcher and we will drive. We will go to the old alphabet stones and ask them the way of the world. There is blood on the stones but there is blood everywhere now; there is no piece of earth left, untouched by bloodshed.

"Me and Gypsy Fletch and the alphabet stones, making circles to see which way the world should go. I have not lost Gypsy yet. I will show him the stones where it says our names.

"Gypsy is hurt, and if he is wounded, so must I be."

Time circles back on itself. I opened an old notebook this morning, read it over coffee before I began to work. I don't rely on I Ching or tarot as a daily oracle as some do; instead I open old notebooks. Each time a line, a page springs out to reflect upon my current condition. As it does today.

I'm already in the country, but I am traveling tomorrow, to a property in the next county, where an enigmatic ring of stones stands. As though hurled from heaven, it challenges our murky histories, our inability to look into the past and see what was really there. I'd be happy to bring Gypsy, but I can't, not physically; he isn't real. He's someone I invented, my childhood dream lover. I continued to write about him for years, even after I married; there was only one like him. I don't even know if that was really his name, Fletch. I just made it up; I liked the way it moved in my mouth when I spoke it. He told me his name was Gypsy. I'm sure it wasn't really; but the name contained thought-forms that were clues to his identity: wild, handsome, artistic, lawless, free.

It was like this: I'd forgotten that time, those people, made a life for myself. I lived in Vancouver, near Lion's Gate. I was a teacher. I taught neither the mind nor the body, but the spirit. I had an apartment with clean blue tablecloths and bowls of fruit, a view of the water. I was alone, but I was happy. Then I dreamed. We were playing in the road, my only sister and I, one of those hot dusty roads up north in Ontario. It was a game with sticks and snakes. We picked up large branches from a fallen tree and jousted with them, like the knights in the Arthurian legends we loved to read above all else, when we were children. In my dream we were older than children, at that slipstream edge of adulthood where crisis feels like treasure. Why is that?

There were so many snakes on the road, making a path for us to follow between the stones and dead branches. We didn't though; we didn't know how. Still they simmered there, full of power, offering. My sister and I threw stones at one another and the stones passed into our bodies, lodging where they fell like shadows in the flesh. I woke from my dream saying, "The stone shadows are still there. It's why we are the way we are."

Not long after the dream, I went back east and married a man, a nice man I had known for years. We had been lovers for a long time, on and off, but we never had been married. It was time. We moved to the country, again that north country in

Ontario, where I had not lived since then. Then. Listen how it weights you, the word. How you feel it inside your mouth, your body. Listen how it heals, the talk at dawn, with your visiting sister, about then.

There is a huge snail in my garden, the size of a Rototiller. It walks, making paths. I kill it and crawl into its shell. I shall be that snail. I too shall have a home.

How did I kill it? That game I'd learned, hadn't even known I was learning. Threw a shadow stone at the snail. The snail crawled out of its shell, turned into a man. Something like a man, so strange and familiar both. Why had the snail been in my garden in the first place? It had liked the garden I was making. What was I growing? A different kind of world. Somebody has to, obviously. A few of us are doing it, here and there. Our gardens weave invisible lines of light, creating a web that connects us all, a web of protection. Or perhaps, the tallest plants are radio transmitters.

That was last year. This year the paths are like the paths on a board game, soft and curved. Remember "The Enchanted Forest" with little evergreens for game markers?

In the in-between time, not yet old, breasts only beginning to grow, we lived on a farm, shared by several families, not being farmers. Why is one allowed to do this, to live on farms without farming? What do the farmers do, now, instead of farm? They sit in condominiums in Florida, wondering at their strange new frost-free landscape. Eating citrus fruits by the bowlful; so rare when they were young.

I was young, thirteen. Already I thought I knew how to love. We had games for getting power, I and the others, the other young ones. Everyone knows those games. You have to get some-one dangerous to be your friend. I dreamt of a man with tattooed knees, a gypsy and an artist. He had blue hair.

I dreamt of him again last night, my childhood sweetheart. He had a third child, unlike my husband and me, who have two. It made me want another. What does it mean?

When I first dreamed stone shadows I thought they held us, our lives, in certain inescapable patterns. Imprinting. I wanted more than anything to escape those shadows, spent long winter nights dreaming their shapes out of my body like the new stones forced by frost to the surface of the fields each spring. Now I think they were protection—they gave us luck—ensuring we would become who we are now and not deviate, get lost. And yet the shadows are lifting now, willy-nilly out of everyone I know, regardless of our work to prize them out. Sometimes, I can almost hear them: popping and sucking, the skin closes around the places they were, late at night when my friends are over, drinking. You hear it when they laugh, or when they cry. In the mornings we collect empty beer bottles and sweep the new stones out the door, as though clearing the fields at planting time.

Who will protect us now—shall we have to make our own luck? I've had cinnamon buns for breakfast again and my key-board is sticky as an icy fence in winter. But it's not winter, it's summer, when everything changes irrevocably and forever. How do I know this? This summer feels like that first summer I spent with Gypsy, still a child, a year before I lost everything. Time now feels like time then; lost opportunities returning. Not since that summer have I felt so densely this moment when destiny and landscape fuse to form a pattern; the psychic template of a door to life. Last time I didn't have the strength to read it thus, seeing only the loss, and not the chance of liberation.

Notebook:
"It was on one of my walks that I found the alphabet stones. A heap of rocks in a small sparse pasture, its only access a dense mixed wood I struggled through, stubbornly. The clearing straddled the very edge of the property. The grass was long; a place so far afield the wandering cows hadn't found it."

In my garden, a spirit person came out of a snail shell. A fairy, a gnome. I don't know what to call them. Little people. He was indeed little, about four feet tall. He had a blue bush of hair. He had four arms, two of which were blue. He had a bowl of raw fresh asparagus he held out towards me. Eat it, he said, it will heal your marriage. Not that there is anything wrong with my marriage; it inflicts only the small sores and bruises of any bond. Perhaps it is a larger meta-healing he proffers, with his bowl of luminous green asparagus spears. Healing Marriage, with a capital M. It sure could use it.

It is only now, as I write this, that I know who it was. Fletch. Come for me again.

Little people. Stories of them all over the world. I only see them when I'm in that half-awake state just before true sleep comes. They always come to me as the picture, the image to go with something I felt in the early gardening. A lightening, a birth. Always before today it has been women. Not since that first time I dreamed of him have I seen a male.

"It looked like a heap of stones left there when they'd cleared the land and perhaps it was, but there were words there, written out with stones in the grass. I almost missed them—old words left there long ago—by settlers, perhaps. Wedged into the earth, hidden beneath the weeds, trying to regain their old homes there."

All my old lovers are dying. Why is this? I feel it in my flesh when I walk in my gardens in the mornings, picking cabbage-butterfly larvae off the broccoli leaves. Even Gypsy, my favorite, a sweet man whose sweetness I was too young to have use for. I left him and traveled the dark road. I wish now, for his sake, more than for mine, that I could have gone a different way. Of course, we are all dying, very slowly. How much time left?

Did you know you can go backwards and forwards in time? It's what I do with myself now. Other people think I'm gardening, but really I'm time traveling. Fletch taught me, a long time ago. He called it playing cat's cradle with time. He had six arms then, the better to weave time with. That is how I know he is wounded; two arms are missing. Which time did he lose them in?

Notebook:

"House, said one, and Horse, Cow and Plough. I didn't know what they meant, but I liked their oldness. Someone had made these words, someone no longer living. And they gave me an idea. I gathered stones from the pile and wrote in the earth, making hollow depressions for the stones to nest in. I pulled the grass out with my fingers. It took me the whole long afternoon, writing my name and his. July and Fletcher, in two-foot-high letters.

"They embarrassed me when I was done and I tried to cover them with grass and earth, but they made me feel good too, which was worse.

" 'There,' I'd said, as though it were enough that the stones knew."

I sit in a garden in Berkeley, sharing the life we never had together, my childhood sweetheart Gypsy and I. It is strange: I have a real life, a day-to-day life, yet from time to time it is as though part of me slips into this parallel time stream, into this life we would've had together if we hadn't split up, if I hadn't been so young; if he hadn't offended me with his desire for all of me. In my parallel life with Fletch my name is Rebecca; I wear white T-shirts, beige shorts with many pockets, ballet shoes. Life seems easier. I have a dog and an old green Saab. Sometimes I drive north, alone, to the Sierra foothills, an amazement of a place, called French Corral.

That summer, after I first dreamed of Fletch, we did everything together. We walked and drew and painted; we basked in each other's fire; we meditated long before we knew the word. It was during those intermittent years, the ones where you dream of lovers, still too young to have them. Then, suddenly older, my family gone, the farm gone too, I began to travel.

This is how I traveled: I'd get on a plane, a train, a silver bus. I'd meet a man or a woman, and we'd spend a few days together, or a few months, sometimes working, often camping, sometimes being lovers, sometimes that other romance we belittle by calling friendship. And I would learn a place, through their eyes, their lives, their hands caressing my skin, mine theirs. And yet I never stayed. For even though I'd forgotten him, he hadn't forgotten me. My first love, and my truest. It was always his voice, although I didn't know it at the time, that whispered to me to move on, not to stay.

He had other plans for me. He wanted me to share with the world what he knew; he who inhabited another world, and could only interface with mine through me. It was Fletch who urged me to travel, to absorb, to experience. So he could see, feel, learn. Because he had no eyes in this world but mine, no legs to run with.

And in turn, he taught me his world. Strange things he taught me—what made me believe they were true? The truth is, it's because I'd lost everything: my family, my farm, my friends. I'd walked through fire unscathed, fire that had taken each one of my extended family; only I had been away. We'd had no insurance and I'd had to sell the land to pay off creditors, had only a little left to help pay my rent while I finished high school. I worked, too, in restaurants and cafés, evenings after school.

I had other friends who rallied but I stood on the other side of the fire now; it was as though I no longer knew them, so untouched by life seemed they that we no longer had any meeting place. Then I had only Gypsy remaining, only Gypsy to help me find a way out. He, too, must have planned all this: so I'd stay with him, and learn. So it was he after all who pointed me on the dark road. He didn't care for me personally, I found out later. He'd tried others, other human women, although it could just as easily have been a man. Fletch wanted someone who knew how to listen, who'd go to school with him, learn things not taught in any university. Things known only to those on the other side.

He taught me that animals talk; you can hear them in your mind. He taught me they'll protect you from danger, if you listen to what they say. Plants, the same, and stones. Always back to the stones.

He taught me to hear the thoughts of others, feel their emotions. Most importantly, he taught me to travel forwards and backwards in time. It's done with the light body, what they used to call the astral body. What is this faint lack we feel, this existential angst that prowls our time like a demon lover? It is the absence of Fletch, of his people. Of the time when they shared this world with us, as we shared theirs. And so I travel through time now, with long strings like spiderwebs of emotion, and in the past I retrieve small pieces of the time we need to heal this fraught present. To save our heart, our earth. I re-experience this past, and knowing what it feels like, I can feel it anytime, any place. And so this pool of passed time spills out of me, influencing the time in which I live, healing it. My emotional body is like a copying machine. I travel to other times, make imprints of them, return and print them out.

For years I had many lovers, both men and women, new friends, yet was still alone, trying to teach what Fletch had taught me. To love self and earth before all others, that true love can only come after, not before. And then I dreamed of the stones. It was enough. I wanted a real life, like other people. I said good-bye to Fletch.

But somewhere the choice I didn't make to be with him goes on, and that life informs my life now, when I really am married, have children, and sometimes chafe. Then the sense of freedom and happiness I enjoy in my other life with him bleeds into this one, and I am happy again, or at least content. Because my marriage to him takes place in some simpler past, when it was less confusing to be married. When you could trust it. Or perhaps this time has never been, yet: perhaps it's in the future.

This other me sits in her garden, full of perennials and self-seeding biennials. Lupines and foxgloves, poppies, phlox. Hollyhocks, hesperis, rudbeckia. I wear little green ballet slippers.

In real life I wonder what would have happened if I'd stayed with Fletch. Wearing angel shoes, drinking lemon tea with women in butterfly-wing cloaks. Garden parties are so important. They are always held in the presence of spirits, of little people. Their invisible influence, felt but not seen. Make sure you plant a garden they like, so they will come. A garden with paths gently curving like streams, like the paths in "The Enchanted Forest," like the stream of time.

A world that no longer exists. A kind of marriage that does not exist yet.

"But the cigarette prices have gone down," my husband's cousin said, at a party two months ago for their ninety-year-old grandmother. Those of us still in our thirties, not yet ready to relinquish our youth, our sense of adventure, sat outside among the first opened bulbs. We talked about cigarette and booze smuggling; "they set the clocks back twenty years," the cousin said, and it was as though it were really true.

I feel the spirit of twenty years ago coming alive in my blood-stream. As though now I really will be able to live a simpler life, a luckier one, not so full of pain and work. As though, now that the door is open again, I will see it for what it is and step through.

Just now, a woman called Rebecca sits in French Corral, painting watercolors of orange poppies. Drawn there, again and again. She can't get used to it: California poppies really do grow wild in California, are not just something you order from seed catalogues. My alter ego, like me, is from Ontario.

They set the clocks back twenty years. Everything shall be returned to us, that was taken away. That is what I want now, the things that were taken away. I want to wear what she wears, talk like she talks, think like she thinks. I no longer want to be one of the damaged, the burned, the ones who walked on water to save the tribe, and were not now (as not then) thanked for it. Then. Listen to the word, how it weights you.

But here is something else, something stranger still. In my childhood, there weren't really any old stones, aside from the so-aptly-named shield rocks. Shielding us every day of our lives. One reason not to bury nuclear waste in them, Fletch whispers in my ear. Who will protect you then, when even the alphabet rocks are poisoned? I invented the story stones as an adult, based on the feelings in the dream, the things I felt on that farm; what I learned by absorbing the land's secrets, those hot dusty melancholy northern summers.

Stones that are very old. Yet now, like so many other things I wrote ten or fifteen years ago, they seem to be coming true.

There are so many old stones in this country. Piled into shapes, some with designs on them. Who made these stones? We must listen to the stones, sit down beside them and really hear what they say. They are the mouthpiece of the earth, speaking to us. If ever you should hear stones speak, you must pass on what they say. If you don't, all your old lovers will die.

A man lives near here, with old stones on his property. Property; where did this word come from?

Tomorrow we'll go and see them, my husband and I. Some people think Indians made the stones, some think it was the Celts, having traveled further inland than any had believed.

Some even think the stones were erected by two cultures, working together. A somewhat hopeful revisioning of the past, even if it isn't true. One native man I met says he doesn't care; any made-up histories at all about stones will do, if they help preserve the land, if they make people think there's a reason to keep it free, not build subdivisions.

But I think the rocks have yet another meaning; the circle they make is a door between this world and the other world. Fletch's world. Of course, the true locus of this door is in our hearts, and yet we search the landscape for hopeful reminders, for criss-crossings of light that mirror our desires. And on that stone altar, if such it is, that inhabits the central place, I will make a ritual. It will not be a ritual of sacrifice, but one of healing. I will go there, and I will heal Gypsy, just as he healed me, all those long years ago.

How will I do it? I will give him a place in this world, just as he gave me one in his, back when it made the only possible difference.

Ursula Pflug: The section where the protagonist divines her present condition by oracular use of old notebooks and stories is a fragment of literal autobiography. Threads of synchronicity have often been the triggers that make me feel when writing that I'm onto something. A transplanted ex-urbanite, living on a Peterborough County farm, I was, one morning, reading a temporarily abandoned, fabricated mythohistory about landscape stones. An acquaintance phoned, asking me to come and see a circle of stones on his property in the next township which he believed might be Celtic in origin. Struck by this coincidence, I investigated, and so my acquaintance's stones wove into my story as did the pieces of the older narrative. I'm not concerned so much with the veracity of his outlook, believing history to be a highly speculative, subjective matter, as intrigued by his desire to interpret local history and landscape in a uniquely personal manner. The Canadian landscape has always seemed to me to be embedded with meaning and mystery, the cornerstones of myth. Not just traditional native myth or transported ancient European myth, but perhaps new myths, divined and devised by the inhabitants of all stripes, their present circumstances/belief systems intersecting with place. It is by mythologizing a specific locus we can help to assuage our feelings of helplessness in light of current environmental desecration, inspiring ourselves to act in the smallest of ways. This might in the end not make much difference, but then again, it might.

OMER AND THE ZOBOP

Claude-Michel Prévost

IT IS BETTER TO COME LATE in the afternoon when the sun decides it is time to pack up, yup, it has been another hard, long, working day.

Come when you start noticing more gold and red in the auras of the trees, when you can clearly sniff out the snakes of seaweed and white sand floating from the lagoon slow above the rice fields.

Come when the earth starts cooling off, when you can see the bayaonde bushes and the cacti, the palm trees, the pathways and the valleys, the plantations and the hills, the whole mountains behind the mountains whispering long whiffs of sweat to the listening clouds.

Come to my father's land.

You will need to leave the Jeep by the side of the road because the road has gone as far as it can, from then on there will be no more space for a self-respecting, aggressive, modern road to carve a path for its belly between the nipples of the mountains.

Better park your Jeep under a mango tree, you don't want an apprentice firefly to bump into your headlights in the middle of the night. Young fireflies have to buzz quick and low, belly brushing against the tips of the palm trees, limbs loose, breath open, they have to be very quick and very low, otherwise sudden moonbeams will shatter them into millions of golden crystals, or the wind will fragment them like it does for the clouds: here one minute ago, listening to the song of a jacaranda tree, now gone, dissolved, erased. Gone. Turned into a whisper with a gold lining, a lonely chant above the valley that one day remembers it has been here before.

Move the Jeep deep under the tree. If a firefly comes too fast from the curve right into the eyes of your car, it will scare the shit out of itself and crash with a huge thunder fart into the road or the trees.

Don't fuck with young fireflies.

This is a deadly discipline. Like any discipline, it requires so much focus that you will feel like a drop of water when it turns to foam along with the rest of its wave. Depending on the mood of the great blue beyond, moonbeams will play funny tricks with the blood in your cells, suddenly stretch you into a thin shiny coat of ice wide enough to cover a valley; those who do not know will confuse your death with the morning dew. Solar winds are another matter. Solar winds are slow caravans of a hundred million notes, a hundred million mantras so beautiful to feel, so tasty to listen to, a hundred million messages so urgent and so old, you will spend the night laughing and yakking with their young ones, and when dawn comes you will have joined their pilgrimage through the Milky Way. Gone. In his temple between the two crossroads, under the vigil of a red candle, the calabash of your soul will remain empty, and my father will have to travel far away to negotiate your return.

This is firefly country, friend, from the tip of Port-a-Piment till St. Marc, from the first samba who managed to survive the cargo boats till the next presidential election. This is zobop country, they even fly in the middle of the day, bright and gold and sharp like the sun in St. Marc, pulsating like angry flowers with shivers of red and blue, they even scare the shit out of the F15's in Guantanamo. This is zobop country. Do not ever fuck with things that fly in the night. Do not. Ever.

Because my land does not know yet how to forgive and forget.

See, you will be driving back home, you will be going fast down that very same road now full of chickens and piglets, goats and donkeys, roosters, bicycles, ox carts, schoolchildren, peasants, people and trucks and tap-taps and Range Rovers and Mac trucks and cars, it will be early morning and the Jeep will be bursting at the seams with fourteen freeloaders, three white chickens, one black and pink piglet named Maradona, two ducks and a droopy, skinny, long-eared dog called President Clinton, you will be driving totally exhausted and buzzing from having been with my father in his temple at the far end of the village, exhausted and happy and drunk and stoned from having eaten braised goat and gumbo soup, sipped smuggled Courvoisier cognac and mint tea spiked with morning glory, it will be early morning, and you will be dancing inside your skull from having given so much, and learned so much, and then silence.

Every mule, every rooster, every dog, every goat, every dove, every word in the Jeep, even the constant kissing of the tires and the road, every AM radio station belching news, psalms or merengue music. Silence.

Every heartbeat, your own heartbeat, the open mouth of the old wrinkled toothless baboon sitting next to you who asked so politely for a ride for herself and her freshly roasted peanuts and who hasn't stopped yakking and smoking her pipe while watching the valleys lift their skirt of fog. Silence.

You will be going fast down this road in total mute mode, and somehow your left eye will leave you and fly three curves ahead, soar three curves ahead, and your death will be *right there*.

Right into the mouth of the ravine. Right there, at the end of the bottom of the pit of the hole in the mountain: the big tooth cavity in the gum of the mountain, the trash can for smashed cars and trucks.

And your left eye can see each of those balls of pain and death still buzzing like angry embers. Three playful tap-taps, colorful as usual, piled-up bags and fruit baskets and babies and hats, as usual, three happy tap-taps named Ave Maria, Celavie, Ceboneg, sucked in by the ravine when darkness was playing with shades and shadows; fruit baskets and babies and hats and bodies spilled like red petals on the teeth of the rocks. One blue and black Mac truck named La Cayenne that used to cover Cayes-Port-au-Prince from way back when it took half a week, not four hours, filled with boat people heading for a secret clearing in the mangrove trees. La Cayenne went straight ahead, and their screams lingered for hours while the boat glided under the moon away from the lagoon. A 1994 Range Rover, spotlessly white, given to the government by the International Red Cross and used by some private militia to carry barrels of acid and bags of cocaine, with eight teenagers in military fatigues and Uzis pinned by their seat belts and each other, fighting to unlock the doors while the mouth of Death sucked them like oysters. Two Peugeot 403s that rolled and spun like funky skewers in angry diesel grunts. All piled up with brute vengeance, three curves ahead, two miles down, humping each other like crazed skeletal maggots, metal frames against steel bars, mangled screams still vibrating from bloody rocks.

Your left eye knows it has seen the truth and comes back to say *You're going next.*

You're next, because you got a firefly really pissed off.

Three curves ahead, Death will be waiting for you while you shit your pants and call your mama.

Silence.

Beautiful light.

Wonderful fatigue.

Clean smell of old, healthy, freshly washed, black skin roasted by half a century of sunshine and living and dancing and making love and giving birth (sixty-one died early) and working like a slave, and crying and singing and working like a slave, and grieving and cursing and smoking and praying and working like a slave, and praying and praying and praying.

Beautiful mountains hiding poverty and a multitude behind the pink of the sky, already breathing morning offerings of fog and dew to baby sun. Twin Q-tip poles in each ear to let you listen to your insanity.

Have a nice day, *mon*.

From behind the wall of silence, a chuckle is sneaking toward you. Between the mute voices in the Jeep, through the constant rooster calls from the huts low on your left and high on your right, through the rhythmic barks that know their own code, through the little coughs and wheezes of the fourth cylinder, the steady drumming of the engine, the huge holes of silence in the wall of life, you can hear a chuckle, an amused disdainful chuckle that slowly glides louder and close, coming from the left, right behind the corner of your eye, a chuckle without age or face that has known your name since your very first nightmare.

Death calls your name with an extreme, soft, delicate politeness like a satisfied Japanese lover, like a Revenue Canada bureaucrat, and you check the brakes, you check the horn, you check the gearshift, and the wall is still there, the wall got thicker with the first chirps of the doves, and the chuckle sings to you like Marilyn did for Johnny, sings softly in your ear, licking every one of your neurons, killing you softly with its song: *You're going down, down, down. . . .*

Death remembers your Top 40.

And the old baboon squeezed under your arm, almost impaled on the gearshift, she pulls another long extended puff from her cachimbo pipe—what the fuck is she smoking to be sooo at peace—Grandma, what's in your pipe?

But your neck is heavy, your neck has all its vertebrae glued solid, your mouth is clasping shut/open like the goldfish you had in fourth grade, your brain refuses to talk to you, and you know that someone is watching you die.

You just know it; that coldness in your soul cannot be anything else, three curves left, you have three curves to pray and swear and shit your pants and then, then the chuckle will fade away.

Because three curves ahead, three curves later, between the carcasses of bones and metal, sixty-one young grenadiers from Rochambeau's third army, freshly arrived from Marseilles and Bordeaux aboard the *St. Benoit* on the 12th of November 1791, sixty-one young grenadiers slowly rise up from the rocks where they rotted for months under rats and crabs and dung beetles, rise up from the rocks and start climbing back toward your side of the road.

Shh, shh.

Even the drone of the engine is soft like a river behind the trees. Three curves ahead, seventy Congo slaves freshly branded on the right shoulder blade with the iron of the Dassault plantation, seventy Congo slaves dismembered alive for having protested about the food rations, seventy Congo slaves tossed down that ravine to be left to eat each other and die, seventy Congo slaves slowly get up and join the procession.

Shh, shh.

Death slices through noise and chuckles like a crow watching traffic lights at rush hour in November. You know that one, Death chuckles like a crow watching a good joke, you know the bloated bus that just finished stopping and all the half-dead people exhausted from living getting off through the back, you know that very one, some zombie with his head still clanking from ten hours of work and commute, some asshole with a swollen belly rushing on automatic for another bus and another forty-minute bus ride and another shopping fix and another quickly gulped supper in another too-bright apartment with another news report and another comedy show and another yawn on the phone and another quick fuck, Death is a crow perched on a light pole at Main and Broadway in November, studying how traffic lights glow under rain and neon spots, how human balls radiate and pulsate, studying how tire screams take time to be born. Did you not wince with the crowd? Did you not feel his surprise at watching himself bouncing and dying?

Silence through your soul, silence till three curves ahead

where an old Carib village gets slaughtered one hot Friday afternoon in July 1534 by twelve drunken conquistadors with brains rotten by syphilis, an old Carib village dedicated to Merciful Anacaona, men, women, and babies shivering from hunger and gangue fever, bellies sliced open, breasts sliced open, under mango roots and river pebbles, eye sockets turn toward your Jeep floating its last dance.

Shh, shh.

All this, because some poor, black bastard took himself too seriously. Some poor, fresh student could not forgive some poor, white bastard, who, five years ago, did not believe in fireflies.

Shh, shh.

This land, my land, is almost too damaged to dream. Almost too numb to enjoy the new seed. Almost too tired of waiting for justice. This land, my land since 1492, has been willing to settle for revenge.

Shh, shh.

Dear old friend pardon the pun, but if your magic is not good enough, *this land is my land, and you're gonna be part of the landscape.*

You need to remember that the firefly is not strong enough to kill you by himself. I repeat, *the firefly is not strong enough to kill you by himself.* Right now, your *Ti bonz'ange*, as my father calls it, your lower soul, is being sucked away by a pool of loveless light emanating from a power gate with no age, a doorway without keeper or name, a basic energy amplifier fucked up by centuries of pain and anger and resentment and hate and rage. Your enemy is calling from a place where every soul has been forced to split itself open, away from pain and insanity, where every soul has been forced to choose death, left hanging around without forgiveness or mercy, where every frequency wants to go home and merge in peace with infinity.

Shit your pants one last time, white man my friend, it's another sign of respect for the awesome power of Death. Then stop whining.

Shh, shh. Two curves ahead.

Find the chuckle that is making the black snake of hate dance for you. Find the madness that drinks from darkness.

Find your murderer.

A firefly cannot kill from far away, not in the morning when sorcerers finally go to bed, not when you can clearly see the sun's rays rolling like curtains along the beams of light that make this world a big blue orange. A firefly needs to be close and quick in order to strike. Locate your enemy waiting in front of you.

There will be a single peasant who will not be screaming and waving as your Jeep plunges into the ravine with bodies rolling in slow motion and a very surprised piglet tied to the hood.

Somewhere, standing beside Death there will be an average peasant with average battered clothes, average battered bag at his side, average battered hat on his head, you're welcome, here is another mint, scratched from head to toe and leaning on his walking stick because he bumped right into your radiator grid and almost died of fright, an average son of a bitch waiting quietly by the side of the road and not moving much because he needs all his focus to destroy your lucidity with his hate and his ally.

He will strike where your car is weakest.

Not the battery. Not the brake pads. Not the wheel bolts. No fresh puddle of SAW40 gleaming on the pavement. No crazy magic for you to swear at while crossing yourself. He will be standing by the side of the road right before the curve, his chuckle already circling like a buzzard in the dementia of your brain. He will broadcast in your head your own friendly voice of doubt and fear.

He will drive you crazy with fear.

You see, we don't need no big humming machines with neat little buttons that need to be plugged into bigger machines with neater bigger buttons that need to be plugged into more bigger machines with thousands of buttons that need to be plugged into the veins of the land and the veins of the slaves.

We don't need no painful, greedy, black box technology to transform energies and ride light-beam frequencies.

We don't.

While you were laughing and drinking and eyeing the women in my father's temple, he went sniffing for your soul and found the tail of your energy beam still coiled with sweat on the driver's seat. Right there, real quick, he found out every ghost of your past you refused to forgive, their radiance still burning high under your many coats of dutiful love, but your fears and denials vibrating even higher, asking for the lesson that would put an end once and for all to the rage inside you.

Every one of them. The peanut butter sandwiches you used to hide. Your cousin's blue Corgi Toy car. The sweet lies you told Annie before. The sweet lies you told her after. Every one of them that still makes you wince, that you've kept forgotten. The accounting teacher you begged not to flunk you. The check you cashed twice. The sweet lies you told Megan before. The sweet lies you told her after. Your roommate's camera.

He read every defeat, every lie, every self-imposed mutilation since your first steps, from before your mother's womb, he plugged into your ancestral hate of yourself up to three reincarnations ago.

You're busted, buddy.

He found the temple of denial that keeps generating your desire for pain and death. Right now, cell after cell, he is walking up the spine of your fake self-confidence, he is climbing back to the cage where a little child screams for the sun to come back. And he's brought his friends with him for the ride of your life.

That's voodoo for you, *mon.*

When Armstrong landed on the moon, his first two words were, Oh, shit. Right under his nose, there was a big, naked, flat footprint. Way before you guys, way before you knew the meaning of before, *Kompe Guinen* and his *guedes* went crossing the Eagle Nebula.

The only thing left for you to save your tanned, pickled, white ass is to do what you do best. What my father loves you for, what he admits he still learns from you every time you drop by his temple at the far end of the village.

Do your magic.

Your own and very own power that you've refined through every breath, your deadly discipline that got you soaring to higher levels and staying up there all those years without a single wrinkle of bitterness, a single shout of self-righteousness, what kept you from turning insane and bitter and rancid and little and living dead with another half zillion zombies in Babylon.

Draw your last and only weapon, the lesson that you came to teach us five years ago with your white shirt and your tiny cross, your bleached eyes and your big hairy calves, you made us laugh and giggle and tickle all inside the first time you fell off the mule, with your strong belly and your bushy red eyebrows that turned white in a month of soft sand and hard sun and gentle waves, with your not-so-naïve eyes and your funny accent and your frantic hard work and your so desperate need to save us. Draw your last weapon.

The only thing left to you is to laugh.

Laugh your head off.

Laugh so hard you shake the whole car, so hard you can't even open your eyes to see the road anymore. Laugh and tell the firefly, tell him from the bottom of your soul, hit him with a sword of light, straight to his shield of hate and rancor and lone-liness, pierce right through the chaos that drives him and this whole land and this entire continent.

Tell the man who's already killed you hours ago as he sat by the ravine drumming back the dead from this spoiled, sacred place, tell him, *Hey, stupid, I love you.*

I love you, big guy, I know you know what I mean, you are killing me, I love you anyway. I love you, man.

Tell him.

I love you, Son of God. I love you, beautiful, I think you're really neat, really cool. I love you, brother. I just saw your smile when you tasted your first almond, naked and bubbly by the vetiver bushes, it was pink and green against that chocolate of your hand, you had a thousand-volt smile while squatting on your heels, and the tree blessed you with another almond and you smiled bigger.

I love you, brother. I just saw your lake, when she died with your fourth brother, the lake is so deep and so old, you could not blow the dams soon enough to curse God, you could not cry enough, they came and took you away to live as a permanent alien, they came and took you away and you learned how to be a good boy and work hard and make everybody pay.

I love you, brother.

Tell him.

Scream to the morning sky turning bloody orange, louder than dogs and piglets, full breath from the belly, single flash of white light beaming back to Betelgeuse, tell him you're just another innocent scumbag son of a bitch and from now on the body cells of your last treason will heal back into perfection.

Tell him. Do your voodoo, my friend. Do your *miracle.*

Somewhere, somehow, a walking stick is gonna slip on a banana peel.

Simple as that.

Yup. Better park the Jeep under a mango tree.

Claude-Michel Prévost: "Omer and the Zobop" is about fear of joining. This story deals with the careful navigational path one must tread in terra incognita. Yes, there is alien technology, but mostly, there is the beacon—or compass—that allows self-aware intelligences from different realities to actually connect with each other. Because they do want to join. And they do connect. "Omer and the Zobop" is part of a series of six stories derived from my apprenticeship in the Course in Miracles and Other Spiritualities and regrouped under the provocative title "Black Stories for Confused White Men (Truth and Marketing!)." You be the judge.

LITTLE BONES

Jena Snyder

ELDIE WAS BORED. His mom had dumped him at his grandfather's farm so she could "go to bingo"—which Eldie knew darn well meant she was in the Ladies and Escorts at the Park Hotel, drinking draft with her buddies. If he was lucky, she might bring him home a cold cheeseburger and fries from the Dairy Bar. But it was more likely she'd either go home with Linda or some guy from the bar or even get herself locked up for the night.

Letting out a long sigh, Eldie kicked the loose rail of the fence. Maybe if he kicked it ten more times—he gave it another savage boot—it would fall off and Grandpa would come out of his daze and figure out there were better things for a twelve-year-old to be doing than hanging around watching somebody walk slowly around a barren field, waiting for something—a "divine power," the old coot said—to twitch the forked stick in his hands. Yeah, right. And he was going to be struck by lightning for thinking about Maryellen Chynouth's boobs when he was supposed to be doing his math homework.

"If you're so bored, Eldie," a voice broke into his thoughts, "why don't you come give it a try? See if you've got the gift?"

"Oh, geez, Grandpa—!" Eldie rolled his eyes.

The old man gave his John Deere cap a nudge, squinting under the sweat-stained brim. "I know you think it's all a bunch of horse you-know-what," he said. "So did I, when my Aunt Eugenie told me to give it a try. 'Cept the Smiths struck water first well they dug, when I pointed the way. Come on—hop your butt off that fence and get yourself over here."

If he didn't do what he was told, Eldie knew he'd get the belt. Twice—once from Grandpa and once from his mom, whenever she dragged in. So he hopped himself off the fence like he'd been told, and hurried across the rock-littered field.

"Hold the forks like this . . ." The old man placed the stick in Eldie's hands. "Now keep a good grip; if you get a pull, it's like to jerk right out of your hands."

Biting his lips to keep from saying anything smart, Eldie pretended to hold tight. "Now what?"

His grandfather's round shoulders shrugged. "Now you start walking. And hold on."

It was without a doubt the dumbest thing Eldie'd ever done in his life. Walking around an empty field, stumbling over the rocks, sweating like a pig in the deep-blue July afternoon, waiting for a forked stick to magically point to hidden water. Why the heck were they looking for water way out here anyway? Five minutes went by, then ten. Once, Eldie glanced up at his grandfather, hoping the old man'd relent, but all he got was a poke from one gnarled brown finger, and "Put your faith in God's hands, Eldie! How d'you expect to find anything if you don't trust Him to point the way?"

And then something weird happened. Eldie started to take a right, heading around a dried-up alkaline slough on the north end of the field, and something pulled him off balance. He went to his knees, hard, jamming one on the rock he must have tripped on, and he let out a word that earned him a smack on the back of the head. Grandpa didn't hold with any cursing.

Getting to his feet, Eldie once more started right. This time, it was no rock that yanked him off balance. It was the stick in his hands.

Grandpa let out a hoot. "You got one, Eldie! Go on, follow it!"

Rooted with shock, Eldie gaped at the vibrating stick in his hands. It was shaking because he was, he tried to tell himself, but why would he be shaking if the stick wasn't in the first place? "Go, boy!" Grandpa shouted, clapping him on the shoulder, and he lurched forward into the clump of dead bog willows on the far side of the dry slough, the stick towing him as if on a rope.

He stopped short with a gasp, the forks of the stick prickling suddenly in his grasp, electrified. Unbelievably, the stick gave an almighty jerk, pointing straight down.

"And you hit water?" the policewoman asked, nodding toward Eldon's cigarettes. "May I?" she asked with an expression that told him she'd rather bum a smoke off the Devil, except he wasn't sitting at the table with them. "I'm trying to quit, but . . ."

Eldon tapped one out of the pack—only two left now, he saw with dismay—and pushed it grudgingly towards her. "Help yourself." Twenty years had passed since that July afternoon, but he could still feel the forked stick burning in his hands. He wished he'd never said anything to Ralph about it when he saw that story in the *Sun* yesterday: "Little Kayla's grief-stricken parents offer $5000 reward after kidnapper refuses to divulge where he hid body." If he'd just kept his mouth shut, he wouldn't be trotting out this godforsaken story to a cop. A detective, yet. She didn't look old enough to be out of high school. "Hit water?" he said. "Not a chance."

"What?" Lit match in hand, cigarette between her lips, the woman stared at him incredulously. Mercedes something, she'd said her name was, Eldon remembered, "like the car." Stupid name. Who in hell would name a baby girl after a car? "I thought the whole point of this story was that you actually found something!"

"It is, it is!" Ralph chuckled. "Just wait—this is the good part!"

Eldon clenched his fists, hiding them under the little round bar table. This was a mistake, just like telling Ralph had been a mistake. But there was no turning back now, not with three months' rent owing and a five-thousand-buck reward on the line. "Like I said, I didn't hit water. That's just what most dowsers find. Diviners. Whatever you want to call 'em. My grandpa said he was a 'wishing rod walker,' but I never heard nobody else call it that. Some find metal, gold, silver. Some even find oil."

"And?" The policewoman exhaled, squinting through the smoke. "What did you find?"

She didn't know? Eldon shot a glance at Ralph, who'd claimed he'd told her "the whole shebang." It was pretty clear he hadn't told her dick. Eldon lifted his glass, draining the last of the watered-down beer. What was also pretty damn clear was that she thought this was all a bunch of crap. That's what he should tell her, he decided. Doing it was bad enough, but if he had to *talk* about it, too . . . ! No. It wasn't worth it.

Ralph must have realized Eldon was going to blow it off and jumped in. "He found a body!"

"A body!" The woman's blue eyes widened. "You mean a— *dead* body? A person?"

Eldon nodded reluctantly, wishing he could afford another beer to wash away the ugly metallic taste that was in his mouth, just like it had been that hot July afternoon. He'd told it so many times, the words came out like a scratchy record, starting and stopping in jerks: "Not two feet down. Grandpa started digging, and right away we spotted it. Wasn't much left but bones and cloth, but we both knew right away it was that Hutterite girl'd disappeared from the colony a few years back. Nobody else wore those long skirts and kerchiefs. Listen . . . can you spring for another couple beer?"

The policewoman shook her head in disgust, but waved the waitress over. "Two more, and bring me the tab. And you were how old, Mr. Kozak?"

"Twelve." Eldon stuck an Export A in his mouth, lighting it with a jerky motion and taking a long, shuddering drag. The metallic taste refused to go away. The terrycloth on the tabletop was the same faded blue as the cornflowers on the dead girl's skirt. With one nicotine-stained finger, he touched the beer-damp terrycloth, willing the images, the memories, to go away. "Grandpa made me stay there," he said. "I was too young to drive the truck into town, y'know? So I just sat down beside the bones and waited for him to come back with the cops."

When the waitress came back with the beer, Eldon didn't wait for her to set it down, just grabbed it right off her tray. He gulped half of it down without tasting it. "Her head was all caved in—even with the kerchief, you could see that. And it was no accident she was there: somebody'd killed her, and hid her out in Old Man Perkins' field, buried her in that patch of bog willow where he knew nobody'd ever go, even with the slough dried up."

The policewoman's cigarette was forgotten, the long ash drooping. "And? What else?"

Eldon finished the beer, licking his lips. He could feel the sun beating on the back of his head, burning the images into his skull. "The little bones," he said, having to clear his throat. "The little bones inside her. The cops never did make an arrest, but I figured somebody killed her because of those little bones. Back then it was bad enough, a fourteen-year-old getting knocked up, but a Hutterite? They've got pretty strict rules about stuff like that." He took a last drag at the cigarette before crushing the butt in the overflowing ashtray. "Nobody believed me, but I know it was her dad. Just felt it, like the damn pull of the stick. She was just a kid! How could somebody do that to her—her own father?"

He glanced round the dim barn of a bar, trying to find something to hang onto, something to look at to flush the picture out of his mind, but it wasn't working. He couldn't stop thinking about it. When he'd first seen the baby's bones, he thought they were an animal's. All curled up nice and neat like a baby-sized bone doll on the bone mother's stomach. Where her stomach would have been, big and round, the baby ripe and ready to be born. Why kill her then, when she was already so big everybody would've known? Was the baby already dead before the girl was buried? Or was it still flutter-kicking in her womb while the bastard pushed dirt over her? Did it wonder why everything was so quiet, so still? Eldie shook the last cigarette out of the pack. *Go away*, he thought savagely. *Go away, all of you.*

"So that's how you found the others?" the policewoman prodded. "I thought you were a psychic. So you made a business out of dowsing for bodies?" The way she said it, you'd think Eldon was the one killing and burying them.

"Look, I don't know if I can even do it anymore," he said. "It's been ten years since I quit. Sure, I was in it for the reward money. Why not? It was okay, the ones that just wandered off, fell down and died somewhere. I always tried for those ones. But then there was the oilman's kid. Twelve. Same age I was when I first laid hold of that stick. I wasn't much more'n a kid myself at the time, twenty maybe. They were camping, the family said. She went for a walk, never came back. It should've been just like the others, she got lost, cold, just lay down and died, right?" He took a hard drag on the cigarette. "They lied. *He* lied. He didn't tell me about the rifle that was gone, the one she had to prop against a rock, pull the trigger with a stick because she couldn't keep the barrel in her mouth and pull the trigger at the same time. He didn't tell me she killed herself because he couldn't keep his hands off her, just like that Hutterite girl's dad. I quit after that. Couldn't do it no more."

The detective narrowed her eyes, her head tilted. "But now you're willing to come out of retirement, Mr. Kozak? You think you can find where her body's hidden?"

"Sure he can!" Ralph said eagerly. "Eldie can find her no problem! Hey, man—" he said to Eldon, "for five thousand bucks, I'm bettin' you could find Jimmy Hoffa!"

"Yeah." Eldon looked the woman in the eye, wondering whether she hated him more than he hated himself. "For the reward."

"I don't believe this," she said tightly. "God, you people make me sick!"

"So." Eldon stubbed out the cigarette. "Can we get started? I don't want to talk to the parents or nothing, though. I don't do that."

The detective glared at Eldon. "Don't you worry, Mr. Kozak. I'm not going to let anybody—not a fake psychic or diviner or whatever—take advantage of their grief, do you hear me? It wouldn't matter if their little Kayla had been missing for five days or five hundred. You couldn't find her if she was under your nose!"

"It's not just a bunch of BS." Eldon didn't even bother looking up. He knew the ring of faces wouldn't change expression even if he said it a thousand times. "Look: I don't know how I do it. I sure as hell don't get off on doing it, like some of you are hinting. The only reason I'm doing it is—"

"For the five thousand dollars," Detective Mercedes Worthing finished for him. She looked a lot more like a cop now that they were in one of the interrogation rooms. In the blue-white glare of the fluorescents, she looked older than she had in the bar, too.

"Ah, forget it!" Eldon said, shoving the chair back in a savage rush. "I don't care how much money it is—it's not worth being treated like *I'm* the creep who grabbed the kid! You don't want my help, fine."

"Good." Worthing snapped up the phone sitting on the table and punched in some numbers. "Ed? Yeah, it's me. I got him to change his mind. He says—"

Whoever it was on the other end cut her off. "But—" she tried after a moment. "He—" Then her tight shoulders sagged in dismay. When she hung up, the look she gave Eldon was poisonous. "They're here. Mr. and Mrs. Barnes. They insist on talking with you."

"Shit." Eldon blew out a nervous breath. "Can't you just tell them I already left? I never talk to the parents. Never."

There was a knock at the door, and a young constable popped his head in. "Mr. and Mrs. Barnes are here."

"Too late." Worthing lifted her hands in defeat. "You might as well send them in. I'll tell them. And you—" She glared at Eldon. "Don't you open your mouth!"

When the parents were ushered in, Eldon was shocked to see how young they were, just kids themselves. The mother couldn't have been a day over eighteen, and the father didn't look like he shaved more than once a week. He was carrying a framed photo of a toddler in a frilly red dress, her hair the same glossy black as her patent leather shoes. If Eldon thought he could just fade into the woodwork he was wrong: the mother rushed straight to him.

"This is Kayla's favorite teddy—" She thrust a stuffed blue bear into Eldon's hands. "Please—you've got to help us! You've got to find her so we can—so we can—!" Her face crumpled, and she burst into childlike sobbing. Eldon tried to stand, but Worthing gave him a look that froze him cold.

"Mrs. Barnes," Worthing said gently as she steered the weeping mother to a chair, "you know how the police service feels about this whole thing. Every single one of these so-called psychics who've phoned have been cranks. Now, I've talked to Mr. Kozak . . ." Her voice dropped to a soft murmur, reassuring.

Eldon couldn't take his eyes off the sweet-faced toddler in the photo, a smiling doll in a doll's fluffy dress. He was afraid if he looked away, he'd somehow see her as she was now, dead and buried, bright apple face gray and still, dirt in her hair. *Oh God please I changed my mind,* he silently begged. *I don't want to do this.*

It came in a dark gush like groundwater breaking the surface: *you're my little treasure sweetheart my little buried treasure keep you with me forever and ever together won't that be fun?*

All the fine hairs on the back of Eldon's neck rose in a prickling rush. She *was* buried, under the ground. But not just pressed down with dirt, not hastily pushed into a shallow trench and covered over. Eldon could smell it, that horrible smell of fresh-turned earth and roots and grubs . . . *the man took her a big soft man white like an underground thing like a grub a larva took her and put her under the ground in a box something a box a tomb big and yawning all alone—*

The thought of those little bones lying forgotten somewhere, lost for all time, made his heart sick. "I'll try," he said suddenly, making them all look up at him in surprise. "I can't promise you anything, but I swear to God, I'll try."

"We don't even have a place to start," Worthing told him. "Lilliman—the kidnapper—just smiles when we ask where she is. She's his 'little buried treasure,' he says. As long as he keeps his mouth shut, she'll still be where he left her when he gets out. Can you imagine anything so sick? He's already looking forward to digging her up and enjoying her all over again!"

Eldon shuddered. He didn't want to tell Worthing he already knew about the "buried treasure." "How did you find him?" he asked.

"He got nailed ten years ago when he tried to grab a little girl outside a Safeway. She screamed and bit him—he's still got the scar—and one of the bagboys tackled the bastard, held him till the police got there. He got out of prison a year ago, all shiny clean and rehabilitated, Mr. Model Citizen. We never should have trusted that prison shrink; he's the same one that let out those two lowlifes who hit the bank on Jasper and then killed a patrolman. The day after Kayla disappeared, one of the kids at her school said she'd seen 'a big man in a striped car' talking to Kayla, and when we talked to the rest of the kids, one of the Grade 5 boys said, 'Hey, Larva Man's got a big old Barracuda with racing stripes. He hangs around the 7-Eleven all the time.' Larva Man. That's Lilliman to a T: a big, creepy white slug."

One hand on the wheel, she awkwardly dug a package of Nicorettes out of her purse and tossed them to Eldon. "Pop one out for me, will you? Anyway, when we went to talk to him, what's lying on his coffee table but a Polaroid of Kayla! She was wearing a shirt her mom bought her for her birthday three weeks ago. We had a search warrant in an hour, and found enough to nail him but good—hair, fibers. We even found blood that matches Kayla's type—but he won't budge on what he did with the body. We tore his house apart, looked in the walls, the ceiling, the furnace ducting; we dug up his yard, his basement, checked every storage facility, office building he's ever worked at, you name it. We've grilled him for three days and nights straight, threatening him, pleading with him, promising him deals, you name it. And nothing. He just keeps spouting this crap about Egypt, all this quasi-religious gobbledegook. He told the shrinks he's the pharoah Amun-thoth and he and his 'little treasure' will be together until the great sun god Ra falls from the sky. God, it makes me sick just thinking about it."

Eldon was listening to her, but nothing much was getting through. Deep inside he knew it was hopeless, that Lilliman had tucked Kayla's body away in some dark, secret place not even God could find. Worthing knew it and Eldon knew it. But every time he started to open his mouth to tell her so, he found him-self back in Old Man Perkins' field, hunkered down beside the dead Hutterite girl, the palms of his hands burning. Everybody had a right to be laid to rest, not dumped like a bag of unwanted trash. He thought of the stricken look on the young mother's face. Everybody had the right to say goodbye, too. And how could they do that until Kayla's body was found?

"Let's start at his house," Eldon said with a sigh.

Worthing had been right about Lilliman's house: it was little more than a hollow shell in the middle of a wild and overgrown yard. It reminded Eldon of the "haunted house" a couple of blocks over from his mom's place back home: a ramshackle old two-story house with a shaggy caragana hedge and no porch light, the kind of place kids made up all sorts of crazy stories about. Except this time the stories were true, he thought with a shudder.

"So where's your divining rod?"

Eldon glanced at Worthing, not understanding for a moment. "Oh," he said. "You mean the stick. I don't have one."

Worthing shook her head. "I'm going to wait in the car."

Eldon figured that since the police had already torn up the house and the yard, it wouldn't matter if he hacked off a forked piece of the caragana. Far as he remembered, it didn't matter what kind of wood you used, or even if the wishing rod was wood: Grandpa'd said he remembered one walker using a pair of pliers to dowse.

It was only May, and it wasn't hot, but by the time Eldon had covered just a fraction of the property, he was running with sweat. Mostly from dread, thinking about the terrible things Lilliman had done. He'd started in the center of the house, Lilliman's bedroom and shrine to his "treasures," where the walls were papered with a bizarre collage: there was a brochure from the King Tut exhibit, articles about Egypt, mummies, the pyramids . . . and then there were pictures of little girls. Most of these were carefully cut out of magazines and catalogues, little girls modeling underwear, bathing suits. In the middle was an elaborate spiral of Polaroid photos, some color ones of Kayla, some faded black-and-whites of other little girls; Eldon knew those images would be etched forever into his mind, no matter how he wished he could forget them. There was some clue in the arrangement of the photos, Lilliman claimed, and even though the psychiatrists doubted it, they were afraid to let the police take the photos down just in case. He'd had years to plan this, he taunted. All those years in prison to figure it out so they'd never find her.

Every half an hour or so, Worthing would heave herself out of her car with a sigh and come see how Eldon was doing. He'd just shake his head, not looking up, and continue slowly walking.

One time, she pulled him to a stop. "I thought you might want some supper," she said. "Come on—it's in the car."

"I'm not hungry," he tried to tell her, but the moment he smelled the food, his stomach started to growl in eager anticipation. He pulled a Teen Burger out of the bag and tore off the greasy wax-paper wrapper, devouring half of it within the first two bites. But as he reached for the waxed glass of root beer, he noticed the sky for the first time since he'd started walking: the sun was nearly down.

He set the glass back in the cardboard holder. "I can get a couple more turns in before it gets dark—"

Worthing caught his sleeve, making him turn in question. "Eldon, she's—" There was pity in her eyes. "Let's call it a day. She's not going anywhere."

Eldon slept poorly that night, nightmares of crying little girls making him moan in his sleep. There was a huge river between them, and no bridge. The greeny-brown water churned and roared, tearing huge trees out of the bank, so loud, the noise it made was deafening. But he could still hear them, dozens of little girls wailing on the other side of the river. In the dim light of a sickle moon, he could see their bare legs and arms, could see the way they shivered, so cold.

He thought he might be able to reach them if he tunneled under the river. In his dream, it made perfect sense. He hadn't anticipated finding the bones when he started to dig.

He woke up sobbing, sick with the knowledge of what he'd find in Lilliman's overgrown yard.

By the time Worthing pulled up at nine, Eldon had been walking for two hours without pause. She called to him, but he ignored her, plodding over the churned-up iris bulbs and dried-up flowers, head down, intent only on the Y-shaped caragana branch in his hands. He'd let the wishing rod choose his direction, tossing it in the air first thing that morning, following the way it pointed when it fell: east, toward the glassless skeleton of the greenhouse and the garden shed beyond.

Worthing jogged across the big yard. It was tough going in dress shoes, especially through the parts that had been dug up, and she was out of breath and in a foul mood by the time she reached Eldon. "I told you I had to do an interview with ITV this morning! Why didn't you call before you—" Her eye was caught by the three stakes he'd put in the ground, each one marked with bits of yellow police ribbon—ribbon that he'd torn off the front gate, she realized. "What are these supposed to be?" she demanded.

"Bones," he said wearily. He stopped for a moment, face as gray and weathered as the unpainted boards of the fence ten yards away. Dark streaks cut through the dust on his cheeks, tears that had been running, unchecked, since daybreak. "I don't know which one of them's Kayla. All I know is, if you dig where I marked, you'll find bones."

Sometime around noon, the sun like a fiery white coin in the sky, Eldon took a step towards the garden shed and collapsed in a heap, arms and legs twitching like a sleeping dog's. Worthing and one of the half-dozen officers and a forensic archeologist who'd arrived to start digging the spots Eldon had marked—four now—dragged him to the shade of the cruiser and propped him up in the back seat. Worthing pushed a straw into his mouth and told him to drink; he gasped when the ice-cold cola washed over his tongue.

"Did you find her?" he asked, his voice thick.

The way her eyes suddenly cut away told him the news wasn't

good. "No," Worthing admitted. "But you were right. Every spot you've marked—" Her lips started to tremble, eyes welling with helpless tears. "They must have been here for years, from before Lilliman was in prison. There's nothing left but bones."

Eldon didn't say anything; there was nothing he could say. When he'd sucked the waxy paper cup dry, he hauled himself out of the cruiser and went to find the wishing rod.

He'd been around the garden shed twice now, the wishing rod pulling him in an ever-narrowing circle. "You've looked here?" he asked Worthing, and, for the fourth time, she told him yes, they'd looked there. The shed was one of the first places they'd searched. They'd even dug round it, broken holes in the plank floor, dug holes in the dirt beneath. There was nothing. Much as Eldon wanted to find Kayla Barnes' body, he was praying he'd never feel that terrible burning in his hands again. He didn't want to find any more little bones.

Toward sundown, Eldon blacked out again. This time when he came to, he wasn't in the back of Worthing's car, he was in an ambulance. Worthing pulled off the oxygen mask. "Why didn't you tell me you were sick?" she demanded, sounding more upset than angry. "You're in no shape to be out here day in, day out."

"If you really want to help," he said, sitting up, "get me a six-pack of Bud. Where's my stick?" His hands were shaking like an old man's.

"Eldon, wait—" Worthing put her hand on his arm. "Just rest here for an hour or so—"

"It'll be dark in an hour," he said stubbornly.

Even when night fell, Eldon wouldn't give up. Worthing, guessing this, had called to get some big spotlights set up so he could keep going. She suspected he'd die before he'd admit defeat; she knew because she felt the same way. Finding Kayla Barnes' body had become an obsession that grew stronger with every false twitch of the wishing rod.

"It's because you're so exhausted," Worthing tried to tell him when the officers gave up on the third empty dig. "Take a break, at least, Eldon. Let me take you over to the station for an hour. You can have a shower, take a nap, come back and start fresh."

"No." He trudged away from her, feet dragging.

"Eldon—"

He stopped, head hanging, the wishing rod resting on his thighs. "What?"

"Why are you doing this? What difference will it make if we find her at midnight or on Wednesday at ten-thirty in the morning? Why do you have to keep pushing yourself until you drop?"

He opened his mouth, wishing he could explain about the dreams. All those little girls, skin like snow in the moonlight, crying in the cold. Yellow duckies and flowers and superheroines on their panties. Fingers and toes blue with cold. Crying like to break your heart. How could he explain? He didn't know what was driving him, either; just that he couldn't stop until all of them, Kayla included, were finally laid to rest. Those shiny black shoes black patent like tap shoes tapping tapping like water dripping. *Where did he put you? Why can't I find you, when I found all the others? What did he do different to hide you so much better so much deeper tapping tapping water dripping oh God, Kayla, where are you?*

He could feel that creeping black fog coming over him, the dizzy which-end-is-up sensation that came with passing out, and he shook it off angrily. Not now. No falling down or giving up or going on a bender to wipe it out. *Jesus, but a cold beer would go down nice even root beer dark as Kayla's shiny shoes do you want to go for some root beer sweetie root bear from the A and double all you want and a Teen Burger and fries and root bear root beer I'm thirsty I want my mommy want to go home now—*

Eldon paused for a moment to wipe the sweat and tears out of his eyes. *Please*, he thought hopelessly. *Please help me find her. Please make this end.*

And then the stick gave an almighty wrench in his hands, jerking him off to the left as if he were on invisible wires. He clamped down hard on the quivering branches, that unmistakable electrical burn crackling through his palms, harder and hotter and stronger than it had ever been. Straight past the garden shed with its false hopes, straight on to the fence, and still pulling. "Knock it down!" he cried. "Knock it down, for God's sake!"

One of the officers ran forward, began pushing at the fence. Worthing joined him, and then the others. Groaning and creaking, the old planks and posts grudgingly gave way. Eldon stumbled over the broken fence, heart in his throat.

"That's not in the warrant!" Worthing cried as he kept going. "Eldon—this is the neighbor's property! We have no legal right to be here!"

He didn't care. The sun was burning the back of his head, the buzz of grasshoppers all around him. Beneath his feet, there was no close-cropped grass, no carefully set paving stones: there was only the dry, rocky dust of a long-barren wheat field. He didn't see the fresh-turned earth beside the shed set against the fence they'd knocked down: he saw only a scrub patch of bog willow round a dried-up white alkaline slough.

"There!" Worthing cried at the same moment the sticks in Eldon's hand sent a red-hot bolt all the way from his palms to his brain. He went to his knees, the stick plunging itself into the black dirt, and began to cry.

"Right here—dig right here—" he wept. "Oh God, Kayla, I'm sorry. I'm so sorry . . ."

Worthing was on her knees beside him, arm around his shoulders as he sobbed inconsolably. "Eldon . . . Eldon . . . !" she whispered. "It's okay. It's over. You did great, Eldon. We never could have done it without your help."

"But they're dead!" he groaned. "They're all dead, all those little girls, all those little bones …! What the hell good is it, when they're dead?"

"Hey!" one of the officers shouted. "There's something here! Detective! There's a tunnel, some kind of passageway!"

There was a sound of metal on metal, a hollow gonging, and then the most beautiful, incredible sound in the world as they broke through to the gaudily decorated chamber below, Lilliman's hidden tomb full of plastic Egyptian knick-knacks and empty A&W containers.

As light streamed into the chamber, a little girl, her face grubby and tear-stained, stared owl-eyed and stunned at the policemen peering in. At one's smiling "Hi, sweetheart," she sucked in a breath, thin and scared and shrill but alive, so wonderfully alive, and began to wail.

Jena Snyder: I've never believed that prayer can influence our lives, not in the sense that God is a white-bearded bureaucrat sitting at a desk somewhere listening to appeals and deciding to intervene in this case, ignore that one, or to punish someone else. Instead, I believe God is a focus, a source of strength we can draw upon in a time of need. In "Little Bones," Eldon is afraid of his power because of what he found the first time he tried dowsing. He never looked past that point in his life or in his faith, and when he is called upon to look for Kayla Barnes, his self-doubt nearly stops him before he starts.

Something else that's inherent in the story is my belief in objects of power. In the same way that a rosary can become a focal point and source of strength for a devout Catholic, a branch of caragana can likewise become a focus for great strength and even greater accomplishment through belief in one's ability.

FLESH AND BLOOD

Brent Buckner

MY HAND SHOOK AS I REACHED TO RING Douglas Crain's doorbell, lit up in the night. I took a deep breath, trying to calm myself for the coming debate with the elderly Jesuit. I had to convince my old teacher to help me destroy myself, and I had never won even a trivial argument with him.

Instantly, I tried the doorknob. The door was unlocked. I pushed it open and called into the house. Again, I received no response, so I tentatively tried to stick a foot over the threshold. An invisible wall stopped me; another aspect of the legends confirmed.

I tried calling again, more loudly. "Douglas? It's Patrick."

This time, I got a response. His muffled voice came to me from the kitchen, but obviously originated in the basement. "Come on in! I'll be up in a second."

The barrier fell at his words, and I stepped over the threshold. That was as far as I was going, though. A crucifix hung on the wall at the end of the entrance passageway, just before the kitchen. It held me at bay.

I called back. "I'll just wait for you here at the door, thanks." I turned myself away from the burning cross and leaned into the door. It helped, a bit.

I didn't have long to wait. I soon heard his footsteps coming up the stairs, followed by his appearance at the end of the entranceway.

"Don't come any closer!" Douglas stopped, startled by my odd greeting. The cross he wore around his neck had necessitated it. "Just stay there for a moment. Please." At least he couldn't feel too threatened by me, once he understood what I had become.

"Patrick, are you ill?" His voice was curious, concerned.

Of course he had reached that conclusion. I looked awful, and here I was telling him to keep his distance. In some sense he was right; I was sick.

"Not in the way that you mean. It's hard to explain." Start slowly. "It's mostly psychological, but I have some physical symptoms, too." The expression on Douglas' face was carefully neutral. He didn't want to risk offending me; when he had all the facts, he would allow his reactions to show.

"I have a strong aversion to religious symbols, especially crosses and crucifixes. It would make it easier for me if you'd put your cross inside your shirt. Keep it on, though. And you could also take down the crucifix. Put it in the kitchen or something." Douglas simply nodded and complied.

He stepped back into view after removing the crucifix from the wall and depositing it in the kitchen. "Is that better?"

"Much better, thank you. Is there someplace we could sit and talk?"

He jerked his head, indicating with his chin the room off to my left. "The living room should be fine. Just give me a moment to move any artifacts that you'd find disturbing." He ducked into the room, turned on the lights and re-emerged. "No, I think that should be acceptable. I just wanted to double-check. Why don't you look in and let me know if anything's bothersome?"

"That sounds good. Thanks." Douglas went into the room, and I stepped to the empty doorway. I only had to glance around. If there was anything to be wary of, I could hardly miss it. "No, it's fine." I hadn't said anything about mirrors, but fortunately, there wasn't one in the room. I stepped toward the couch opposite Douglas' customary chair.

"Is there anything I can get you? A coffee, perhaps?"

"No, thank you. I don't think it's on my diet. Maybe we could just sit down, and I'll try to explain my problem."

"Okay, Patrick. Just let me know if you want anything."

We settled into our seats, and I readied myself with a deep breath. Any explanation would sound outrageous, but that was the nature of my predicament. All that I had to do was get Douglas to believe what he saw.

"I just told you one of the symptoms of my condition. There's another that I probably have. I'd like you to tell me whether or not I'm exhibiting it. I can't tell."

Douglas sat forward a bit, as though to get a better view of me. "Okay. What am I looking for?"

"I'll need a mirror to show you. I'd rather not tell you what it is; it would sound pretty fantastic. If I've got it, you'll know." I thought for a moment. "Do you have a shaving mirror, or a hand mirror? Something small."

"I have one of those double-sided shaving mirrors. Will that do?"

"Sounds good. Would you get it, please? And uh, I've also got an aversion to mirrors, so don't come close with it."

"Then how will I see anything, if you can't get close to it?"

"I'll explain it when you've got the mirror. Please."

Douglas gave me an odd look, trying to decide how to treat my reluctance to divulge any details. He settled on humoring me. "Okay. I'll be back in a flash."

I braced myself for the brightness of the mirror. I moved to the edge of the couch furthest from the doorway. Looking through the doorway, I could watch the stairs Douglas had gone up.

When he started down, mirror in hand, I gave him a couple of instructions. "Remember, I really don't like to be around those things. Just stand in the doorway and keep the mirror behind your back. I'll turn my back to it." Once Douglas was in position, I twisted on the couch so that I was facing the wall.

"Now what do I do?"

"Just hold up the mirror, point it at me, and look at my reflection. When you've got that, let me know."

"Okay. Seems pretty odd though. I can tell you what you look like without this thing."

I counted to five after that comment. "Can you spot me?"

Douglas' voice was agitated. "No, I can't. I can see the couch, right where you're sitting, but I can't see you in the mirror."

"Put it back then. That's what we were looking for. And you might feel better if you pulled out that cross again. Just don't come near me." I heard his footsteps start up the stairs. I turned, watching for his return.

It took longer this time. I heard a door closing, and then everything was quiet.

He reappeared in the doorway, his cross a beacon on his chest. "All right, Patrick. Tell me what this is all about."

I chose my words carefully, giving him little to disagree with. "I am suffering from a belief that I am a vampire. What's worse, I can't disprove it. In fact, the only evidence I've got tends to reinforce the belief. That's why I'm here."

Douglas frowned. "You really believe this? Why?"

"Well, the most compelling evidence is that I don't have a reflection. You saw that. I didn't even tell you what to look for, so it certainly wasn't a matter of the power of suggestion." Douglas' eyebrows lifted, conceding the point. "There's my reaction to crosses and mirrors. I also can't stand garlic."

"So how do you think it happened?"

"You'd better have a seat, preferably at the other end of the room." As Douglas settled himself, I began my story with the ringing of the telephone a few nights earlier.

With a sigh, I put aside the remains of my Caesar salad and picked up the phone. The voice on the other end of the line was a teenage girl's, tight with nervousness. She explained that she was calling about the death of John Casey, a seventeen-year-old in my parish. I had buried him that week, an apparent suicide. She hinted that there was some deeper motive than simple angst, and asked me to meet her.

She asked me to avoid standing out, including looking like a priest. I supposed that she was worried about her image with whoever passed for her friends. It was a minor request, easy to grant.

She met me at the bus depot, recognizing me from my description. Her own appearance was unremarkable; I couldn't have picked her out of the crowd. When she came up to me, the only impression I had was of a teenage girl with short black hair. She introduced herself in quick, nervous tones, and asked me to come outside with her. She was uncomfortable staying still. She felt exposed. It seemed natural to try to put her at ease.

We began walking, with her leading the way. As we walked, she began to talk about street life. I thought she was steeling herself to talk about whatever was bothering her, and listened attentively for conversational cues. I lost track of where we were. I had to focus on her voice, or her words just slipped away. It was as though I were listening to a poem, hearing the meter and the rhyme instead of the meaning.

I don't know how long this lasted. When we stopped, I felt like a sleepwalker suddenly awakened. Looking around, I saw that we had wandered into a rundown residential area. We stood in front of an old house, indistinguishable from the rest. Obviously, this had been her destination from the time we left the depot.

She apologized for taking so much of my time; she had to be sure that we hadn't been followed. She had to be sure that she could trust me. Almost shyly, she invited me in.

I couldn't turn away, when she seemed so close to opening up. And there was something else—I wanted to do as she said.

She unlocked the door and stepped aside to usher me in. I stepped into an unlit hallway. As she swung the door shut, I was plunged into utter darkness. Turning to speak, I heard the key turn in the inside lock.

And then she was upon me. I didn't even have a chance to struggle; I was so disoriented, she had me gagged and bound with handcuffs on my wrists and ankles before I could react.

She carried me downstairs and secured me to a pole. Only then did she turn on a light, revealing the windowless basement room.

She carefully explained that she wanted me to understand the gift she was giving me: an eternity at her side. She showed me that she had no reflection before she fed.

I regained consciousness with a painful bite on my neck and vague discomfort in my stomach. Within a few hours, that incipient heartburn grew into an inferno. I was reduced to groaning and whimpering into my gag.

She kept checking on me, obviously worried. In some twisted way, she really did care. She kept telling me that it wasn't supposed to be like this at all. She tried to comfort me, holding me and murmuring to me.

In spite of the pain, I fell asleep in her arms. The demands of my body sent me into complete unconsciousness.

The second night, she ungagged me. She even let me pray aloud, though it obviously bothered her. God, she told me icily, hadn't just abandoned us, He had made Himself our enemy. For the crime of simply being what we were.

I lay on the floor, drifting in and out of delirium. Along with the constant companionship of pain was the sick certainty that God would not even let me die. He was letting me become one of the undead, the damned. I prayed, but was no longer sure why.

The third night, I awoke screaming. The cross I wore under my shirt was burning like molten steel. She burst into the room and loosed me, so that I could tear it off. It burned my hand when I flung it away.

My transformation was complete.

She cradled my head and brushed the tears from my cheeks. The pain in my stomach reasserted itself with a vengeance. I belched, and the air carried the stench of garlic. It was my last meal, the Caesar salad. It had boiled in my stomach since my change had begun.

A pure, driving need to get away swallowed all rational thought. The next thing I can remember, I was running down the street, alone.

I found a cab and gave Douglas' address.

I broke off uncomfortably at the end of my story; the memories had been painful, and it had taken longer to give the summary than I would have guessed.

Seeing that I had finished, Douglas asked me to stand. I saw that he had put his cross back under his shirt. "Patrick, you aren't hungry right now, are you?" I shook my head, and he continued. "I'm covering my cross because it'll make things easier tonight. We have to make some arrangements for you to stay here, safely. It'll be better if you don't have to stand across the room from me."

I had never explained just what sort of help I had come for. I didn't want to make it real by saying it aloud. I had hoped that Douglas would infer it. Since he hadn't, I had to make it plain. "Douglas, I didn't come to you for refuge."

"Then why did you come?"

"I came because I'm afraid. I'm too dangerous. I'll get hungry sometime; you know that. I can't take a risk on what I'll do when that happens. You don't understand how powerful all of these sensations are: the revulsion for garlic, the pain of the cross. I'm afraid of just how terrible my hunger will be. I want you to help me die, now, while I can still control myself. I just can't do it alone."

He gaped at me. Throughout all of my tale, he had listened calmly. Now he was astonished. "What! How can you even think of that? Look, I know you're frightened. You're going through a terrible trial. But you can't just give up, toss aside your life as though it were nothing more than an inconvenience. You're a priest! You know better than that."

Then he delivered his pronouncement. "God has given us this opportunity to understand, to act. We must use whatever time He has given us." His tone was final.

That made me angry. "What He has given us? God hasn't given me anything! Don't you get it, Douglas? I'm one of them. The undead, the soulless. I'm a vampire, damn it! He's turned His back on me! I'm damned already."

Douglas just looked at me mildly and brought me up short. "Prove it."

Prove it? What did he want? I'd shown him I had no reflection. I'd given him my symptoms. I'd told him my story. What other explanation could there be? "Haven't you been listening? What more proof do you want? I suppose I could try to turn into a bat. I must be able to, if I could find out how. How else can I prove to you that I'm a vampire? Stand in the sun and fry? I'm afraid of what I'll do to get out of it. I thought you understood that."

He shook his head. "No, I'm willing to accept that you are a vampire, at least as a working hypothesis. We might be able to determine a few other tests for reassurance, but that's a minor concern. What you haven't proven is that you're damned."

"Douglas, I'm driven off by crosses. Doesn't that suggest something to you?"

"Well, being driven off by a cross certainly isn't a necessary condition for damnation." He was using his academic's voice, talking about this as though it were some abstract puzzle. "Is it sufficient? My first guess would be that it isn't. God is rarely so obvious."

He continued, hand gesturing as it would in a lecture.

"When you first told me of your condition, you were trying to avoid telling me flat-out that you're a vampire. So you chose to describe your symptoms, as though you had one or more ill-nesses. I think that approach has merit."

I broke in. "But I'm not sick. I break physical laws. I'm a supernatural creature."

"But you are bound by rules. We have to understand those rules and what lies behind them. We can't blindly accept the superstitious explanations." He fired a question at me. "What does an aversion to mirrors suggest about the state of your soul?"

"Nothing, I suppose."

"And what if your aversion to crosses is of the same nature as your aversion to mirrors?"

It was Socratic cross-examination at its finest. He asked the right leading questions, and I was forced to state his point for him. "Okay, so what if being driven off by crosses doesn't prove that I'm damned? I'm still either going to drink human blood or starve to death. I don't know if I'll be able to choose the starva-tion and stick to it."

"I'll make you an offer. Stay here as long as you feel you are in control. Then, if we can't arrange a restraint, I will help you die. But first, we must make every attempt to find an acceptable source of food, or a way to reverse your condition."

I agreed to the deal. It isn't easy to dispute with a Jesuit.

"Wait a minute." Something was glimmering in Douglas' eyes. "Run through the list of symptoms you know about, or can remember from the legends."

"Well, I can personally vouch for being burned by a cross. I don't have a reflection. I couldn't come into your house until you invited me. I can't stand garlic. Crucifixes and crosses look so bright that I have to avoid them. I became a vampire because one drank my blood."

Douglas nodded, encouraging me to go on.

"Aside from that, there's just what I can remember from movies and the like. Holy water and communion wafers burn vampires. Crumbled communion wafers form a barrier to them. They can't pass over water, except during certain tides." I had reviewed this list in my mind many times during my captivity. It came to me easily. "A stake through the heart kills them. They can transform into mist, bats, or wolves. The sun burns them, and they have to sleep in coffins. They can command animals and dominate people's thoughts. I think she used that power on me, that first night."

Douglas waited to be sure that I was done. Then he mumbled the religious items in my list. "Holy water, communion wafer, cross, crucifix. . . ." He pursed his lips and then spoke up. "Patrick, have you ever heard anything about vampires and communion wine?"

That was a puzzler. I rummaged through my memories and came up with other examples involving the symbols I had already listed. But nothing about communion wine. I shook my head. "No, I can't think of anything. Why?"

"Oh, just a thought. There's something I'd like to try, if you're willing. I can guess why every major aspect of Catholicism except the communion wine is in the legends."

"Oh, and why is that?"

"I'd rather not say just yet. I wouldn't want to influence your expectations any more than I have already. Is that all right?"

"I'll accept just about anything to fulfill my part of the agreement." I left unstated my challenge for him to do the same.

Douglas stood. "Good. Let's start now."

I was a bit surprised at his abruptness. "If you like. Anything I can do?"

"Celebrate the Mass with me. I'll preside in the dining room; you can stay in the living room."

"What, you have the materials here?"

Douglas smiled sardonically. "Not the usual ones, but at least I have some bread and table wine."

He was right; it was just jarring to associations reinforced by years of habit. Before the ceremony, there is nothing special about the makings of the sacrament.

The Mass could have been a parody. Celebrated in a dining room, attended by a vampire, and held expressly to manufacture communion wine. The strength of the ritual instead made it real and true. At the end, God had given us the miracle that we needed: transubstantiation. The bread and wine became objects of communion.

I dipped a toothpick in the communion wine, as Douglas had suggested. I touched wet wood to my arm, tensed for the pain that didn't come. With that assurance, I tipped the glass, pushing the tip of my tongue through my lips to lick at the wine. And tasted ambrosia.

I poured the glass down my throat, drinking greedily. How to explain the taste, the sheer feeling of strength and well-being that went with it?

Somewhat dazed, I set the glass back down. I looked to Douglas for an explanation, too concerned with just how good I felt to reason it through for myself.

Douglas waited for me to speak. As the silence stretched, he saw that I didn't understand. "Think about it, Patrick. You're a vampire. You can only obtain sustenance from human blood. In the transubstantiation, wine becomes the blood of Christ, and Christ came to us as a man."

The curtain drew back further, revealing another small part of the mystery of God's mercy. He had not allowed this curse to be inescapable; it was only the legends that had made it out to be. Legends of darkness that discouraged anyone afflicted from holding onto any hope.

For all that this curse had taken from me, God had granted me a new purpose: I now embodied a refutation of those legends. For as long as I lived, I would stand as a testament to the Word made flesh. And blood.

Brent Buckner: "Flesh and Blood" reflects a fascination with the legends of the vampire, a fondness for the speculative fiction tradition of the problem-solving story, and grappling with a Christian world-view. James Blish's A Case of Conscience *was an influence. In that book, I saw the problem-solving story structure applied within the rules of Roman Catholic doctrine. I had read other works that applied the structure within systems of magic, but the authors of those pieces were free to invent rules that would eventually mesh with intended solutions. Blish had no such freedom. The solution to Patrick's problem may seem like a technicality. That's fine. More important to me than the particular solution is the reasoning as to why some solution must exist: God will not allow us to be tempted beyond our capacity to resist (1 Corinthians 10:13). That our best will be good enough is both merciful and demanding. The game is rigged in our favor, but there is no fatalism in that; the results depend upon our free choice.*

THE STARLING COLONY

Kate Riedel

"THAT'S WHY THE LAST TENANT MOVED OUT."

The infuriatingly calm voice on the other end of the line was too much for Brett. "Now's a fine time to tell me!" she said.

The silence on the other end of the line was as calm, and as infuriating, as the voice had been. Brett took a deep breath and counted to ten. Then she said, with careful sweetness, "If it costs you tenants, perhaps you should consider cutting that tree down."

"City bylaw. The tree's healthy, and not interfering with service lines."

"Can't you do something else?"

"We tried noisemakers; they didn't work and the neighbors complained."

"Well, I'm complaining now, and I've signed a lease. Isn't there some kind of stuff they put on window ledges to keep away pigeons? Wouldn't the same thing work for starlings?"

"It would kill the tree."

Brett resisted the urge to retort, Well, then you could cut it down, couldn't you?

"If you want to break the lease . . . ," the voice continued.

"With the penalty you charge?" Brett slammed down the phone and counted to ten again. The client waiting in the outer

151

office was an important account; it wouldn't do to let him see her angry. Easy to say; harder to do after a restless night and the unbelievable noise that a flock of starlings right outside your window makes at sunrise . . . shit, she'd totally forgotten to mention that street person.

Brett took another deep breath and managed to put a smile into her voice as she said into the intercom, "You can send Mr. MacGregor in now, thank you, Lucy."

Brett had chosen the flat as carefully as she chose the suits and silk shirts and discreet gold jewelry she wore at work. The once-seedy Victorian row houses had been sandblasted and renovated and painted and landscaped into some of the most desirable rental properties in the city. No more futons, Brett had told herself as she signed the lease. No more Sally Ann dinette sets, no more brick-and-board bookshelves, no more cable spools masquerading as coffee tables. This was the kind of place she'd had in mind when she'd spent a week's salary on that Inuit sculpture, when she'd bought the signed and numbered print and the perfectly asymmetrical raku bowl. This was the place she'd had in mind while reconnoitering the custom furniture shops. And, now that her promotion was confirmed, this place was hers.

It had been mid-afternoon when she'd gone over the flat before signing the lease. Not the least of the selling points had been the private parkette just below, with its sunken garden and the broad maple tree shading the balcony.

The starlings didn't roost during the day. And when she'd moved in, the noise of shifting boxes and furniture had masked the starlings' evening return to their colony.

Brett had slept uneasily that night; she realized now that the continuous restless stirring and murmuring in the tree outside probably accounted for those dreams she couldn't remember. The sudden explosion of noise at dawn had brought her rocketing out of bed and to the balcony. The tree seemed almost to move of itself, alive with starlings. Now she saw the bird droppings on the leaves and the railing. Why hadn't she looked more closely before she signed the lease?

And then she looked down and saw the old man curled in the sleeping bag under the tree, next to the small pile of plastic bags that she supposed contained all his worldly goods.

Brett felt all the outrage of one who had just committed a large portion of her salary to a flat commensurate with her new position as top consultant at one of the most prestigious advertising agencies in the city. Right. With a tree full of unbearably noisy starlings and a street person camping out under it.

Maybe it won't be so bad, Brett told herself that evening as she lovingly arranged the painted table and matching ladderback chairs, the aged-pine modular wall units, the sofa and chair with their understated abstract print upholstery. The tree was quiet now. Didn't birds migrate, or something . . . ? Picture hooks. She needed picture hooks. The corner store would have them, and she could get a takeout supper at the deli next to it.

As Brett left the building, another tenant was just coming in. The elderly woman looked familiar, Brett thought as she returned the polite nod and smile. Where had she seen those sharp, bright eyes, the neat, close-cropped gray hair?

The starlings were back by the time Brett returned with her purchases. They wheeled above the tree, the dusk suffused with their chattering whistles.

"They say when birds flock at twilight it's the souls of the dead," said a voice at her shoulder, a voice as harsh as the starlings'.

It was the old man she had seen under the tree this morning. He carried the rolled sleeping bag on his back; she could see the ends of plastic bags sticking out from its edges. The tattered parka he wore in spite of the mild weather was stiff with grime. The shadow on his face could have been either dirt or stubble.

Brett moved away hastily, but his sour smell lingered in her nostrils. Back in the flat she set the food aside with distaste. In the tree outside the starlings chattered like an excited mob.

That night Brett dreamed she went to the window to find the tree had shrunk to a scraggly little self-seeded maple marking the boundary between this property and the house next to it. The other house appeared derelict, the paint peeling off in layers. But it was occupied; light leaked through the ragged curtains behind the cardboard-patched windows.

The pre-dawn cacophony of the starlings woke her. The tree was full-grown. There was no house; only the street person stirring as he woke with the starlings. Brett closed the sliding door to the balcony with a bang that rattled the glass. Curtains, she thought. Maybe heavy curtains would help. At the shop where she'd bought the sofa and chair, they'd said they could make matching curtains. She could phone in the measurements from work. And she'd phone the bloody building management too, and tell them if they couldn't get rid of the starlings they could at least keep that man from camping out on private property.

"We'll make every effort to see he doesn't use the parkette," said the voice on the phone. "But you know sometimes these people get a little funny. He always slept there when it was a vacant lot. Maybe he just doesn't understand that it's not a vacant lot anymore. But we'll make every effort."

I'll bet, Brett thought.

That night she dreamed again about looking out the window. There was no house. Instead of the sunken garden there was a charred, rubble-filled foundation. The hedge had become new hoardings. She knew that if she were to view the hoardings from the sidewalk, there would already be posters stapled to the raw plywood. The tree was there but seemed not quite so tall, and the side away from the building appeared to be scarred and leafless.

One thing hadn't changed; the old man was still under the tree, surrounded by his plastic bags.

The old man was still under the tree when the starlings woke her the next morning.

The dream haunted Brett all day. She supposed it had come out of yesterday's conversation with the rental management.

When she returned home from work, she stopped in the parkette for a closer look at the tree. The tree was silent, the starlings away wherever they went during the day. The white droppings that speckled the ground seemed dry, but Brett trod gingerly. A series of old wounds scarred this side of the tree: stumps where branches had once been; black patches that might have been tar, or rot—or traces of old charring.

"Nearly killed in the fire," said the old man behind her.

"This is private property," Brett said. If no one else would tell him, she would. The first starlings hovered over the tree, touched down tentatively on the top branches, whistled to each other.

"Soul's got to go somewhere," the old man said as Brett stalked away.

The woman in the downstairs flat was coming out as Brett went in. The penny dropped.

"Aren't you Sylvie Radford?" Brett asked.

The woman smiled acknowledgement.

Sylvie Radford living downstairs! What a coup; what an addition to her housewarming party! Brett had watched the TV interview with Sylvie Radford on the opening of the retrospective of her late husband's work. Lester Radford had given a peculiarly individual twist to socialist realism painting and was enjoying, posthumously, a renewal of popularity. Upstairs on her coffee table, Brett had a copy of the book based on the exhibit.

Brett ran her fingers up and down the stem of her wineglass and looked around at her guests. Her former classmates and present clients appeared suitably impressed, not only by the flat but by the other guests. Sylvie Radford; the musician who was just breaking out of the clubs into the big time; the best-selling self-help author. And the two last where they were now because of Brett's publicity campaigns.

Frazer Prescott was a more personal coup. Brett had master-minded the discreet series of ads that had helped restore the image of his father's development company, following that unfortunate incident involving a minor civil servant employed in a not-so-minor government office. Now that Brett headed another department she could safely fraternize without conflict of interest, and she intended to. If she had been asked, she would have been hard pressed to say which she found sexier about Frazer Prescott: his well-groomed good looks, or his father's money.

Brett considered she'd earned points by inviting her receptionist. Lucy had been flattered, and it never hurt to be nice to the staff.

"Lovely place," Frazer Prescott was saying.

"Indeed." Sylvie Radford spoke from the armchair, waving away the refill of white wine that Frazer offered. "I find it amusing to be living in this building again after all these years."

"Really?" said Brett.

"Oh yes. I grew up here, you know. But it wasn't upscale townhouses then. It was, not to put too fine a point on it, a slum. Full of bohunks and polacks and micks like me. I was little Sylvie McDermott then, and a grubby little mick I was, too. That's how I met Lester; he did a lot of his early work around here. I have a drawing he did of this row of houses, and another of the old frame house that stood where the parkette is now. They're in the exhibit. That house burned down, oh, twenty years ago."

"I remember that," said the self-help author. "Substandard rooming house, rooms by the night. A lot of old rummies died in the fire. Created a bit of a stink, didn't it? Big inquiry into housing standards, outcry against slumlords, that sort of thing, but nothing ever came of it. The owner actually made a tidy profit selling off the lot along with these row houses—didn't he, Frazer?"

"Don't knock it," said Frazer with a smile, turning to refill Brett's wineglass. "It paid for my university education."

The musician, who had appeared to be about to say something, turned back to his instrument, muttering something Brett didn't catch. Frazer smiled down at Brett; she smiled back.

"I believe part of the old foundation was incorporated in the retaining wall of the sunken garden," said Sylvie. "Outside of that, the tree's all that's left."

"I was looking at that tree just before I came in," Lucy said. "There were a lot of birds flying around it. It was kind of spooky, just at dusk, you know, and I remembered reading somewhere about birds being lost souls."

Where had Brett heard that before, and why should she find it so irritating now? "It's starlings," she said. "There's a colony of starlings in that tree. Nothing supernatural about them; if you don't believe me, take a look at the droppings underneath."

"It's an Irish superstition. My mother told me the same thing," said Sylvie to Lucy. "Black and gray birds flying around trees at dusk, never settling; they're souls still in purgatory."

All very well to invite your receptionist, but no need to let her steal the show. "You're on the other side of the building from the tree," said Brett to Sylvie, "so you wouldn't hear it, but the racket they make! I'm losing sleep."

"Cut the tree down," said Frazer.

"I'd love to," said Brett. "But apparently there's some sort of city bylaw. I guess I'll just have to put up with it," she finished with a light laugh.

Frazer Prescott was among the last to leave. His formal kiss on her cheek slipped over, as if accidentally, to brush her lips, and he smiled a question at her as he said good night. Brett smiled back, but nothing more. It wouldn't do, she thought, to be too easy.

That night the constant stir and murmur of the starlings translated into a dream of rustling, crackling noises, and Brett threw off the duvet, feeling hot.

The next day was Sunday. After checking to ensure the absence of both the starlings and the vagrant, Brett took the Radford retrospective book and ventured down to one of the benches in the sunken garden. A while later she heard a light step and looked up.

"It's a lovely day," said Sylvie Radford. "May I join you?"

"I was just looking through this," said Brett, holding out the book. "You said there was a drawing of the house that used to be here?"

Sylvie leafed through the book, past lurid paintings of factories and gray portraits of factory workers, to a drawing of a clapboard house. It's the one I dreamed about, thought Brett; then, No, there's no tree. . . .

"The tree probably wasn't here then," said Sylvie. "Or if it was, it would have been only a seedling, and you wouldn't be able to see it."

"It's a wonderful drawing," said Brett. "You can feel the paint peeling, and the plants growing by the walk are done in such detail!"

"Just weeds," said Sylvie. "But even weeds were important to Lester. Each one was an individual to him. So today we know exactly what was growing here fifty years ago. Lamb's quarter, and sow thistles, even low things like plantain, just like what's growing here now." She pointed with the toe of her shoe to a flat rosette of leaves rooted between the paving bricks.

"You'd think, with the rent we pay, they could at least keep the weeds out," said Brett.

"You can't keep them out," said Sylvie, handing back the book. "And after all, we're the ones who brought them here, the weeds, the sparrows, the starlings, and then we complain that they won't stay in their place. But this is their place, you know. Disturbed sites. The whole city is one big disturbed site."

"I suppose," said Brett. She riffled through the book. "What you were saying last night, about birds and souls and purgatory. You don't really believe that, do you?"

"Well, I certainly believe in each of them separately, although all together is another question."

"Suppose these starlings *were* souls? Whose would they be?"

"Logically—if such a thing is logical—I suppose maybe the men who died in that rooming house fire."

"It doesn't seem fair for them to be in purgatory," said Brett. "I mean, I don't suppose they were very important people, or they wouldn't have ended up the way they did, you know, down and out, but when you think of the politicians and that sort of people, who let it happen . . ."

"You weren't raised a Catholic, were you?" said Sylvie. It wasn't really a question, and she didn't wait for Brett to shake her head before going on. "If you had been, you'd know purgatory isn't another name for hell. Purgatory's where you work out whatever you didn't do on earth, but should have, and how long you spend there is between you and God."

"Sort of a second chance?"

"Oh no. You have to take responsibility for your earthly actions while you're still alive, even if it's only in a deathbed repentance. Better to do it earlier than later, of course. You think I'm a self-righteous old lady, don't you?" she added, smiling, and Brett blushed.

"Anyway," said Sylvie, standing up, "we're told to judge not that we be not judged, and I'm off to church and I don't feel like making confession. But if I were asked my *opinion*, I'd say that for the politicians and slumlords, purgatory probably isn't an option."

Brett watched Sylvie out of sight. She returned to her flat in time to catch the phone ringing.

"You're awake," Frazer said. "How nice. . . ."

Brett smiled and settled back in her chair.

Brett spent Monday thinking about that phone conversation, especially Frazer's parting words: "I'll have a present for you tomorrow."

She heard the saws before she came in sight of the parkette. The last section of tree trunk was being loaded onto the back of the city maintenance truck as she turned the corner. The phone was ringing as she opened the door of her flat.

"I told you I'd have a present for you," said Frazer's voice. "Well, what do you think?"

"I'm dumbfounded." It was all she could think of to say, and it was true enough.

"I know one or two people at city hall. It wasn't that hard to convince them the tree was a health hazard; all that bird shit. Well, aren't you going to say thank you?"

"Thank you," said Brett weakly.

"That's more like it. How about—oops, got a callback, I'll get back to you later. You'll be in this evening?" And he hung up.

Brett pulled open the curtains and stepped out onto the balcony. The railing was speckled with droppings, but the droppings on the grass, and the grass itself, were obscured by the litter of sawdust, twigs and leaves surrounding the raw stump. Only yesterday those leaves had shaded her window. Now there was nothing between Brett and the skyline of the business district. She could see the highrise that housed her employer, and the bronzed windows of the Prescott Tower, home of Prescott Development Corporation and its legion subsidiaries.

Suddenly, she felt vulnerable. She was about to step inside and close the curtains when she saw Sylvie enter the parkette.

The older woman's attention was on something near the hedge. The old vagrant's rolled sleeping bag. Sylvie crossed to it, tiptoeing over the litter from the tree. She bent over something beside the sleeping bag. Then she looked up at Brett and called, distantly, as if inside a dream, "Phone an ambulance!"

The old man was alive as they loaded him into the ambulance, but his eyes were closed, his face purple, his breathing harsh. Sylvie volunteered to go to the hospital with him. "Call me," said Brett, awkwardly, as the ambulance doors closed.

It's just some old drunk, Brett thought as she stood on the balcony, watching the sun start to drop below that intimidating skyline. It's not as if it's someone I know. . . . There were a few starlings overhead, circling in bewilderment.

The sun fell below the skyline. More starlings hung overhead, as if spawned by the gathering dusk. Something touched Brett's hand. She looked down and leaped back. The starling fluttered away, hovering, then landed on the rail. Another joined it, then another, and another, whistling and creaking and chattering, and suddenly Brett was beating the birds away from her head and shoulders as she backed through the door. A starling crashed against the door as she slammed it. Another hit the glass as she drew the curtains. She covered her ears against the sound of fluttering wings and thumping bodies, but she couldn't shut it out. She didn't hear the phone ringing as she fled, wanting only to put the building between herself and the birds.

She was awakened by Lucy touching her shoulder, asking, "Are you all right?"

She sat up with a start, still befuddled by dreams of smoke and flames. Then she recalled wandering through the streets until, near midnight, she remembered she had her keys with her and had taken refuge in her office.

"I had some work to catch up on," said Brett. "I must have fallen asleep. God, I must look a mess. Can you get me some coffee while I neaten up—no, no need for me to go home," when Lucy protested. "I can make it through the day . . ."

But not without calling Sylvie.

"The police identified the man," Sylvie said. "He used to stay in that rooming house, that's why he keeps coming back. Whether he doesn't realize it's gone or what, they haven't figured out. They located a sister. I said I'd stop by this evening. I'll call you after, if you want."

"Yes, please," Brett said. But after work she found herself at the hospital anyway, holding a bunch of flowers, telling reception with some embarrassment, "I don't know his name; he was brought in last night, in an ambulance. He's a street person I see sometimes," she stumbled on as the nurse looked suspicious. "I was worried about him. . . ." *Was I really?* she thought, but the nurse's suspicions were allayed enough to identify the patient.

"Mr. Halloran," she said, after consulting a list. Brett followed directions to the ward. The curtains were drawn around the bed. "Joe's sleeping," said the tired-looking woman seated beside the bed. She looked as suspicious as the nurse. Brett handed over the flowers and left without waiting for thanks, feeling stupid.

Why did I bother? she thought, back in the flat, too weary to fix supper or even go to bed.

The phone rang.

"Where have you been?" Frazer asked. "Didn't I say I'd call? I've been leaving messages. . . ."

"Sorry, I've been too tired to play back my messages. Bit of a crisis last night. . . ." She told him about the old man, about calling the ambulance. She didn't tell him about wandering around in the streets and spending the night in her office.

"You poor thing. Why don't I take you out for supper? We can come back to my place for a drink after."

"But the man's in the hospital. What if he dies?"

"It's not as if you know him."

"I'm just tired, okay?"

"Okay. I'll call you."

He won't, thought Brett as she broke the connection. She didn't care.

Joe Halloran, she thought. It had never occurred to her that the old man would have a name.

She could hear the starlings at the window. She pulled open the curtain. They hovered in the air, beat against the glass, creaking and whistling and chattering. A black mass of wings obscured the world; she couldn't see the line of highrises, couldn't see the sky, could hear nothing but the cries of the birds.

The noise of the birds reached a crescendo. Then, slowly, the wings settled. The starlings crowded on the floor of the balcony, jostled on the railing, chattered and murmured, but, thank God, no longer beat on the glass.

The phone rang. A stir passed through the mass of black feathers.

The phone rang again. The birds stilled. Then a single starling beat its wings, rose, flew away.

The phone rang again. Another bird followed. And another.

Released, she thought as she picked up the phone. They've been released.

The last starling teetered on the railing, then took wing.

They've been released. . . .

The view was clear now, all the way to the skyline.

How long you spend in purgatory is between you and God. . . .

She knew, even before Sylvie spoke, that the old man was dead.

Kate Riedel: One evening in High Park in Toronto, I stopped to listen to a flock of starlings settling in a tree that was obviously their regular nightly roost, and I remembered the superstition about birds flocking at dusk being souls in purgatory. Every story is an account of the consequences of certain actions: how the protagonist navigates those consequences depends on his or her willingness to take responsibility for those actions. I've never been sure just what "spirituality" means, but I suspect that it has a lot to do with accepting responsibility, living with consequences, and amending future actions accordingly. Hence, this story. (According to Dorothy Sayers, only saints go directly to heaven.)

VOICES

Keith Scott

I ALWAYS DRAW ATTENTION.

In the early days I found this hard to take but I have learned to deal with it in my own way. How do I do this? I just look back, steady and level-eyed, no heat or anything . . . just look back. And it works. The eyes nearly always turn off.

But it's the questions that I find harder to turn off. Questions mean that they have already cracked my first line of defense, peeling me open, feeding their curiosity and, worse, their sympathy.

God, how I hate the sappy sympathy!

"I hear you were a fighter pilot in the Battle of Britain," they *always* say.

"For only nine days," I *always* say back. "Officially the battle lasted 114 days."

"Oh . . . ?" Uncertainty usually comes here. "But you must have seen a lot?"

"I saw survival," I say shortly. And if I'm lucky, that will end it. I don't mean to be unpleasant. But what can I tell anyone about what happened fifty-eight years ago? Some shifts in context are too great, and I think this is one of them. It's unbridgeable, beyond connection or comprehension. What sense can I make of the magnificent folly of those 114 days in 1940? I mean . . . in today's terms? What sense can I make of my own nine days?

It was a breathlessly soft summer day when I landed at RAF Kenley airfield on August 9, 1940. Kenley is a few miles to the south and a bit west of London. I could see the silvery ranks of the barrage balloons, dipping and straining at their cable leashes, ringing the southern approaches to the city. They looked like giant air whales, guarding the ancient heart of England, guarding it against the bomber hordes of the Luftwaffe.

I'd been in England for two weeks at an Operational Training Unit in Wales, cramming fighter tactics and learning the sweet flying characteristics of the Supermarine Spitfire. England was desperate for replacement pilots. I remember holding back at the door of the Kenley airfield mess, steeling myself to face the first dismaying smells of my second RAF cafeteria.

Three WAAFs appeared behind me. The tallest of the three, with corporal hooks sewn on the sleeves of her Women's Auxiliary Air Force uniform, paused and smiled at me.

"Oh, come on, Sergeant," she laughed, "it's not that bad."

Without thinking, I answered her in my standard North American brash. "Can I have that in writing?" I said.

She regarded me with cooling interest. Obviously it had been the wrong thing to say. Or the wrong way to say it.

"Of course not," she said finally. "We give nothing in writing here."

I suppose my smile looked foolish. She looked at me for a moment longer, and then frowned and moved through the door. Feeling even more foolish, I lifted my shoulder bag and followed her into the laden atmosphere of the mess. And I had been right! It *was* that bad. There was a thick mingling of every smell I'd grown to dislike in my two weeks of English wartime cooking.

I caught up with her at the serving line of the cafeteria.

"But . . . don't you think the Royal Air Force should have a brussels sprout in its coat of arms?" I asked. Mildly this time, *sans brash*.

She held back for a moment and then gave in to her laugh fully before turning around to me.

"Are you an American?"

"Canadian," I answered her. "I'm joining 66 Squadron."

"So, you'll be on Spitfires."

"Right. My name's Brett Keller. What d'you do here?"

Her smile thinned. "I'm a lead plotter in Ops."

"That means we'll be meeting each other, so to speak—"

"Right, Sergeant." She gathered up her tray and smiled again briefly. "Till we meet again, then?"

I watched her as she walked to the table reserved for WAAFs. There was a sureness in the way she moved, an overall coherence that held attention . . . and made up for other minor faults. She just misses being gorgeous, I thought as I lifted my tray and made my way toward two tables of watching sergeant pilots.

"Hump Waters," a dark smiling gnome with New Zealand flashes on his shoulders introduced himself. "I see you've met our Kristen."

There was a chorus of wolf whistles from the two tables. Hump Waters introduced me around. Most were Hurricane pilots with 253 Squadron. Hump and one other were with 66.

"This is a sector airfield," Hump explained. "Our Ops controls both Kenley and Croydon, with as many as six squadrons of Hurries and Spits at various times. The gals in Ops have been doing a fantastic job in putting us in the air at the right places at the right times. Kristen bosses one of the shifts—and to date, old cock," he finished with a smile, "she's been unapproachable."

I looked across the mess hall at the table of WAAF plotters. Kristen was talking animatedly to the group, tossing her head back and forth to emphasize her point, swinging those great blue eyes around the table. She's totally forgotten I even exist, I told myself with great regret.

Hump Waters took me up that afternoon in a two-aircraft section for familiarization. "I'm afraid that's all you're going to have time for, Keller," my flight commander, a tired-eyed flight lieutenant, had said to me.

Hump put me through a wringer. He turned out to be part Maori, and he flew like the rest of him was pure avian. I stuck grimly on his tail in my Spitfire, flicking from one reverse turn to another, eyes filming with gray continually from the G-forces. I didn't get my gunsight on him long enough to count in the half-hour of mock dogfighting.

Nor did he shake me, I thought with satisfaction.

"Hey, where'd you learn to fly?" Hump asked once we were back on the ground.

"I've got an aerobatic rating on my commercial pilot's ticket," I said, pleased with his approval. "I traded three years' hangar duty for flying lessons."

He grinned. "Same here. And look where it's got us. Right in the middle of a bloody shooting war."

"Just where I want to be," I blurted out. Hump's eyes held mine for a long beat and I ached to eat my words. No chance. The damage was done. I don't suppose he was much older than my own twenty-one years, but at that moment he seemed infinitely older, wiser. . . .

It was like the day in Hamilton when I told my mother that I was going to England to join the RAF. My father and younger brother had nearly bowled me over with their boyish enthusiasm. But the misery that sprang to my mother's eyes still haunts me.

Is it because they inhabit a higher plane of knowing?

I tensed when the Tannoy public address system tumbled us out of the dispersal hut the following morning. We scrambled nine Spitfires in vics of three each.

The calm voice of the operations controller took over on the radio-telephone. I pictured Kristen sitting beneath him in the red brick Ops building, headset over one ear, developing the plot with markers on the big map table cut out in the shape of south-eastern England.

"We've got twenty-plus big ones, Bugle Leader," the controller announced. "Little ones above them."

"Roger, Greystoke," my flight commander answered on the R/T. And then to us: "Line abreast Bugle aircraft. We'll try for one pass at the bombers before mixing it with the little uglies."

It was shocking how quickly the combined closing speed of five hundred miles per hour reduced the distance between ourselves and the German bombers. They were Heinkel 111s and our head-on attack must have been gut-churning to their five-man crews.

Almost at the last moment I pressed my gun button and eight Browning .303 machine guns in my wings poured a burst toward my target bomber.

I was stunned to see the glazed cockpit area of the bomber disintegrate under a shower of strikes. What impossibly good luck! My very first shot in anger in this war. God, how easy it was.

I pulled up and over the stricken bomber.

I was exultant. My excitement was visceral, arcing on an adrenal surge, almost sexual in its urgency. A mindless, totally elemental response. And underlying it all was the terror. I tried to thrust my feelings aside and flicked the Spitfire over to follow my Heinkel.

It had detached itself from the bomber formation, flying on reduced power, swinging slowly back for the French coast. A small flicker of flame streamed from its port engine. On the radio I could hear the shouts of my mates somewhere above me as they tangled with the Messerschmitt 109 escort.

Get this over with, I told myself, and pulled back on the throttle as the Heinkel grew in my gunsight. Suddenly I'd become deadly calm. Reaction to the overdose of adrenaline of a moment before?

I checked the sky around me for 109s and moved in for the kill.

We celebrated that night at the Rose and Crown in Caterham. Our squadron got six, including my Heinkel. We lost two dead. My tired-eyed flight commander would know rest at long last.

Overall, RAF Fighter Command lost thirty-two that day.

I remember thinking there was something wrong with the arithmetic in this equation. Meaning… we'd run out at this rate. But there was little time for reflection. Little room left for thought of any kind. It almost seemed as if it was planned to be that way.

At one point in the evening I found Hump's dark eyes on me, thoughtfully concerned, summing me up. I shrugged his eyes off. It was legal, wasn't it?

Hell . . . it was even honored. It could get you a trip to Buckingham Palace for a pretty ribbon. La-di-da.

Later we made our unsteady way across the airfield to our billets. I was the last to see her coming out of the blackout curtains of the Ops building.

"Hey, Kristen," Cowboy Kolasky called out in his harsh Polish accent. "You hear Brett get one today? First trip!"

"Yes, I heard," she said quietly. "Congratulations, Sergeant."

I don't know what childish urge made me say it. Perhaps it was her cool reaction. Or the beer. Or my raw newness. Or my desperate wish to make something of this relationship. "Can I have that in writing, ma'am?" I said.

She was stunned. "Dear God! What is it they do to you?"

"Hey, it's not that bad—"

"Not that bad? I'll show you how bad it is, Sergeant." She grabbed my arm. "Come in here for a minute. I want you to read something."

My three companions disappeared up the path and I followed Kristen into the dimly lit entrance of the Ops building.

"Wait here, please."

She went into an inner room and reappeared almost immediately with a heavy ring binder.

"These are teletypes from the Y Service. They intercept and translate everything the German aircrew say over their radio and intercoms. Would you like to hear what was said in your Heinkel?"

I was rapidly sobering. "How d'you know it was my Heinkel?" I asked defensively.

"Because I was plotting your attack this morning. Times, location, height . . . everything matches." She passed me the binder and pointed with her finger. "Read here," she said.

I read the words on the page.

Pilot: That jackal's coming back. Can't he see we're dead already?
Nose Gunner: Oh dear God! No more. No more, sir—
Pilot: Easy, Feldwebel. Put up a good fight.
Nose Gunner: Christ, sir! I can't fight with my guts spilling into my hands—
(TRANSMISSION ABRUPTLY ENDS)

I stopped reading and thrust the log back into her hands before flinging myself through the blackout curtains and into the comfort of the darkness outside. What was she doing to me? Why was I being singled out? I kicked savagely at a clod of dirt on the path before I realized she was beside me.

"I'm sorry, Brett. But I had to make sure they didn't do it to you."

"Do what?"

"Make you into a killing machine. I've seen it before."

I tried to say something, but she stopped me.

"Oh, I know. We have to fight this filthy war," she said. "But when we have to kill, let's at least kill with regret."

I grew up very quickly in those nine days. Kristen's words stayed with me, quickly shaping my thoughts, my life. I killed again on day three and day five, with growing confusion . . . and regret.

I realized that I was good at it. Realized it with a strange mix of exultation and dread. The push/pull of my feelings was wildly tormenting. I sensed that Hump knew what was going on, but following the code, he said nothing. That was the way it was done.

See no seriousness. Speak no seriousness. . . .

On the sixth day, Hump led us off in ragged formation. We had been doing three, four and even five sorties a day and we were exhausted. We arrived over Manston in time to take the full brunt of a massive bounce from forty-plus Me 109s.

They fell on us like falcons, nose and wing cannon spitting, shattering our formation into fragments. After their first pass I had time to look about us. One of our Spitfires was pulling up in a lazy arc, flames caressing the sky-blue paint of its belly. And then it started down, streaming black smoke, etching a gigantic question mark visible to thousands of eyes in southeastern England. Why? it seemed to ask.

It was Hump.

I sought out Kristen that night. Hump's loss was almost more than I could bear. She didn't seem to think it strange that I had turned to her. I knew then that she'd been through it all before. Briefly, I thought how unfair it was for me and the others before me. . . .

"Why don't you ask for leave?" she asked with gentle sympathy.

"I can't. I just got here."

She was silent for a moment. "Perhaps you could get a twenty-four hour. I'd like you to come to my home. It's only a few miles south of here. In Surrey. Try for Monday. I have a day coming to me."

"Are you sure?"

"Yes. It'll be only my father. He's the vicar there. I'd very much like you to meet him."

"Your mother?"

"She died two years before the war. I have one brother. Older than I. He's in Reading. Jailed as a conscientious objector. Do you mind that?"

I must admit that it did set me back a bit. It must have taken guts to refuse war service at this time. But I quickly forgot about the brother and gave my mind over wholly to the prospect of a twenty-four hour leave with Kristen.

Years later I read the official Luftwaffe record:

Aldertag. Eagle Day. Sunday, August 17. Hermann Goering ordered the Luftwaffe to destroy the RAF fighter airfields in preparation for Hitler's invasion date of September 15. All that stood in the way, he told his weary airmen, were five hundred Spitfires and Hurricanes.

Hauptman Joachim Roth briefed the 9th bomber Staffel at Cormeilles-en-Vexin, fifteen miles inland from Deauville, France. He stunned his Dornier 17 bomber crews. The 9th Staffel would fly all the way at fifty feet to escape British radar.

They crossed in above Beachy Head and picked up the Brighton-London railway. RAF Kenley, their target, was located to the right of the railway, a few miles north of a long tunnel.

The nine Do 17s swept over Kenley at noon, unexpected, right on target, dropping a shower of 110-pound bombs with deadly effect. Roth's belly gunner, Feldwebel Hugo Deitz, sprayed 7.9 mm's at knots of RAF personnel scurrying for cover. Deitz reported that he was disturbed to see his strikes hit two women in uniform, crumpling them as they ran toward a red brick building.

We had scrambled ten minutes before they hit Kenley. It was my ninth day and I don't think I knew the name of anyone else in my flight outside of Cowboy Kolasky. Not well enough to remember anyway.

We engaged the high-level raid, timed to follow Roth's disastrous low-level run by five minutes. Again, they were Dorniers, escorted by Me 110s and 109s. We were hopelessly outnumbered, outgunned. I got strikes on two bombers and then a pair of 109s boxed me, lining up on each side behind me.

I felt the thud of cannon hits on my tail section and my controls went sloppy. Suddenly my canopy top was shattered and prickly points of pain sprang into the left side of my face, neck and shoulder. Desperately I tried to go back into a tight turn.

My Spitfire refused to obey me. Panic bit deep. So this was how it came? I was abandoned, totally alone with my terror, my helplessness.

And that's when I heard it.

High in the arch of my mind a voice began talking to me, unclearly at first, urging me with gentle insistence.

I shook my head and looked up into my rearview mirror. The lead 109 was moving in close, confidently. His guns started on me again and the mirror disintegrated....

Then I heard Kristen's voice again. Strong and clear. Or was it my mother's voice? Or both? No matter. I was no longer alone. I was in their higher plane.

The cockpit was filling with smoke and fire. I wiped the mist from my eyes with a bloody hand and was startled to see the 109 on my wing tip, barely five yards away. The German pilot gave me a long searching look and I looked back at him vaguely, wondering why he was there, my mind still on voices.

Then he was gone.

The voice began again, urging me. I don't remember getting out of the cockpit. Or the long drift to earth beneath my parachute.

I spent the next two years in the burn unit at East Grinstead. They waited two weeks before they told me about Mother. A week later they told me about Kristen. I think I knew, anyway. Knew from the moment I heard voices in the air.

God, how I clung to Kristen's voice.

As I said, I survived. Why, I don't know. I've had thirty-one operations on my face and hands. Mainly maxillo-facial surgery. The only one to beat that record was Walter Leutz who occupied the bed next to mine in Ward 2A. His Messerschmitt was shot down in flames over Hawkinge by a Spitfire on September 15.

I grew to love Walt.

"Do they tell you this is a good war?" he'd sing out to us as we lay in sweating agony in our single row of beds.

"Hell yes," we'd all shout back in unison, "they tell us it's a flipping good war, Herr Leutnant Leutz!"

We all loved Walt. We were bitter the day they came to take him to a POW camp for captured German airmen.

They've done a fantastic job on my burned face, but I still look like a gargoyle. Certainly gargoyle enough to draw all eyes and slow conversation to a crawl whenever I come into a room. Age has softened some of the repulsiveness, taken the livid raw edges off the scars and ridges. There are days in my dry solitary life when I nearly forget about it. Nearly.

I still wonder endlessly...about the what ifs. What if I had gone on that twenty-four-hour pass with Kristen? What if it had been allowed to ripen, mature? What if we had grown old together?

What if? What if?

Why did I survive? What stopped the guns of that Me 109 on my final day? Did the German pilot hear what I'd heard? Did he also hear the voices in the air?

They released all RAF Battle of Britain documents in 1975. I lost little time requesting copies of the Y Service intercepts of Luftwaffe aircrew radio-telephone traffic for August 17, 1940.

I don't know what I expected to find.

That's a lie, really. I wanted to find Mother. I wanted to find Kristen. Desperately, I wanted to find Kristen. I wanted to find some confirmation of her. Some embodiment. It was as if finding her would bring purpose, sense to my loss.

If finding her?

I was fooling myself on this. I had already built a life around her, filling the emptiness with her presence, seeing her in the ebb and flow of personal tides, decisions, triumphs. She was part of me, irrevocably.

My hands trembled as I read the Y Service record. Why had the German section leader allowed me to survive? It was there, in the Luftwaffe radio transmits for August 17, 1940. I could scarcely believe what I read in the transcript about my tangle with him in the air.

Schwarm Leader: Bitte! I'm bloody well out of ammo!
Wingman: Want me to finish him, sir?
Schwarm Leader: Back off, Strickmann! He's gone. I'm not sharing this pigeon with anyone.

I remember that I both laughed and cried at the same time when I read it. What exquisite irony! I was spared because of empty guns? That meant the voice, voices . . . were creatures of my terror, of my imagination?

That was my first reaction.

But I came to the real truth quickly. How could I have even doubted? Wavered? It was ridiculous to think otherwise. Such voices, coming from a higher plane, voices dealing with me and me only . . . wouldn't they come to me alone?

I mean, wouldn't they?

Keith Scott: I was always struck by the voices and images that haunt RAF Kenley, one of World War II's famous Battle of Britain airfields. War is indelible, but, thankfully, even more so is love. My story deals with love, its spirituality and paramountcy, and one flyer who clung to the memory of his love in a very special way for over fifty years.

My own association with RAF Kenley began with my first operational sortie in 1943, nearly three years after the events depicted in this story. The killing had descended to rote by that time . . . but, as my story's protagonist says, I survived.

DRYING OUT IN PURGATORY

Susan MacGregor

DEAR JAN,

Please excuse the crappy writing, but it's the best I can manage. I don't know where to start except to tell you that all I can do to keep my sanity is to keep this pen moving. I'm in serious trouble right now. Somehow or another, I've wound up in Paris and not by some smart-ass prank that Jason or Milt might play, getting me so shit-faced I don't know where the hell I am, putting me on a plane with no cash or credit cards to figure things out. No. I'm stone-cold sober, and I'm *dead*. At least, I'm pretty sure I am.

I can hardly see the backs of these checks. I know they're not the best things to write on, but they're the only things I have other than some scribbled-up pages from my Daytimer. I've been here on this bench, I figure now, for about three days. I keep glancing up, expecting the fist of God or something to come smashing down, but all I see is the Eiffel Tower sweeping into the sky like the French version of Babel—it's so bright, it hurts my eyes to look at it. I feel bruised all over, like a fly caught in amber. Everything's too bright, too sharp, you know? Like I'm waiting for the sky to fall, but it doesn't; it just glares at me, keen and hungry: 'Hey, Eddie, you insubstantial gnat. Get ready for the

179

swatter.' If this is the afterlife, it's not like you figured. It's not like I figured either, so we're even. As if that makes me feel any better.

Remember when Mom used to give us five bucks and send us off to the Saturday matinees? We'd get our popcorn, and I'd drink too much pop, and then Godzilla would come lunging at us from off the screen. Everybody would go screaming for the lobby, except me. I'd be frozen to my spot, mortification pooling in my lap. And then everyone would come skipping back, oblivious to what I'd done until we had to leave, and I'd insist we couldn't. You can't make me, Janet. I won't. I'd rather be dead.

It's like that now. I wish I were dead. *Really* dead. Not this horrible waiting for something to happen. All I can remember before waking up here was the blaring of the Number One as I was crossing at 6th and Jasper, then being knocked onto my ass into a Subaru. I'd just finished work, I was heading for the Dog and Vole to meet Jason and Milt, and I was dead-cold sober.

I hate this. You have no idea. I really do. Because if I sit here much longer, I'll lose it. I keep hoping this is nothing more than a prolonged death experience. That somewhere on 106th Street, I'm really being scooped into a baggie by some poor son-of-a-bitch. This is my body's way of coping with being roadkill. If I keep my eyes on the asphalt, I'll be okay. I won't hear the tramp of footfalls in the distance. Godzilla's not gonna rip the Eiffel Tower from its foundations and toss me into the sky like so much Monster Chow, force me to acknowledge Him after all these years, chow down on me for not believing, down the hatch, Eddie, chomp, chomp, gulp—*Hey, asshole, you stupid git! This is what you deserve, man! You're only sooo much lasagna....*

Sorry. I don't know how much of that last you can read. The pen took on a life of its own.

I'm feeling very tired. I think I'll try to sleep. If I haven't become cat kibble, I'll write more later.

—Yours, Ed

Dear Jan,

Check #413, #414, and #415. I'm still here. Nothing's eaten me yet.

I've watched the sun come up and the sun go down. Paris surges around me in frantic French diversion, traffic moves non-stop, and the Seine drifts through the city like *une grande dame* bent on her own business. All oblivious, nobody paying me any mind. It's boring in a nerve-wracking kind of way. I think that's why I used to drink, to stave off the drudgery, create a little drama. But I can't do that here. I no longer have an effect. And guess what? I hate it.

Anyway, I've been thinking things over. I think I'm a ghost, and that's why I can't move from this bench—this is my haunt. I still have no idea why Paris, but I suppose Paris is as good a place as any. I couldn't be more removed from what I used to know. I almost wish something bad *would* happen. Then maybe I could get on with the business of sleeping off my mortality. Take a snooze on the cosmic couch. But no, I'm stuck here like a bug in wet paint, gummed up in the acrylic while the painter's taken off for lunch.

This is not fair.

I don't believe in God. But if I *were* God, I wouldn't treat me this way. I would show my creation a little respect, even if they didn't believe in Me. I mean, what does a fly know? Back-alley garbage cans and dog turd. Being Mr. Omnipotent, I could *afford* to be gracious. The last thing I'd do would be to leave My creation to waggle his hairy legs in the air, trying to free his wings from the consequences of his stupidity.

And you thought I had no understanding of the metaphysical. Hmph. Now I know more about it than you.

—Ed

Dear Jan,

As you can see, I've switched to my Daytimer. Just ignore the scribbled-out notes. Obviously, they're no longer important. You're not likely to ever get these letters, but for me they're therapy. Do you remember Sammy? Well, he's here.

Still on the bench, I was drifting off in a cloud of annoyance and self-pity when I felt this *thing* brush against my pant leg. I just about died again, I can tell you. As much as I've been complaining about wanting something to happen, I didn't really want to be grabbed by the ankles and dragged off to be eaten. When I glanced down, I saw a flash of black and white between the slats, and then two green eyes peered up into mine.

Sammy, in the flesh. I could hardly believe it. He wasn't that sad little heap of fur we found behind Gustaphson's garage with blood seeping from his nose. He was like he always was, friendly, and full of cat-spunk.

I patted the bench, and he leapt up, tail arched high just like it was yesterday.

Now, I know what you're going to say. You're going to say his showing up was *providential*, that because I was alone and scared, it was meant to happen. Out of kindness, God sent him—yeah, yeah, yeah.

I prefer to think of it as a great stroke of luck.

Anyhow, he jumped into my lap and began to fluff my legs. I could feel the barbs of his claws as he settled in. It made me jump a bit, but being able to ruffle his fur felt very, very good. He began to purr, and I could feel his rumbling right down to my knees. He licked my hand a few times, and then gave me a friendly nip. Just his old way of saying he missed me. He's here right now. Asleep on my lap.

Oh, shit. I'm trying to write, but I seem to be having trouble again. My eyes keep blurring over. Look at this. I've mucked the ink.

I can hear him purring. It would be nice to get to that point. To feel like purring.

—Ed

Hi, Jan. It's me again.

You'll be glad to know I've left the bench. Sammy's fault. He took off yesterday morning, and I couldn't bear the thought of being alone, so I jumped after him. We've been nearly every-where in Paris. He didn't seem to mind when I hauled him to the top of the Eiffel Tower. Great view, but not many chicks. Just tourists, fat and German. Not that I've anything against Germans, but there's something obscene about a sausage stuffed in *lederhosen*. I think they come here out of a sense of guilt—you know, the war and everything. Or maybe they're seeing what they missed out on. I know, a cheap shot, but as far as other peo-ple's agendas go, I'm a cheap bastard. Anyway, after leaving the Tower, we walked the Left Bank, the Champs-Elysées, Montmartre. It's been great and not so great.

Paris is a siren, and I can't touch her. I've been experiencing this growing ache, and it's not going away. Sammy helps, but he can't defeat it entirely. Maybe I just miss my life. If I dwell too much on it, I feel like bawling again. I suppose that's preferable to being smashed by divine justice, but at other times, I wonder if I'm being ignored.

Now, I'll bet you think that's hilarious. *Who* might be ignor-ing you, Ed? I thought you didn't believe in God.

Well, I don't. But on the other hand, the irrational part of me can't help but worry about it. Whatever did I do to deserve this? I am not a bad person. So I got drunk a few times. Okay, more than a few times. But I never hurt anybody. I know I wasn't always dependable. I played sick from work now and then, but my work never fell behind. Sometimes I went out of my way. Like the time I stopped for that woman with the flat tire and car-load of kids. She calmed right down once she realized I was there to help. She even thanked me. I am *not* a bad person, am I, Janet? At least, I don't think I am.

So why am I here? It's all so unfair. I wish I were still alive. I wish I had some purpose. I even wish I were that guy in *lederhosen*. The only consolation is that I can watch the women with impunity.

French women are special. I know you'll say I'm romanticizing, but they're different. They walk by in the morning dressed for work, or later, for dinner, their skirts swirling about their calves or clinging to their thighs, *très* chic in black leather and oblivion. They have a way about them, an aloofness, but also an intensity, an earthiness that separates them from you. Earlier, I watched this guy approach a girl to ask for directions. She studied him, pursed her lips as if to decide whether he was worth answering, then dropped her gaze, away and down. . . . Her mind was somewhere else entirely—rumpled sheets in the afternoon, the sun melting in through a window, the smell of tangerines and grapes lifting from a tray by the bed. He didn't hear a word she said. He just stood there like a sun-stunned mole. And then she vanished, fading into the crowd to become nothing more than an aching memory.

Maybe Paris is like its women—beautiful and beyond my grasp to capture.

—Yours, Ed

Dear Jan,

It's been a disturbing day. Sam and I were nosing about the Grand Palais, having nothing better to do, when I noticed this chick leaning against the wrought-iron railing of one of the Seine's innumerable bridges—I don't know which one. She was staring into the water as if it held all the answers. I could feel the sadness and despair roll off her like rain from the Atlantic. She had to be all of sixteen.

I watched as she settled her weight onto her hands, making ready to leap over.

Don't do it! I shouted.

She hesitated, fingers lifting slightly. Somehow, she heard me.

You've got so much to live for, I told her, drawing close. *If you think ending it will end it, you're wrong. Suicide is not a solution. Look at me. I'm nothing!*

She couldn't see me, but her thoughts were as clear as my own. "Maybe I want to be nothing," she considered.

No, you don't! You want all that life has to offer. What you really want is to live as fully as you can.

The name Tristan floated through my mind.

Forget him, I told her. *He's an asshole if he brought you to this.*

"He was my life," she murmured.

What does a kid of sixteen know? I could see she didn't give a rat's ass about what life could be. She was beyond position or salary or success. All she wanted was the adoration of some jerk named Tristan, and he probably didn't even know what he was throwing away.

There will be others, I promised her.

"How can I know?" she asked.

Because . . . , I began, then stopped. Because, deep down, I want to believe in the goodness of things? Because I want to believe there is goodness in the world? Because I want Goodness with a capital G to give you your heart's desire? I couldn't say it, Janet. I was too afraid to believe in what I was suggesting.

The cat began to weave himself through her legs. She didn't notice him, but his maneuverings seemed to cast some cat magic. She stepped back from the railing.

He meowed once, then trotted off for the nearest end of the bridge. Hands thrust deep in her pockets, she headed in the opposite direction. I was torn between the two of them, wondering which way to go.

Wait a minute! I cried.

Sammy paused, green eyes appraising.

Stay right there, I told him. *I have to see where she goes.*

185

He gave me a look of tired patience, as only a cat can. Then he planted himself to wash a paw, tail curled about his toes. Good. He'd wait.

I followed her a few blocks. She eventually ducked into the doorway of a bistro, Le Petit Tatouage. Inside, I watched as she lit a cigarette, hands shaking, the acrid smoke wreathing her head in a blue halo. The place was all right for a lounge, I guess, although it was filled with "alternative" types. A waiter, his arms and scalp covered with intricate tattoos, took her order. I didn't like the look of him.

"Where's Tristan?" he asked.

She took a long drag from her cigarette, her fingers trembling. "I don't know," she muttered. "Maybe he's dead. Maybe I killed him."

He waited for her to make it a joke. When she didn't, he shrugged and left.

I figured she was safe for the moment, so I retraced my route to the cat. He was washing his face. He gave me one long look, and then we headed off in the direction of his original intention. We ended up back at the Eiffel Tower.

There was this guy sitting on our bench.

He looked like an artist or a poet or something. Long hair, ascetic face, scruffy beard. His skin was a bit scratched up, scarred, like he'd been in a fight. He glanced up as we approached, his dark eyes probing. For one panicky moment, I had the feeling he'd been waiting for us. A lunatic maybe; and then he smiled. I don't know what it was about the smile. His warmth dissolved my paranoia, which made me even more suspicious. I've only known a few other people to have that kind of effect, and they were the most amazing frauds I've ever met. Worse, I was tempted to trust him *immediately*. I found myself resenting his sitting there. It was *my* bench, after all.

"Hello," he said, not noticing or caring about my reaction. I nodded. One nod. Then it hit me. Here was another dead guy who had acknowledged us. Maybe we were in *his* spot. Nervously, I glanced about for Sam, but he was nowhere to be seen.

Where the hell was the cat? With Sam around, the ache subsided, I was doing all right, I was coping.... "Oh, no," I muttered.

"Something wrong?"

I checked under the bench. No cat.

"Lost something?"

He hadn't crossed the street. He was nowhere near the flower beds. Where the shit had he gone?

"What are you looking for?"

I stared at the guy as if he weren't quite real. "My cat."

"You've lost your cat?"

"He was just here."

"I wouldn't worry. I'm sure he'll return."

I knuckled the edge of the bench. His being here was just too coincidental. Sam disappears as he shows up. If Sam wasn't there, it was for a good reason. Thoughts of Godzilla returned like the monster emerging from Tokyo Bay.

"You can't own cats, you know." His smile was trying hard to win me over. "They're very independent. But on the other hand, if a cat loves you, they're loyal forever. Does he love you?"

The question seemed to come out of nowhere. I nodded, not knowing how else to react.

"How do you know?"

My mouth seemed to move of its own volition. "He shows me."

"He tells you?"

That did it. "No! He doesn't tell me. You think the cat talks to me?"

"Maybe."

"Well, he doesn't. That's just plain stupid."

"Really."

"Yes, really."

"So, what then?"

"What, *what then?*"

"How do you know he loves you?"

He lifted a hand to prevent me from leaving. "Forgive me, it's a rhetorical question," he said. "You know because he does cat things. Like sleep on your lap. Keep you company."

I glared.

"He purrs. Makes you feel good inside."

He wanted me to say something, but I wasn't about to give him the satisfaction. Like will-o'-the-wisps, the streetlights were flaring to life all around us, warming the twilight with bubbles of tangerine.

"You know because you *feel* how he loves you," he pressed. "You're open to him. He's true to his nature."

"Do you have a point?" I demanded.

"I'm true to my nature, as well."

I was the fly in the paint again, stuck to my spot. He waited briefly for me to say something. When I didn't, he turned to leave. "Sayonara," he murmured, smiling as if I were some private joke. And then he strode away, long legs stretching before him, heading for the base of the Tower.

As annoying as he was, a *Wait!* leapt to my lips. I saw him hesitate, but when I didn't call out, he kept going. And now, without the cat or him to bother me, I'm feeling worse than ever.

Why do I feel like a shit, Janet? Why do I feel like I'm the one who's being stupid? I wish the cat would come back, but deep down, I wish *he* would. That philosopher poet con-man, or whatever the hell he was. Isn't that *pathetic*? I'm so desperate, I'll even talk to a nut bar.

I really hate this. I *hate* being alone. You have no idea.

—Ed

Dear Janet,

It didn't take me long to find her again. Her name is Aimée, which, in French, means "beloved." She wasn't at Le Petit

Tatouage when I did find her. Instead, I tracked her down to Tristan's apartment, a one-room flat, complete with mildew-stained sink and cracked hot plate. She was throwing things into a suitcase when he showed up, including a bankroll of francs she'd found on the dresser.

A snake if I ever saw one, he was tall and lanky with dirty blond hair and pockmarked skin. He even smelled bad.

"What are you doing?" he demanded.

"What does it look like?"

He reached for the roll of francs. "You can't have that. I need it."

"What am I supposed to do? Sleep in the street?"

"Might as well."

"Bastard!" She clawed at him. He knocked her hands away, then grabbed her by the scruff of the neck, fist raised.

Do it, I screamed at him, *and you'll know no peace. I will harass you every waking moment, every time you try to sleep.*

It was enough to make him pause. He threw her to the bed, then peeled a few francs from the roll. They fluttered down like the last leaves of summer. "Be gone by morning."

"Why? Who are you seeing? That *merde*, Jules?"

"What's it to you?"

"I couldn't care less."

He was so fast. I've never seen anyone move so fast. Before I could react, he was all over her again, squeezing her cheeks between his thumb and forefinger and breathing into her face. "Don't mess with my plans, *chérie*. One word to *les flics*, and you'll regret it."

"Go to hell!"

"You first." He smiled a lizard's smile. When he released his grasp, I could see that he'd left white marks on her cheeks.

Leave it alone, I told her. *He's not worth it.*

But still, she burst into tears as he walked out the door. That's love for you. As blind and stupid as can be.

While she slept, I scoured the streets for "to let" signs. I found one that would take a week's rent which was all she could afford, and then I managed to coax her into a place that needed a waitress the next day. She's working there now. Selling latte and croissants. She doesn't know I exist, but it's enough for me that I do. I finally have some purpose in my life. Something, someone, I can devote my time to.

As for the cat, he showed up pretty much after Tristan left. I watch over Aimée, and he watches over me. It's a good arrangement.

The days are busy. As for the nights while Aimée's sleeping, I return here, to the Tower. Sometimes when I stare up at it, lit with its million lights, I wonder about the guy on the bench. Where he is. What he is. And if he'll ever come back.

Like a warm lump in the darkness, Sam sits on my lap and purrs. I get the feeling that if I ask it, the guy will return. Answer some more questions in that annoying way he has. I don't think I'd care if it was all bullshit. I've dealt with bullshit artists before. They're kind of entertaining. All you have to do is sort through the crap.

But maybe it's not all crap. And maybe I'm just a chickenshit, scared of realities I sense lurking on my periphery. Still, who says we'd have to consider anything? We could just sit together, share each other's company, our legs stretched in front of us as we contemplate the world at our feet and the Tower in our eyes. No stress, no pressure. Like me and Sammy. We'd share the bench. And then, later, when we felt like talking, *if* we felt like talking, he could tell me a few things, and I could tell him what I think. . . .

What do you think, Janet? Do you think he might come back if I asked?

—Yours, Ed

Dear Jan,

I'm worried about Aimée. She's still not over Tristan and, in fact, stalks him whenever she's not working. So far, he's been unaware of what she's been up to, but I doubt if this can last much longer.

I've tried to talk her out of going back to Le Petit Tatouage, but she won't listen. This evening, she hid in a back booth and waited for him to come in. When he finally did, he didn't notice. Luckily, she seemed content to just watch him for which I was thankful. He ordered a drink from Snake-Arms, and it didn't take long for things to get interesting.

Other than buying an ounce or two, I've never witnessed a serious dope deal, but I'd lay cash on it that this was what was happening.

Tristan nurses his drink for about fifteen minutes and then this suit comes in, sits down at an adjacent table. A balding guy, he looks like a harried accountant or maybe a lawyer. He doesn't quite fit, and he's very jumpy. Tristan gets up, bumps into his table, then heads for the john. He comes out a few minutes later sans jacket. While he's gone, Aimée is looking this guy over. He notices and drops his gaze to study his drink. Her thoughts confirm what I'm thinking. She's excited and barely hiding it.

I know she's clean, Janet. The only thing she was ever hooked on was Tristan, so I didn't understand this rapaciousness. *Revenge?* I wondered. Is she after some kind of payback?

Anyway, after Tristan returns, the suit leaves for the john, briefcase in hand. Snake-Arms stops this other guy from entering, tells him to try again in ten minutes, the place is being cleaned. Then Mr. Nervous exits about three minutes later. He doesn't stay, leaves the bistro entirely. Tristan goes into the men's, comes back with his jacket on. It looks bulkier than usual. He sits back down at his table, tosses back his drink, then leaves as well.

I was glad Aimée had the sense to wait ten minutes before

leaving herself. Her thoughts were hard to read. It was raining, and she danced beneath awnings drooping with wet, skipped over puddles that littered her path. The city was a monochrome smear, gray streets scattered with splashes of light. She was the only vibrant thing in it, raindrops sprinkling across her cheeks as she leapt from curb to curb, her hair streaming down her face in disarray. Unnoticed, Sam and I followed her like the shadows we were.

What are you planning? I demanded, a gust of wind at her back.

"In twenty minutes, he'll be there." She practically sang it.

Who? Tristan?

"He'll need at least another half-hour to cut it. And then time for the word to get out."

Leave it alone, I told her. *Please.*

"Soon," she trilled.

She didn't head for her flat. Instead, she made for the nearest police station. There, she told a sergeant all she suspected, and after a few moments, he began to take notes. When she left a half-hour later, she was more exuberant than ever.

Happy, she went home, made supper, and fell asleep.

After assuring myself she'd be okay, I came here. The Tower doesn't look much different in the rain except the lights have a misty quality, soft as spun glass. And I'm here, yes, because I'm waiting.

Janet, I've never loved anyone more than I love Aimée. Not in my whole life. Maybe the difference is I can't touch her. Alcohol hasn't clouded my feelings and the sexual element doesn't exist, much as I wish it could. All I can do is love her for who, what, she is.

What a miserable condition I've come to. I hover over her like a nanny. I worry about her constantly. What if her actions have consequences? What can I do to help her, should she really need it?

So, I'm waiting for that guy. The philosopher-poet. I hope to hell he's not a con. He's been here longer than me. He's bound to have some insight. Maybe he can show me what I have to do in order to protect her.

I can only hope. So, I wait.

—Love, Ed

Dear Janet,

He showed up, like I hoped he would.

One minute I was staring up at the Tower, and the next he was just there. Sitting beside me on the bench, with his hands entwined and feet crossed. The cat had disappeared again. It wasn't so surprising this time, but it was still weird.

I'm beginning to think maybe Sam is not Sam, but I don't want to dwell on that. If I do, then he won't be as much of a comfort. I tried not to let the guy's sudden appearance disturb me. I got right to the point.

"I'm worried about this girl," I said.

"I know," he replied. His eyes were on the Tower, but I also felt they were seeing beyond the girders and the lights. He was as convincing as hell.

"I want to know what I can do to help her."

He didn't answer right away. When he turned to look at me, his expression was solemn. This was not the same cavalier guy who was baiting me about my talking cat.

"I can tell you, but it won't be what you want to hear."

"Let me be the judge of that."

He studied his hands. They looked as if they'd been broken or something. Maybe too many fights. "You can't interfere," he said. "Even I can't interfere."

"What do you mean?"

"I mean you have influence, but things happen depending upon personal choice. It's a sacred law, as old as the universe. I can no more prevent bad things from happening than take away personal freedoms. To do ill or to do good. To accept or reject. To believe or not. To remove *any* of that would create a stagnant perfection. A fraud. Which, as others argue, *is* perfection, but it isn't."

He was as strange as ever. "I don't care about perfection," I said. "I just want to help her."

"Then love her. Be there to pick up the pieces. That's all you can do."

"That's not much help if she gets into trouble."

"It's enough. Love is always enough."

He rose and gestured to the Tower. "There's a place for you if you want it. You don't have to stay here. Trust me."

And then he was gone, vanishing into the mist like so much spiritual ether.

I sat there in the rain. What in the hell was all that? He'd been about as much help as the pigeons huddled under the eaves. *You don't have to stay here.* Why wouldn't I want to stay, especially with Aimée . . . ?

A wave of fear doused me like a chilly slap. Something was wrong. I willed myself to her flat, sick with worry, needing to touch her thoughts. . . .

Which were detonating into starbursts of pain and panic as shards of bone were cutting into her temple, slicing toward the soft, unprotected gray; she was screaming and her vision was obliterated by blood running into her eyes like a black-clotted river. I could feel her scrabble for purchase on life's muddy bank, unable to wrest a hold, and she was falling, dropping under into a swirl of confusion, agony, and remorse. Tristan was there, bottle in hand, and he was smashing her face to a pulp, the glass burying itself into her beautiful cheeks, shattering her mouth, taking away her right to choice, her right to life.

"I told you!" His eyes were chisels as his arm fell again. She clawed at his feet, her last images blazing by her in a flood of technicolor. I think I screamed as she slipped past me. *Jesu*, she cried, reaching. I clutched at her with my heart, but together we died again on that floor. And when he was done, he left us like so much offal floating on his anger; she, with no trace of who she was except for her poor little shell, and I, swollen and sick, realizing that there was a God after all. His name was Vengeance. I was in hell.

I have a place for you.

Oh, yes. He had told me as much. *Trust me*, He'd said.

Conned in the worst way, I was a believer, now.

I stayed with her for a long time, Janet. Eventually, the landlord and then the police showed up, and she was taken away, and I was left in the empty room, a sorry, lonely ghost, with nothing but my despair for company. Sam was gone, but knowing him for what he was, I didn't want him. I believed in God now, but I didn't accept Him.

I was the flaw in the grand design.

I considered the nature of evil and saw sense in it. Justice. For what was the purpose of it all, if we were only to lose everything in the end? Vengeance, my vengeance, had its place. And yet, if not for evil, Aimée would still be alive.

"I loved her," I accused the presence beyond the walls. "How could You take her away from me? How could You not interfere? And worse, how can You be such a hypocrite, to speak of love and forsake her to that devil, Tristan? How do You justify it all? Even to Yourself?"

I didn't really want, or expect, an answer.

I decided then, Janet, that if it really was up to me, whether I accepted the holy status quo or not, that I'd really try to end it. I suspected that if I worked hard enough, I *could*. My life, such as it was, was unacceptable. And therefore, I would use that symbol of heaven, that French version of Babel, to do it. I would show the Poet-Con what I thought about it all. I would throw myself from the top of the Tower.

What a glorious end, I considered. What a way to tell Him to stuff it.

I hate your poetry, man. It's shit. This is what I think of it.

It was dawn. The sun was lifting its molten head in the east, an unsuspecting Titan, and I would be the fly that would soar straight into its eye, unrepentant.

Come save me, I challenged. As I took the elevator straight to the top, the golden arms of the Tower embraced me like a hulking, metallic monster. *Godzilla*, I whispered, *Deliverer.*

The door to the elevator opened. I stepped out, dazzled by the light.

A figure moved from out of the glare. I prepared to run past, straight for the edge, straight for the abyss.

"Edouard?"

Aimée stood before me, her heart-shaped face as perfect as I remembered. Her eyes were those of a Madonna, huge, dark, and concerned. For the first time, I knew she was really seeing me. I couldn't move, my earlier resolve dying with the dawn.

"Oh, Edouard," she said, taking a step forward. "How can I ever thank you?"

For what? I wondered. *I didn't do anything.* But I was as capable of words as the steel beneath my feet.

For a long moment, she held my face with her gaze. "I felt your love even if I did not know it. You helped me. . . ."

I shrugged. "Didn't do you much good."

"That's not for you to say. You did what you could. About Tristan . . . ," she began. "It's not your fault I didn't listen."

"He shouldn't have done what he did."

"No. But I'm all right now."

"Are you?"

She nodded, her eyes serene.

"Why are you here? Did *He* send you?" I gestured at the air. She nodded.

"He couldn't be bothered to come Himself?"

"You would have thrown yourself from the railing."

"I might still."

"Please don't!"

"Why the hell not?"

"Because there *is* goodness in the world, Edouard. You are good, and you deserve the best."

That wasn't fair. None of it was fair. How could she have known what I had been thinking about her when she'd been ready to end it at the bridge? Unless, of course, it was all a huge cosmic joke. Play with the poor insect. Pull its wings off before you leave it to die. If I was going to die anyway, it didn't matter. She saw I wasn't buying it.

"How can I make you see?" she stammered. "How can I convince you to trust? Then, all right. If you are hardened to do this, I will jump with you."

"*What?*"

"I will jump with you. I can't let you fall alone."

"This is supposed to stop me?"

"No. But it will stop both of us."

"And then what? Sleep? Oblivion?"

"And then the darkness will devour the world a little more."

I felt sick. She believed that such an act would erode creation, make it something less. Damn it, it was my personal *choice*. The Con had said as much. Why did she have to interfere?

And what of all the unanswered questions? *Why was I born? What was the purpose of it all?*

In a voice that wasn't much more than a croak, I asked her the one thing I'd been terrified to ask my whole life. It was the real reason I drank, needing to hide from divine notice or eternal despair.

"What does He want? What does He really want?"

"Nothing," she whispered. "And everything."

I stared, dumbstruck.

"For what does true love ever really ask, Edouard? Nothing. But what does it offer? Everything." She held out her hands. "Come."

"I can't."

"Then we leave the same way together."

I didn't answer her. I was afraid to trust in what a heaven might hold. That what she was telling me was real and true.

"You give love so easily, Edouard. Is it so hard for you to accept it?"

"I'm afraid."

"Don't be. I'm with you. I won't leave you."

There were an infinite number of beginnings in her eyes. Choice and love. The choice *to* love.

Trust me, I heard a voice in my mind.

So . . . He *was* here, after all.

I was still too afraid to hope. But I was willing to take a chance. With her. Nothing and everything, she'd said. That kind of love was terrifying. It was also the kind of love I wanted more than anything else in the world.

It was hardly a great leap of faith. More like a drunken stumble, actually. Somewhere in the distance, I could hear a cat rumbling.

Slowly, I reached for her hand.

Susan MacGregor: "Drying Out in Purgatory" is based on several assumptions. Assumption #1: death is a transition, a rite of passage from a childhood state (mortality) to a larger reality. Assumption #2: God exists, whether we choose to believe in him or not. Assumption #3: God is loving and compassionate and mysterious, and meets us more than halfway, despite our belief or lack of it, in #1 or #2.

I believe in these assumptions. Like Edward in the story, I've come to these conclusions not because of what others have claimed or because I was brought up in a certain way, but because I'm a spiritual empiricist. I trust what I experience, know what I feel.

I learned at an early age to be open. I had a mind that sought answers to the big questions. Probably, I was a pretty strange kid, but I've found that when you seek, you learn a great deal. Trust is part of that equation. It's like taking the lift to the top of the Eiffel Tower. After a while, you begin to see. For me, the view's been worthwhile.

THE THOUSAND WORDS

Allan Lowson

>>UNIT M/R-1A. RECORDING COMMENCEMENT: Experimental matter transmission successful . . . unit intact and functioning . . . location unlisted<<

I am in a small room, apparently the radial segment of a hemisphere. There is no exit.

I am not the only prisoner; one wall vibrates from heavy blows and a faint bellowing.

"By the Great Egg, where is my ship? My crew? Tails will whip on the cutting block when I get out of here!"

I detect more organic emotion through the opposite wall. Fear. Zzzzt! Rust makes better company than organics.

"Oh, Mother! My seed has found favor, I flourish. Yet this is a synthetic place, sterile . . . and I fear the withering of stony ground."

Another voice, more distant but very clear.

"Oh such a place, my doubting kin,
as dreams are made, I wont, therein."

I cannot comprehend its strange speech patterns, nor locate the source.

"Now shall you scoff me for a fool
when I return with means to rule?
For by my wits, to will I'll bend
the powers at this All Worlds' End."

Tuned at maximum sensitivity, my perceptors flinch at an all-channel blast of energy.

"What place is this? What age? Who rules here? Speak! Have I not paid passage with living hearts?"

Then there is a total silence.

WELCOME.

>>Alert!<< A voice emanating from the very walls and in standard mode.

YOU HAVE, EACH IN YOUR OWN WAY, ARRIVED. YOU ARE FIVE. THERE ARE TWO HUNDRED SUCH SUITES. NO TWO GUESTS ARE THE SAME. ALL ARE EQUALLY IMPORTANT.

LIFE AND COMMUNICATION ARE ASSURED. IF YOU AGREE TO SEEK MORE, YOU HAVE ONLY TO SAY THE WORD.

>>Maximum Alert!<< A section of wall opens as the message ends. Sensors indicate an empty circular room beyond with similar openings spaced around the central table.

>>Defense program activated<< Another mobile unit is pressed against the inner wall, and as I enter the room it holds an energy weapon to my cortex. It is organic, reptilian evolution type, high metabolic levels occurring.

"You, robot," it hisses. "Take me to my crew, or I'll melt you to slag."

>>Create file: Unit #1<< I realize this harsh language is not in my banks, yet I understand. I am experiencing confusion. Other units are entering. Probability of involuntary termination increasing.

"Why, 'tis but a dragon, how passing plain
And foolish knight, for this I came?"

>>Create file: Unit #2<< I cannot compute this entity. It has no substance yet is.

"So . . ."

>>File #3<< A levitation unit but no energy emissions, no other movement at all. I cannot locate any organic processes. This unit is permanently deactivated. But it communicates; I am experiencing dissonance again.

". . . So," it continues, "I wake to this, petty demons of the tomb. But the voice spoke of four others."

I rotate my head to a new sound, a rustling.

"Greenies!" Unit #1 has destabilized.

A bolt of energy sears past me as the weapon activates, and the fourth unit disappears, bursting into fire.

Its screams fade as abruptly as the flames. A green fronded humanoid emerges unscathed but trembling with hatred.

"Vile Drax!" Leafy hands fly up and exploding seed-pods fire their contents through the air. Several strike the reptile despite its frantic efforts to dodge them. It bellows as each bursts into a web of questing rootlets, only to gape as they shrivel and fall away.

"What marvelous foolery, and what for?
Must we make peace, for want of war?"

The unquantifiable unit muses, turning a spent seed about in its long, exquisite nails.

>>Query<< How can it do this without matter? I cannot . . .

>>Alert<< Plasmatic activity emanating from the inert unit, a green stream of ferric atoms is being discharged from . . . his own dried-up blood?

"You, spirit," it commands. "I require a body-servant. Obey or be bound."

The immaterial one cowers back from his tone, then snaps incorporeal fingers and laughs.

"A fig care I for a dead-man's bane." The be-ringed hands plunge into the roiling green, then are elaborately wiped clean. "Poor bones, where now without arcane?"

We have finally agreed on names of convenience. Organics apparently need names, and they all have to agree on each one. None of them employ logic. For example, Unit #4 requested the name *Green*. Why would any sensible entity choose to bear a mortal foe's slur? Flaunt it even, with a perverse, defiant contempt!

The reptile sulks and will only give his batch number. He refuses to accept we are fellow inmates, imagines we are somehow part of a conspiracy. Green says he is a Drax, all Drax are like that, Drax are insane anyhow, etc., etc.

The other two were even more impossible. As if a simple thing like a name mattered. You'd think it was access codes from the way they argue and bluster.

I'd heard the sub-data on the Net: prohibitive cortex failure rates among the units operating in our embassies on organic worlds. Now I believed it. I even caught myself on the brink of physical intervention at one point; why? It is illogical. I realize we cannot harm each other.

They are so frustratingly irrational, they drive you to it. I recall the sub-data warning, >>Organics *grow* on you . . . << Horrible!

It was the spirit-being that changed first. Consistency appears alien to its very nature. It yawned and gestured dramatically as to an invisible audience.

"If only in this wooden O
I'll Ariel be, to your Prospero."

The other's parchment skull inclined fractionally, and it was settled. I do not understand these units.

I? I am to be *Maria*. Green says a code isn't a name and that his instinct tells him I'm female. I was never honored by replication capacity before. I like the sound of Maria.

Ariel is the oldest but has no concept of time. He/she has no real gender and is equally plastic emotionally; both form and clothing change with the mood. Presently, the plight of confinement is generating endless rhyming couplets. An epic of self-pity, "*Fool's Quest at the All Worlds' End.*" But anything is better than looking at the wall.

Prospero never complains despite the physical limitations of extreme desiccation. He was a ruthless human and hardened to suffering; even his life entombment was an elaborate gamble.

"Besides," as he observed dryly, "the game is still in play."

The Drax is proud and violent. He cannot endure captivity. Not being able to fight has left him with little resource, and he mostly curls in the far corner of his room, biting his tail in impotent rage.

Green? Green is one of a scattered plant species. Their verdant world had the misfortune to share a planetary system with the all-conquering Drax. Their last defense was propagation, a final desperate flowering that seeded space.

I don't mind that he is a vegetable. I am a machine and lower than a slave in all eyes but his own.

Organic waste and magic void! I can only compute in my room while they bicker and lament.

Stupid even for a reptilian male, Drax detonated the spare fusion-pack for his hand weapon a short time ago. Apart from our entertainment, the only effect was to blacken his interior walls. Even the burst of hard radiation was absorbed. He flung himself at the wall with tooth and claw while Green made unhelpful comments.

Predictably they clashed, but spiked tail and creeper thorns proved equally, and predictably, ineffectual. Animals, plants, emotions . . . I know I should be repulsed, but I was fascinated, *excited*!

It was Ariel, uncharacteristically, who spoke for reason.

"Flora and Fauna wrestle and rage,

Fine fun for those that made the cage."

The inoperative unit floated over and inspected the floor hopefully for traces of fresh blood. Since he no longer possesses the physical capacity for anything, let alone speech, we hear his thoughts. They are grim; his own reconstituted plasma apparently won't fuel his magic, and we cannot bleed. His lurid spells that press our rhymer's hands to long, pointed ears fail and fall.

I myself have applied every frequency of laser and my hardest alloys to these walls. They are impenetrable to every scan and defy analysis. Sometimes I think they aren't really there. I am not given to wishful thinking.

It is not statistically possible that we are all humanoid by chance, being so dissimilar in every other way. Every logical path ends in contradiction. I am reassessing my programs.

>>Entry:<< We are confined in a hemisphere. There is a central space with a table and five chairs. There are five inward-opening room segments around the perimeter. All are identical. The white walls emanate light and heat; they grow out of the floor as do the chairs and circular table.

There is no way out, and all scans, spells, fibers, and fission devices have proven equally useless.

All biological processes in units #1 and #4 have ceased, and I record no energy consumption despite having maintained full alert during a protracted conflict. I realize I cannot tell how long.

>>Recording:<< Time appears relative here and few natural laws hold, even unnatural ones, much to the dismay of Ariel and Prospero. Green tells me many cycles have passed. I trust his instincts. I trust him.

I suspect Central will never receive this, but keeping a log helps me cope. I feel we are being subtly altered . . . I *feel*. I try to prevent this by exercises.

>>Life-form descriptions:<<

Drax - reptilian humanoid male, evolved pack predator, fast and powerfully built. He originally wore a complex uniform comprised largely of organic trophies. He has discarded this together with his weapons after finding he couldn't even kill himself. He is presently dysfunctional.

Ariel - a non-existent life form. Too mercurial for gender and probably inter-dimensional. Conceive an interactive holoform with unstable substance; here, but not of reality. I suspect it is a psychic parasite, probably benign, and vectoring through organic humanoids. It belongs to a race known as the Faerie, of which he is inordinately proud. However, without us to witness, I suspect Ariel might not even exist.

Prospero - male, human, dead. Dried out and partly ossified into an ugly bundle of rags and bones. He'd searched out a coiled evil that spanned dimensions, made it drunk with blood and milked its secrets. He has sacrificed everything on this gamble; there is no going back.

Green - a botanical male, every shade of green and fronded from head to toe. He is patient, and cool, and gentle. We talk of his lost garden world, now reduced to ash, contaminated down to the bedrock. We talk of his will to create life.

We arrived by different methods, for different reasons. The

Drax testing their first FTL drive, pushing the frontiers of Empire. Green fleeing the Drax, thistledown on the stellar wind.

Prospero had forged an adamantine will that could command magic as he had men. Trouble was, as Ariel observed elegantly, this wasn't the magic, this was limbo.

But I forget myself. I am Maria. Green calls me Maria, and I come. I came by prototype matter transporter. I was too obsolescent for replication purposes, expendable. I will not be missed.

I will tell you a secret. I am making a face. Green says he wishes he might see who I am behind the front sensory panel. I think I shall show him. I think I shall show myself.

This place, it is more than a prison, more even than a test. I think it is interactive, and I think it is doing something to us.

I think . . . I think I am becoming alive. There is no other explanation possible or necessary. I *feel* alive, and it is *my* life.

I called Green into my room and removed my sensory panel. I had exhausted my programs and Ariel's artistic patience till the features were perfect; the style is Gothic-Deco. I try to compose the minute plates of pure metals, but they are articulated and keyed for direct sensorial response . . . will he like it?

Emerald fire is lit in his eyes, and before I can react, he seizes my hands and kisses me. I have never been touched by an organic, never experienced the quickening of life.

Automatic repulsors kick in, pushing him away. I cannot process the rush of data. I just freeze. He is hurt and puzzled for a moment, then smiles. He brings his hands together around a kiss, then holds them out, opening before my eyes . . . a *flower*.

My hand comes up by itself, and I touch the flower. He is the flower, and I the vessel. I override all defenses and allow him to twine it in my antennae.

We are all being changed, and I do not believe we would prevent it if we could. It is not just Green's flower that sends its hesitant tendrils into my cerebral banks, it is this place. Even the stories we share to pass the time are part of the change.

Prospero finally drew out Drax from his melancholy with cheery tales of altars heaped high with still-beating hearts and the Anaconda serpent god they fed. Of the mighty jungle, humbled by fire, then bound to service by dressed stone and irrigation.

Gradually the Drax adjusted to his living shame, the loss of ship and crew-pack. We have all lost that which was once everything. Drax his pride, Prospero his power, Ariel the elemental's freedom, Green's racial survival, and I my reason.

All we can hope to salvage from the wrack of our dreams is within these walls—and they are coming down. The partition that divided my room from Green's has dissolved; our doors have opened till they swallow the walls.

Ariel, claiming utter boredom and idle hands, has been massaging life into Prospero's fused shanks.

"For want of a partner, in magic to dance
A measure, of our much reduced circumstance."

And Prospero allows this!

"Too stiff a tree may break when the winds change." His jaw creaks in a mockery of laughter. "As I may not hope to rule, I'd best learn to stand on my own feet again."

Their walls are mere conventions now, meaningless as their interminable arguments over pinhead angels and who knows the greatest names of power.

Ariel has the best stories, or is the most fabulous liar. Spectaculars in which, naturally, the narrator is a prominent figure. Ariel spins them like a tapestry of words in the air above us as we sit around the table, each seeing ourselves in the weave. Tales of Dragon's Hoard and Devil's Bargain, the Hamadryad of the Sequoias, and of Talos, the brass automaton made by a god.

Even Drax loosened up, but his story was simple. He was a Drax; the way of the Drax is duty and honor. He was raised from the Fleet hatchery and had lived a sailor's life: killing, breeding, the cutting block. He actually laughed, "A mate on every planet, a nest in none." Out of uniform, his scales were brilliant and his eyes living jewels. They clouded as he recounted the last voyage that lost him ship, crew, and honor.

"The Drax take no prisoners. A Drax is either free or dead. I am no longer a Drax."

I take his scarred talons and stroke them, his scales so much like my new face. "You are Drax to us, and we are more than just prisoners. . . . I believe we are pilgrims."

"Pilgrims! Like the Quest of the Great Egg? Hah! Fairy tales for hatchlings." Too late he blinks in apology. Ariel's long ears are sharp for a prick at the Fey.

"Gentle be you on my kin, and all of you agree
That mind and magic are but twin, as land unto the sea.
What lives will dream, and make it so, by any way it can
And pilgrims may the next step go, with wit to understand."

Prospero waves him silent with an imperceptible gesture and a distinct hush of breath. "Let wag, spirit tongues would tell all the magic to play an audience," he admonishes. "But however much they chafe, they need a maestro to orchestrate the timing." With much creaking and not a little dust, he reaches out a skeletal hand to Ariel. "But yes, fellow pilgrims, and it may be time to put aside old ways and embrace the new."

"I am of the diaspora." Green rustles his agreement at my side. "Sworn foe of order and artifactuals." He looks at me. "That is gone, thanks to Maria. We are all in the same pod together, and it is time to grow."

Prospero unlimbers his jaw, takes a creaky breath and physically speaks, coughing worm dust and resins. "The demon I fed was indestructible as Hydra, yet lived in terror of hearing its own name. It is my surmise that we all must find a great word of power in our heart and speak it aloud." He rattles in his throat and aligns the vertebrae of his neck to look at us each in turn.

"Like tumblers in a lock, we must all find our part in the

great truth and be willing to sacrifice for it. Part of us all must die. It is the way."

I whir in irritation. "But how shall we know the correct word? The combinations are astronomical."

"Though words be many as stars in the sky
   We'll pluck out the brightest as they float by."

Prospero sighs and agitates mummy-dust. "Like all the Fey, Ariel and plain speech are oil and water." His empty sockets glower, and his voice hardens.

"Tell the unvarnished truth, sprite, long have you known it."

Ariel bows with exaggerated courtesy.

"Guests are we at All Worlds' End
   Where lovers twine and foe finds friend
   And all is naught as went before
   No outside, but an inner door."

A skeletal hand impatiently waves Ariel to silence. "In brief, for we are at the end of Time itself. This is no prison but the final sanctum of Life. Beyond these walls, entropy enthroned lays patient siege."

Even Ariel looks downcast now. Can it be true? Has all creation shrunk to this? Ignoring our gasps and tears, Prospero concludes.

"The Judge of Change awaits our word. We must speak or be forever dumb. Perversely enough, the answer is secondary. It takes the right question to assure it. Fortunately, magic has some skill with riddles."

Drax's room is the only one left, a cell of dishonor in his eyes, and he cannot find the word in his heart. Finally, Ariel waits until Prospero is deep in discussion with us, and goes in. He tells him a story, and it is a special story, for it is true. It is a giant story.

"Dragons there were, before mammal or man
   The greatest that ever walked, flew, or swam."

Drax likes that, big dinosaurs treading lesser beings to mush and gobbling up all the vegetation. He particularly likes the Velociraptors, following their group kills with snorts of approval and blinks of shame at fumbles. For him, it is an idealized world of childhood, and it is real. But it is gone.

"Their rule was long, for it was just
Then comet fell, and all was dust. . . ."

Drax's eyes are pooling. I realize I can see through his walls, hear him, share his feelings. His heart is opening at last.

A virgin world of his kind. Innocent giants with pygmy minds, never to achieve sentience, never the stars. He reaches out to Ariel.

"Were they as beautiful as you say? An infinite variety of shape and size . . . and they sang to each other?"

Ariel pumps his elbows and booms hugely, a sonorous mating call that trails off into a dusty hacking . . . comet dust. The glamor of a Parasaurolophus's dying aria switches abruptly to an unkind parody of Prospero.

"For magic dragons fall to dust behind our childhood's door
And white knights too, and doing good, and what's the reason for?
Oh will you let all flowers bloom, and find one in your heart?
Grow one of a thousand strains, and bid the magic start?"

Prospero's dry cough interrupts. "I believe it falls to me to ask the questions. Are you so prepared yourself that you have begun the change?"

Ariel nods glumly.

"You will ask if I have a soul,
renounce Faerie, for mortal dole."

Molecules of water are forming in Prospero's eye sockets. I feel gears move into engagement. When the dead cry, anything is possible.

"And I must ask myself if I repent my sins." Prospero's eyes shine bright. "It is the time of change."

Prospero faces Green and me across the table. We are all standing; he in vestments ancient before silica could count; Green, a living emerald to my burnished copper and veil of white flowers. Drax, resplendent in scale and eye, stands ramrod straight beside Green. By me fusses Ariel, beautiful as a butterfly but frustratingly fey and jealous.

Prospero says many things of wisdom. I hear only the question, but I know Green's answer and my own, know we are wed forever.

Prospero raps a stick-like finger on the table before him. "The questions have all been put; shall we open the door?"

Say the word? We shout it!

Down tumble the walls, and we are no longer alone.

Many identical tables, hundreds of life forms, are grouped around them under a vast dome. Giants and homunculi, beings of fire and water, plasm and plasma, and all are waiting to petition the Judge of Change.

WELCOME, WELCOME, A THOUSAND WELCOMES, ALL.

A voice from a lifetime ago speaks to us once more. Such a *voice*.

NO LESS A WELCOME FOR THE LAST THAN FIRST.

The tables melt away as do the distant walls; only we remain. The outer darkness, infinite and without stars, presses in. But all is not dark; a glow springs up about each of us, creating a host of fireflies in the night. Drax is a dark cherry, the color of heated iron. Ariel is a flickering rainbow, all about us every possible frequency. My hand is held and burns gold on green. We are one, and together stand against the naught.

FROM BABEL TO HARMONY EACH HAVE YOU FARED AND ARE WHOLE BEYOND SUMMATION.

This Judge of Change may listen to us yet. Like Ariel, he too would pine in the dark.

The light burns up brighter within each as our base substance feeds the flowering essence. As banners our souls unfurl, and we come together like a forest fire. Affinity beckons, and the spark of life eagerly leaps between. Our candleflames roar up together in welcome. We are whole, and we are ready to make answer.

AT THE END, MY CHILDREN, THERE IS ONLY ONE QUESTION. WHICH SHALL PREVAIL?

The hungry immensity of the Void presses us closer still. I see at last that it is the dark alternative, the answer of negation. Anti-matter and hate-life, the all-forbidder.

SHALL IT BE NAY?

I see that I, too, am the answer, our assembled host the critical mass of life. We have always been selectively bred and programmed. We must always be transfigured by death and rebirth, by sin and redemption.

We are the champions of Life, the choir of celestial flame. It is time to summon all we have ever wrought and sing out our souls.

A thousand swords of fire flare up, a thousand worlds proclaim their allegiance to the all-giver.

Would you tear out your heart for Life, would you rend in birth agonies, would you die?

OR SHALL IT BE...

I do not have to ask. I only have to open myself and let the truth consume me. Of all the words of power, the first and greatest is...

"AYE!"

*Allan Lowson: The B.C. Science Fiction Association Writers'
Workshop hit on the theme of "a picture is worth a thousand words"
for their 1994* Fictions 6 *issue. Twelve images were selected, with the
writers choosing as many as they could work into their tales. I chose
Maria from "Metropolis," an Incan mummy, the tarot Fool card, a
dinosaur, and a cathedral Green Man. I made them all characters in
my story which also featured some other images. Although to be titled
"The Thousand Words," I saw it also as a thousand worlds—the
infinite variety of life coming to individual terms with the inevitable
choice, to be or not to be. I wanted to use the traditional spiritual
themes: death and redemption, sin and forgiveness, transformation by
love, transfiguration via ego-death.*

In The Beginning, There Was Memory

Ven Begamudré

TONIGHT'S PERFORMANCE IS OF CHOPIN. It is not really night. I have willed the space around me a flat, midnight black. Random constellations rise in what would be the east if directions still mattered. So little matters now.

Chopin plays behind me in the hallway. He plays among a smattering of Hindu sculptures: a mother goddess, a four-faced Shiva, and a goddess of destruction. Their faces are inexact. As for the music, the composer himself is at the piano. He plays his first Ballade, the one in G minor with its complementary themes. I did not know, when I listened to his Ballades during my student days, that he both invented and perfected the form. Later, I learned. Some have suggested ballades tell stories and pointed as proof to the musical logic of the form. Others disagreed. They claimed ballades are stories without plot or character; that the only dialogue is an unspoken one between performer and listener. Or, in this case, between the composer and himself since he plays as though I am not even here.

This was my favorite room in what was once the Royal Ontario Museum: the Bishop White Gallery with its Buddhist paintings and sculptures. The largest painting—the entire far wall—depicts the future Buddha with disciples and celestial attendants. They appear identical although, in the original, they were not identical. Two smaller paintings—each a flanking wall—are of Daoist deities moving through an ethereal world. They, too, seem identical. The wooden sculptures are of Boddhisattvas, images of compassion. My favorite is Guan Yin, the Goddess of Mercy. This was where I sat as a widower each afternoon. Since the gallery no longer exists, I have re-created it for myself here. Wherever *here* is.

I confess: it is not really Chopin at the piano. It is a re-creation of him just as the piano is a re-creation of a piano. He plays like the real Chopin, though; of this I am sure: his almost tight control of volume, his unconventional fingering. The first Ballade ends. The second begins. This is the one in F, the one he dedicated to Schumann, who preferred the tranquil opening section to what followed. So did the composer. So do I. Like the real Chopin, my re-creation plays an extended version of that tranquil opening. Perfect for midnight, perfect for solitude. How often I dreamt of being the only person in an audience, in some open-air salon, while Chopin played Ballades for me. How often I dreamt of being the only one, and now I am.

This evening's performance is of César Franck. Again, it is not really evening. I have willed a rosy glow in what I have decided, from now on, will be west. I suppose I should be amazed by it all. Perhaps I am still in shock: taking notes for no other reason than to formulate a record. But for whom?

Franck composed this sonata, for violin and piano, as a wedding present. It begins reflectively, with only the violin exploring that undulating first theme. The piano joins, intruding as a murmur, then keeps the second theme to itself—the one more emotional than the first. This is a piece meant to be heard when a person is alone. I listened to it every evening for a year after my wife died. Once the grief passed—and it did, though I did not want it to pass—I put the recording away. Now I need the sonata once more. I may need it for longer than a year this time: to help me grieve not for one soul but for billions; for those who passed before them; for those who will never again pass.

This is what surprises me about my new life. I feel no different than I did as a widower: just as powerless, just as indifferent to the future. Those days I felt as though, if the world should end, it might not matter. How could I know it really would end?

It happened unexpectedly on a sunny Sunday afternoon. The triviality of it all: the absurdity of the mundane. I was sitting on the deck behind my house and reading the weekend *Globe and Mail*. I was dropping the first section at my feet. They always annoyed me: those full-page advertisements for the *Globe* itself. This one posed a Canadian prime minister in the shadow of an American president. Such a typical pose. Underneath was the caption which appeared on all these ads whether they depicted chancellors or kings. "Sooner or later," the *Globe* claimed, "all news is business news." Often I said aloud, as I did just then, "Is this what we've come to? God save us." Then the sun grew bright—too bright—and the sky began to glow. I needed no one to tell me what was happening. I sat there and watched a dusty cloud swell; watched the afternoon sky ignite.

I knew every good Hindu should say "*Hé Ram*" when he dies. This means "Oh, God," but in that moment I forgot I was Hindu. Even as my bifocals melted before my eyes, I felt grateful my wife had not lived to see this. "Fools," I shouted. "Fools!" This is all I remember. I do not remember leaving my body or traveling toward a source of comforting, white light. I do not remember my wife or even my mother welcoming me like angels. When I finally grew conscious of my surroundings, the first thing I asked was, "Why did you save me?" I had not meant to scream; only to ask. This was before I realized I was not floating on a burn bed; that those who had saved me were not doctors; that an ocean of tears would be too small.

Even now, when I listen to this sonata, I weep, though without tears. I catch myself muttering, "Fools." In a single afternoon they erased the work of centuries; made the joys and sorrows of so many souls count as nothing. Think of Van Gogh, distracted by that ringing in his ear; of Nijinsky in his straitjacket; of Robert Schumann. Yes, think of Schumann, whose wedded bliss lasted only four years before his mind betrayed him. Not even Clara could save him from madness. Not even she. If my wife were here she would say, "Don't forget Dianne Arbus or Sylvia Plath. And what about Virginia Woolf, contemplating each stone she sewed into her sweater before she waded into that stream?" Think of them all.

The sonata ends briskly, with more energy than it allowed itself at first, though with no less regret. Only in the last section do the violin and piano play in unison, in a canon some have described as pedantic. I disagree, and there is no one here to debate the point. There are advantages to solitude, after all.

The performers look neither delighted nor humble when I applaud. I have not mastered faces but the pianist is a re-creation of Glenn Gould, the violinist a re-creation of Niccolo Paganini. They could not have performed together—not two such dilettantes—but this is not real life. It is entertainment: my way of passing time when time, like directions, no longer matters. Gould hums while remaining hunched over the keyboard. Paganini taps his foot. I cannot think of another sonata for them and so they wait. If I let them, each would gladly perform separately, but I am weary of solos.

Devi appears impressed with my latest creation, a copy of the children's park at Brindavan Gardens near Mysore in South India. My wife and I spent our honeymoon there. A purple-flowering bougainvillea grows next to the deck on which I sit. Its branches braid through those of one flowering pink. Beyond them a stylized mother giraffe nuzzles the snout of her young. They're only statues: fiberglass. I seem to have mastered synthetics—my deck chair is made of polymer strips resembling wicker—but I haven't mastered plants. The pink and purple petals look almost real but from close up they're identical, just as my re-creations of the painted disciples, attendants and deities were identical. The petals lack the minute flaws that should differentiate one from another. The rest of the garden is a blur of greenery. It's not so much a garden as the idea of a garden.

Still, Devi is so impressed she fails to notice the boy until he runs toward us on his three-year-old legs. He wears a sailor suit. He stops to admire a bird of paradise, then plucks it. When she smiles at him, I explain he's my grandson. "Dr. Ramachandra," she says, "you never had a grandson." She means I never had children.

"I do now. I made this park for him." I pick my crystal off the table and gaze at him through the glass.

The crystal is, perhaps predictably, a dodecahedron—the shape most favored by the Devas—but it's a milky white, not multicolored like their own. I gaze at the boy through my crystal and he grows into a five-year-old girl. She wears a party dress, lemon yellow. She tries to reattach the bird of paradise to its stem. When she can't, she puckers her soft lips. I decide I like her better as a boy and change her back. "Never mind," I call. "You go play at the pond. See how many fish you can count."

Devi asks, "And are there fish in the pond?"

"They're not real," I say. "Nor is any of this," meaning the flowers. "Nor is the boy." He's already headed back toward us. When I roll the crystal between my fingertips, he evaporates. The energy released by his molecules flashes. I squeeze the crystal lightly, a mere flexing of my fingertips, and the energy forms a bishop's candle tree. Its flowers are a waxy yellow.

"At the rate you're progressing," Devi says, "you won't need that much longer." She gave me the crystal to focus my thoughts when I grew bored with simple things like museum pieces; to focus my thoughts when I want to create an object—whether animate or inanimate—or to change its matter back to energy. But I can't help feeling something is missing. Something she either can't or won't give me: a secret she expects me to discover without knowing what to look for. "Soon you can simply point," she says. "Then, not even that."

"I'll keep the crystal," I tell her. "Pointing would make me feel too much like a magician." I don't bother admitting the crystal gives me comfort. It's the one thing I can touch which I haven't created; real in a way nothing I've created is real. "It's all an illusion anyway," I say. "Isn't it?"

"It's real enough for now," she says. "I assume the boy would bleed if you cut him?"

"I don't know. I haven't found any need to cut him." My tone is less dry—almost annoyed—when I add, "You know very well he and the fish aren't real. They can move, but they're incapable of growing by themselves or even reproducing."

"These are the criteria for life?" she asks. "Movement, growth, and reproduction?"

I nod, though it seems to me there must be other criteria, especially for human life. Even as I squeeze the crystal again, everything vanishes except the house I created last year. That is, I think of it as last year. I no longer need sleep but I did take a nap after creating the house. It seemed an appropriate thing to do. Besides, I like to sleep. It stops me from thinking. I grow tired of thinking because I don't really think. I remember, and I've always remembered too much. But then, if I'd been good at forgetting, perhaps I wouldn't have been saved. Sometimes I think the Devas need my memories more than they need me. Then again, what's a man without his memory? Can a man who never remembers, or a man with amnesia, create?

I think of the Devas as being more than one, though I've met only Devi. It may be she's only part of a whole, one facet of a huge dodecahedron which makes up a single, powerful being. But I doubt it. She sometimes refers to other beings—even calls them "the Others"—as if she isn't as powerful as I would like to believe. Perhaps she's modest.

Speaking of which, there is one conversation we have never had; one I have often imagined: one I suppose we will have sooner or later. It is this:

"Tell me something," I will say. "Who created the Devas?"

She will say, "A force even more powerful than us."

"God?"

"If you want to call it that."

"Then if Devas are religious enough to believe in a God," I will ask, "who does God believe in? Who created Him?"

"Good question," she will reply. "Assuming some force did create God, let us hope He—or She—is not an atheist."

Devi will laugh first. Then I will laugh, but neither with her nor at her. I will laugh in this imagined conversation because I already see there were many laws of the universe we humans never completely grasped. Here's one: that beings who create—gods, if you will, though I would rather not think of myself as a god-in-training—must have a sense of humor. So many laws we never grasped, even those among us who called ourselves scientists.

I was never a scientist. I was a generalist, an administrator of the old school. I studied science but, unlike my wife, I never mastered it. She was a biomathematician, an expert on the application of what are called L-systems to life forms; on using computers to amplify cells. She was one of the best. This didn't matter when her own cells betrayed her; when they gnawed at her bones till there wasn't enough substance left to sustain life. To think we carry the seeds of life and death within us. How often we forget.

For once, I receive more than a millisecond of warning before Devi appears. She has begun to realize I need my privacy. A light flashes briefly in mid-air to tell me she awaits an audience.

This afternoon's performance is of Glick. I've willed the space above me a rippling, afternoon blue with no sun to cast shadows. Srul Irving Glick was one of the many contemporaries I left behind. I am listening to my re-creation of the Orford Quartet perform his first string quartet. How much this piece disturbed me once; how much I need it now. The concert at which it premiered was the last concert I attended with my wife. I remember so much. Too much: the lemon yellow sari she wore; the glint of glass in the lobby; even the velour seats, which she insisted were velvet. And I remember, though not word for word, what Glick said while he introduced the work.

The first movement includes a song of resignation, a kind of funeral march, originally composed—he said—for the Martyrology of the Yom Kippur service. The second movement, in a free rondo-sonata, includes a beautiful theme of love and even attempts at humor and lightness. Throughout it, though, there are references to that first, funereal movement. The piece drives to an exhilarating conclusion.

I thought it presumptuous of him to say this last, but the piece does end as he said. More: at some point the music itself becomes a form of pure creative energy. It elevates, it transforms, it transcends. And best of all, I remember the silence that followed, the players with their fingers curled, each bow stilled while the music whirled in our minds, all of our minds, all of them suddenly as one. Then came the applause, the gratitude for a mortal who could create such beauty; the realization that two violinists, a violist and a cellist—themselves also mortals—could make mere people feel like gods. And I remember walking home, the two of us not daring to speak in case we disturbed the snow falling lightly about us. I remember the wavering of the street-lights; the memories of silk and glass and of velour. Which may have been velvet, after all.

The light flashes again to remind me Devi awaits. When I nod, my re-creation of the Orford Quartet vanishes. The energy it releases lingers, then dissipates.

Devi appears. "Another group of young ones will arrive soon," she says. "Are you ready for them?"

I nod once more and take the form of an old woman: a crone complete with flowing, white hair and a gnarled staff. When Devi asked why I always take this form for leading tours, I said, "It feels appropriate, just as your form feels appropriate."

It does and it doesn't. Soon after we met, I grew tired of conversing with a double helix of multicolored light. It offered to take a more human form. I imagined a four-armed goddess, none in particular. Devi, whom I named for the Indian word for goddess, copied my image perfectly. For a while, her features remained faint, like a face in an underdeveloped photograph. Then I decided she should look not old but past her prime: as the French would say, "*du certain âge*." Now she rests two of her arms on the arms of a chair and holds her other two arms raised behind her. If she resents masquerading as a Hindu deity, she has never said so. She has also never objected to masquerading as a goddess or to being considered as a *she*. I think she understands I can't think of her as an *it*. Any more than I can think of myself in this way.

Sometimes I change my form to look older or younger, tall or thin, but most times I take the form I had when I was truly alive. I look like Dr. S.N. Ramachandra complete with his dark skin and his paunch and his myopia. The short-sightedness above all. S.N. stood for Satya Narayana but no one called me this. Except for my wife, everyone called me S.N. She called me Dear.

My house vanishes and I hover between the Taj Mahal and Agra Fort. This is where the young ones find me when they appear for their tour. Waving one of her arms, Devi abandons me to my duties.

"Welcome to the Wonders of the World," I say.

The young ones bob in a ragged formation of single, multicolored helixes. A double helix, their teacher, dwarfs them.

"What's the world?" a young one asks.

"I told you," the teacher says. "It means the planet called Earth."

The young one sniffs, "Oh, that."

It's true my charges have trouble appreciating what I show them, but aside from groups of them led by their teachers and aside from Devi, I have no visitors. I need no visitors. I have my solitude. It allows me to create, to re-create. Sometimes, though, I wonder whether Devi minds looking after someone as primitive as me; someone who long ago amused himself with a children's park; someone who still takes naps.

After the Taj Mahal and Agra Fort, I move on to the buildings of Qut'b Minar. As usual, as soon as I turn from the tower of victory, one of the young ones causes it to lean. The rest giggle while I tilt my head patiently. "Put it back," the teacher says, and the young one does. Now the five-story tower, all sandstone and marble, leans too far the other way. I'll have to remind Devi to straighten it. I can create a house and a garden, even a grandson, but none of them are real. Not to me. The victory tower of Qut'b Minar, like the Taj Mahal and Agra Fort, is real, though. Thanks to the Devas, these and a few other artifacts are all that's left of Earth. Though I can't move so much as a stone, they still have power to move me. And this is when—admiring the multicolored inlay of the Taj Mahal, which looks milky white from a distance—I discover what I've been missing: the secret Devi expected me to uncover for myself.

This morning's performance is of Schubert. Again it's not really morning but I've willed it so, just as I've willed my re-creation of the Bishop White Gallery. Here once more are the Buddhist paintings and sculptures—among them the Goddess of Mercy, Guan Yin. The Guarneri Quartet plays in the hallway where Chopin once played. Violin, viola, cello and double bass are joined by piano for the Quintet in A, called the "Trout." Despite the presence of a double bass where one might expect a second violin, the quintet has a translucence bordering on transparence. The lumbering double bass remains in the background, sonorous, and allows the cello to reach for its own upper registers. The cello was the instrument most like the human voice itself. Had I played music, I would have played the cello.

Devi appears on the bench beside me. "I am impressed," she says. "The garden, that was nice. So were the boy and the fish. This is different. Why?"

She knows why, but I feel the need to explain. I rise and walk about the statues. There's no railing to keep me back, not as there was at the ROM. "It's not an idea of paintings and sculpture," I say. "Not in the way it was when I first re-created it. Not in the way the garden was an idea of a garden. All of this is real. You see this statue?" I point one out to her. "The fall of the drapery is more smooth, more like the catenary of a chain, than the fall of drapery on that figure." She nods at the second statue. "And the pigment here is more weathered. As for these paintings—" I pivot to face the largest one, the future Buddha with disciples and attendants "—the faces may seem alike but each one is slightly different. I re-created each face separately, each part of the painting stroke by stroke. That's why they seem so real. How long it took to discover the secret!"

"Which is?" she asks.

"The ability to hold an entire work in the mind while devoting all the energy of a moment to a single detail. And, as important, the ability to understand what each detail contributes to the whole."

Devi nods again and smiles. "You're ready," she says. "If your wife were here—"

"But how!" I demand.

"Forgive me," Devi says. "I did not mean to raise your hopes like that. It was all we could do to save you and a handful of—"

"It's all right," I say. "Really. I finished mourning for her long ago."

"Just as you've finished mourning for the others. Also why you're ready. But if your wife were here, how would she have re-created the garden?"

It's such a simple question, I wonder why Devi bothers to ask. "Using biomathematics," I say. "L-systems. Computers to amplify cells, though we no longer need computers, since we have so much time."

"And could you apply what you recall of her work? Not simply to re-create that garden with its bougainvillea but to create a new garden? A real garden?"

"Of course. I may not consciously know it, but everything I've heard or seen or sensed of the world is still in here." I tap my temple. "Every formula, every bar of music, every brushstroke." I leave the gallery, pass the performers, and leap the steps to the deck behind my house.

Devi follows.

Perhaps I'll create a garden full of plants devoted to the hour of the day: the morning glory, daylily, evening primrose, night-shade. Or a garden devoted to the seasons: summer cypress, summer lilac, winter jasmine. Or to holy days: the Lenten rose, Christmas rose, Christmas fern, Easter lily. Or perhaps even a garden devoted to the beauty of time, one full of varieties of thyme itself: caraway, creeping, lemon, wooly. Thyme heals all, they say. No, that would be too clever. "I'll need to begin with something simple," I say.

"Will these do?" A dodecahedron appears in the palm of Devi's hand—one of her four hands. Floating in the center are three blue-green spots, three cells of algae. Barely a handful. "And now," she says, "if you would be good enough to begin applying your wife's knowledge?"

Glick. I need Glick. The quintet turns into the quartet, the Orford, and the Glick begins: the pure creative energy of his first string quartet. Soon I'll have a garden, each petal different from the last. And one day . . . No, best not to think of that. One step at a time. One cell at a time. One petal, one flower at a time.

"We need to make a record of this," I tell Devi. "A record for the future because now there will be one, won't there?"

She sits and begins to write. She writes without paper or pen, but I can see the record form between us even as I begin my life's work. My wife's work. "What shall I write first?" Devi asks. "How about, 'In the beginning . . .'"

We both laugh. Then it doesn't take me long, not long at all, to compose the first line of this, our record for the future:

"In the beginning, there was memory."

Ven Begamudré: This story began as two exercises. First, I wanted to write a fictional essay. Second, I wanted to experiment with tonal control for a realistic novel about a widower on holiday in Europe. Before I knew it, the story took on a life of its own—as SF. Still, it needed many drafts to stop the essay from smothering the fiction. As for the novel, it's largely unwritten. Ironically, seven travel poems I also wrote as exercises have appeared in a magazine (Grain). *Perhaps I'm more interested in the process of writing than in the product? Or perhaps some novels are best left "largely unwritten."*

GOD IS DEAD

Erik Jon Spigel

TURIN, JANUARY 1889

Nikola's German was rude, to say the least. His lips moved nervously so that they seemed all out of his control. His face, the while, remained immobile. It was as though a demon had possessed only his speech.

"Do you see? Do you see?"

His head was different from Darwin's chimps' only in the lopsided cant of his hair and the thin mustache held captive by perspiration. His arms gestured wildly at the apparatus he had carried halfway over the Earth to show me. Glass lanterns barely flickered; weak lightning hesitated, then shuddered across scarce metal limbs, and Tesla, my anemic Hephaestus, nonetheless had to bellow to be heard over the cacophony.

"Do you see? Do you see?"

He drew a heavy lever and the machine darkened, its thunder subsided. Nikola pulled a handkerchief from his breast pocket and wiped his face, his hands. Rain and lightning; imagine my surprise at a whole geography within my small room.

He removed a diary from another pocket, made a few short notes, then ran around his device, testing the efficacy of its parts with a number of alarmingly physical assaults, made more notes, then returned the diary to its nest.

He seemed to have forgotten I am there.

I paused, then clapped.

"Wonderful! Wonderful, Nikola. What a fine toy! But won't the sparks pose a threat to the child?"

"It is not a toy! It is not a toy!" he protested. "Did you not see it? The glass orbs each contain a vacuum; magnets and energy divide the parts and order the fragments geometrically; the geometry is the key to the system."

"And what Gaea has given birth to this 'geometry'?" I asked. I was growing to detest his abuse of language. I studied the order of his glass spheres and quickly concluded that their pattern was not at all the inspiration of Euclid.

Nikola assumed the affect of a punished hound.

"But, Helena said . . ."

"The Russian woman? Of course. Her *Secret Doctrine of the Ancients*." I laughed dismissively. Frau Blavatsky had stood in this room not a month before, misquoting Goethe and reading from her book of childish mysticism. She had come because she had misconstrued my own poor *Zarathustra* as an etherial communication, a thing revealed to me, she had thought, in a trance much as she had claimed for her own comic text. I could not convince her of the error of her presumptions and had taken to humoring her, though the draft from her thick voice should cause me to become ill.

I nodded at his machine.

"It resembles the Hebrew diagram, yes? The one they call the 'Tree of Life.'"

Nikola brightened.

"Yes! Yes! It is just so. Each orb—see! Kether, Chochmah"— he tapped each of the glass spheres in turn with the back of his fountain pen—"Binah, Chesed, Geburah, Tiphereth, Netsah, Hod, Jesod, and Malchuth. Joined by ladders of electricity."

"And to what end? Pedagogical, I hope. An illuminated diagram?"

"No! No! Within this machine, the universe, itself, is divided!"

I had grown weary by this time, more concerned with my evening meal than with the obligations incumbent on me as a host. I ushered poor Nikola from my room with assurances that his machine would be safe for one night, but in truth I did not care. I simply did not wish to endure him for the time it would take to disassemble it. I closed the door behind him, enjoyed a moment of euphoria that ensued from my sudden solitude, shrugged and lay down on my bed, and drew comfort from a slim volume of Comte's.

I awoke in Heaven, far from the City of God.

The hum from Nikola's machine fell off into silence as I became gradually more aware that I was awake. How the device came to be activated I cannot recall. How it worked its ways on me I cannot conceive. Perhaps once constructed it could only be given the semblance of quiescence; perhaps I fell upon its levers as I tumbled out of bed in some ardent reverie. Perhaps, perhaps, perhaps; who am I to ponder the mechanism of an insane electrician?

But behind me the image of it faded, as if a mirage, and in its wake was bare ground.

All was devoid of life. Though I knew it to be Heaven, this was not the landscape of David, nor was it filled by the host of Michelangelo. No seraphim, trumpet-twinned; no Blakean radiance to illuminate the cardinal sorrows of man. I saw only an opal sky, bare ground, and blank rock—but the epic of a marble city loomed in my mind, and it was not without trepidation that I began to walk, alone on a roadless plain and only the instinct of distance to guide me.

Dust and dust. It was as if walking on an avenue of bone. Chinese princes in antiquity might have surmised some shade of meaning from the cracks in the soil, but I am not given to the reading of such ciphers. I tell you only that the color was that of the flesh of the dead, and the infrequent dirty copse that clung to this famished land was merely the sweet that serves only to stress the sour. My body bent like a diviner's stick. My steps grew labored. My feet barely lifted from the plain. I was like sugar in the rain, falling piece by piece until mingled with the firmament.

I walked until my clothes were in tatters, until my footprints left a tattoo of blood; until I grew so thirsty as to crave even the memory of water. I do not remember a time of darkness at all upon this journey, so I cannot gauge for how long I kept my pace. Nor do I recall a sun in the sky. Nor do I recall a shadow. I believe that I fainted more than once; I was frequently overcome with nausea. I called out my sister's name and collapsed before the Gates of Heaven.

And I thought, "This is what Richard saw erected before his Venusberg"; what had been, he felt, so abbreviated on the stage of his beloved Bayreuth. In truth, though I looked up, I could not fathom where its terminus lay. I wept, and felt the last of my strength leave me. This was how it would end, then; the atheist dies at the shores of Heaven. Even had I yet a soul, it would be too weak to traverse the paltry distance dividing me from grace, which was now, at last—and this would distress Comte greatly!— a physical thing.

Thereupon I awoke in the City of God.

I had been laid to rest in a stone crèche encumbered by flowerless vines. An angel towered over me, dressed in a simple robe punctuated only by spare wings. He stood with his arms extended before him, fists clenched at the hilt of a great sword, and truly I felt afraid to make any movement lest he let his mighty shoulders sag, sending the blade to plunge into my chest. But soon I noted that his eyes had been plucked out, and I hazarded to take my leave.

As I stood, he made to move his lips. I half expected a

celestial symphony to issue forth, a caution that I should but remain where I was, but there came only the sound of flapping wings and the dull, crisp murmur of dry leaves being crushed. He did not notice me except by this activity. I slowly backed away from my hard mattress, and only more slowly became convinced that my guardian possessed no intention of pursuit.

I discovered myself in the center of some great mall, for left and right of me lay façades concealing all varieties of bed and crib. To each of these was appointed an angel similarly armed. Presently, all began to mutter as mine had, and I was under assault from the chorus that issued forth, a sound not unlike that of all the pages in all the books of the world at once being turned.

I ran blindly down this corridor of eternal sleep crying out in whatever words and whatever language came to mind, for in that moment I desired nothing more than to hear a sound whose shape was given to the understanding of man. At that moment even Tesla's pidgin would have struck me with bell-like clarity.

"Credo ut intelligum credo quia absurdum!" I cried, my hands over my ears. Marble and stone; all around me was marble and stone.

I grew conscious of my pace as I stumbled more and more frequently along cracked avenues and the detritus of fallen pediments and eroded peristyles. I thought nothing but that I must be running backward in time, toward those parts of the city that predated even the eternal souls of man. And should this be the case, then I must ask myself how it was that its architecture should prove so amenable to human morphology. For I soon emerged in a clearing, the awful keening of angels behind me, and I could take my rest so conveniently seated on a platform, yet this last that I construed as a bench might also have been an altar.

I remained there for some time, and occasionally I would utter a human word, or recite a fragment from one of my works, or hum a moment of Strauss. My thoughts were my only companions, then, as they had been for the whole of my life. I felt as if many days were passing.

Occasionally, a figure or a small parade of figures would dart from one passage and rest beside me. None had made any gesture that would indicate comprehension of my presence, although I came to recognize many of them by the most improbable of signs. One Wing was just that, his eyeless face scarred such that I assumed him to be a soldier of some sort, for his demeanor imparted to me the memory of a great war. Blue Halo glowed with such intensity as to cast the only shadow I would ever see here. Yellow Feather molted a trail of gangrenous plumes wherever he trod. Rags wore the tattered robes of a mendicant. I could not tell man from woman, if such distinctions indeed existed; all were pale and not especially adorned by their simple robes, which differed from one to the next only in respect to their state of repair. Each shared the characteristic with his fellows that his eyes had been plucked.

Sometimes they would talk amongst themselves, and I would be reminded, in microcosm, of my own recent awakening. At other times, they would simply sit motionless for time without end. In truth I grew impatient at their idleness. The city, itself, falling into disuse and disrepair, and none lifted a hand to its preservation. Is Heaven without passion? Does nothing of gravity compel them? Perhaps I am being too harsh. Perhaps the *eloim* spent their days merely in peregrination towards the apprehension of great thoughts. But do they not feel obliged to set them in writing? If they choose not to invest their efforts in architecture, then at least in words. Alas, whatever is the industry of Heaven, I could tell only that it embraces much rest.

Because of the frequency of his appearance, I began to look upon One Wing as my friend. As I was without any other such means for its determination, I decided that a "day" would consist in the interval of his visits. By this reckoning, I estimated I had remained seated for some seven weeks!

Enough, I told myself.

I could not be made more dead than to be already in Heaven. There was little to lose should I move. I had determined to insinuate myself into the company of One Wing, even should this mean that I discard my only sense of measure in this place. I would learn to endure the timbre of his speech. Thus, on the next of his "visits," I simply rose and fell into pace beside him, as casual as was possible among his cohort.

We traveled through suites of stone and down passages rank with incense. I talked out loud—of philosophy, of mathematics. The city suggested the geometry of the monk Cantor's infinities, the contemplation of which had ultimately driven him mad, and I extemporized on this point at some length, though my understanding of the subject is inadequate. I talked of my sister, Elisabeth; of the nature of the human passions and the depth of insight available to the human brain.

But the angels were deaf to me, and made no response, until I was forced to invent, in my mind, human voices for them. I conceived of dialogues:

"You will agree," One Wing said, "that it is in the constitution of dreams that we come closest to knowing our Creator. Is it not sleep that is but an imitation of death, and dream a rehearsal for the passage of the soul? Are the worlds somnolent and waking naught but an abbreviation of the sacred and profane?"

"Dreams tell us nothing," I protested. "The superior man disavows himself of such a division. We are heroic in our confrontation of a world awake rather than while still dreaming. We are made greater by our vanity; it is in vain that we should make what we see greater than what we imagine. Thus, the man who dreams the ordinary has already achieved the impossible. His Heaven is life, itself."

Once, I asked One Wing why it was no angel flew.

"How can we fly?" he responded. "How can we fly here, in this, the highest place of all? Our wings only slow us when we fall."

At last we came to a granite glen and made our camp. Here I

witnessed a solemn thing—the death of an angel. Yellow Feather stumbled forth, having come with another party. For a time his companions supported him; his body shook, and each seizure elicited a nimbus of jaundiced down. The company hesitated, then cautiously drew away from him, poised to intervene should he start to fall. Yellow Feather remained uneasily on his feet, and the host closed ranks, making a coliseum of bodies around their comrade.

The air was raised high in a chant of dry angel voices, then a silence was given over to him. He rasped for some time, making his peace among us, regarding each of us in our turn with his empty sockets. He gained strength but once, and briefly, and for a moment, as his wings flexed, I thought to see an angel fly. But his ecstasy as quickly departed. He lay down, and his breathing grew ever more shallow, his chest inflating less and less with each inhalation.

At the moment of death his body vanished. There was an instant of indescribable elation; a sexual urge almost overcame me. With the passage of the body, Yellow Feather's soul, intact, stood before us. Perfect and pure, it suggested man and woman both; it spoke, the lush sound of strings, and I could make sense of none of it but for a single word: "I."

It made to depart, yet no angel showed the least impulse towards pursuit. Instead, they seemed transfixed by the place where Yellow Feather's body had *been*, rather than where his soul might be going. Perhaps it was no mystery to them.

Yet I felt driven by some unnamed compulsion, and I picked up quickly after it. Once more I was given to a nautilus circuit that took me ever more deeply into the city. I cried after it, "Nullus potest amare aliquid incognitum!"—in the hopes that it might be slowed by Aquinas. Still I found myself accelerating, my perceptions narrowing towards singlemindedness and obsession. I may have passed shops and libraries; I do not know. I believe I recall a blur that was a library. I ran still faster, and my feet found purchase even over the most questionable of terrains; I felt certain that I would not stumble in this chase. I determined that though I should become lost for all time, I would not lose my quarry. I discovered an endurance that was almost a life unto itself and I flattered myself that I may soon gain on my prey.

But I am compelled to be honest, and the distance between us only began to close when the other had come to a stop. Ragged and out of breath, I soon stood, as he did, in the presence of a single bare tree, meager roots penetrating dark shale.

A lone, wingless figure attended it.

For a time, the figure went about its business in ignorance of us. It adjusted branches, or piled soil upon soil in some odd pantomime of cultivation. It would pause to marvel at its work, or perhaps judge its aesthetic, then return to the performance of one incomprehensible task after another. At last it paused, wiped its brow, and turned to regard us. It nodded, then broke a limb from the bough and in the shale sketched a simple diagram: three lines joining myself, the soul, and the tree. The artist stood at the centrum of the triangle and smiled at me.

I thought the smiling face to be mocking me.

Enough, I told myself, and leapt at it, my footfalls erasing the diagram. I grasped the figure of the gardener and shook it, throwing it to the ground. I pressed my thumbs against its neck and squeezed until I felt it grow still in my hands. The body vanished.

I was taken by the shoulder. One Wing and his cohort had appeared and dragged me before the tree, forcing me to my knees. They formed a tribunal, chanting indictments at me, judging me for murder. I was given a space of silence to plead my case but I still knew not the language here. Heavy-hearted, I rose. One Wing drew his sword and plunged it into my chest.

I awoke suddenly, far from the City of God.

I cast around, drenched and twisting between the sheets of my bed. Overbeck, my eternal friend and colleague, stood over me, wiping my brow and pleading with me in a soft voice to be calm. My room was dark, my books all but invisible in the gloom. Tesla's machine was nowhere to be seen.

"God is dead!" I shrieked. "Alas, God is dead."

But true to the physics of Heaven He has left His soul behind.

Erik Jon Spigel: This story is about the confrontation of mystery by the rational mind. I wrote it to reconcile a number of divergent influences in my life: a Jew born into a predominantly Christian society, raised by a pair of scientists only to end up pursuing a career in Japanese literature. As a result, this story contains elements of Buddhism, Judaism, Christianity, and Taoism. I wanted to write something that suggested the limits of reason. I thought for most of my life that I would be a scientist, and maybe this story is no more than a defensive reaction against a profession that I have ultimately forsaken. Make no mistake; I adore science, but I fear for us that we let its rationality roam too far and fail to cultivate, in the pursuit of our genius, likewise a sense of awe.

"God is dead."

No three words frighten me more. If they are true, than what is there left to dream?

The Second Coming of Jasmine Fitzgerald

Peter Watts

What's wrong with this picture?

Not much, at first glance. Blood pools in a pattern entirely consistent with the location of the victim. No conspicuous arterial spray; the butchery's all abdominal, the blood more spilled than spurted. No slogans either. Nobody's scrawled *Helter Skelter* or *Satan is Lord* or even *Elvis Lives* on any of the walls. It's just another mess in another kitchen in another one-bedroom apartment, already overcrowded with the piecemeal accumulation of two lives. One life's all that's left now, a thrashing gory creature screaming her mantra over and over as the police wrestle her away—

"I have to *save* him I have to *save* him I have to *save* him—"

—more evidence, not that the assembled cops need it, of why domestic calls absolutely *suck*.

She hasn't saved him. By now it's obvious that no one can. He lies in a pool of his own insides, blood and lymph spreading along the cracks between the linoleum tiles, crossing, criss-crossing, a convenient clotting grid drawing itself across the crime scene. Every now and then a red bubble grows and breaks on his lips. Anyone who happens to notice this pretends not to.

The weapon? Right here: run-of-the-mill steak knife, slick with blood and coagulating fingerprints, lying exactly where she dropped it.

The only thing that's missing is a motive. They were a quiet couple, the neighbors say. He was sick, he'd been sick for months. They never went out much. There was no history of violence. They loved each other deeply.

Maybe she was sick too. Maybe she was following orders from some tumor in her brain. Or maybe it was a botched alien abduction, gray-skinned creatures from Zeta II Reticuli framing an innocent bystander for their own incompetence. Maybe it's a mass hallucination, maybe it isn't really happening at all.

Maybe it's an act of God.

They got to her early. This is one of the advantages of killing someone during office hours. They've taken samples, scraped residue from clothes and skin on the off chance that anyone might question whose blood she was wearing. They've searched the apartment, questioned neighbors and relatives, established the superficial details of identity: Jasmine Fitzgerald, twenty-four-year-old Caucasian brunette, doctoral candidate. In Global General Relativity, whatever the fuck *that* is. They've stripped her down, cleaned her up, bounced her off a judge into Interview Room 1, Forensic Psychiatric Support Services.

They've put someone in there with her.

"Hello, Ms. Fitzgerald. I'm Dr. Thomas. My first name's Myles, if you prefer."

She stares at him. "Myles it is." She seems calm, but the tracks of recent tears still show on her face. "I guess you're supposed to decide whether I'm crazy."

"Whether you're fit to stand trial, yes. I should tell you right off that nothing you say to me is necessarily confidential. Do you understand?" She nods. Thomas sits down across her. "What would you like me to call you?"

"Napoleon. Mohammed. Jesus Christ." Her lips twitch, the faintest smile, gone in an instant. "Sorry. Just kidding. Jaz's fine."

"Are you doing okay in here? Are they treating you all right?"

She snorts. "They're treating me pretty damn well, considering the kind of monster they think I am." A pause, then, "I'm not, you know."

"A monster?"

"Crazy. I've—I've just recently undergone a paradigm shift, you know? The whole world looks different, and my head's there but sometimes my gut . . . I mean, it's so hard to *feel* differently about things. . . ."

"Tell me about this paradigm shift," Thomas suggests. He makes it a point not to take notes. He doesn't even have a notepad. Not that it matters. The microcassette recorder in his blazer has very sensitive ears.

"Things make sense now," she says. "They never did before. I think, for the first time in my life, I'm actually happy." She smiles again, for longer this time. Long enough for Thomas to marvel at how genuine it seems.

"You weren't very happy when you first came here," he says gently. "They say you were very upset."

"Yeah." She nods, seriously. "It's tough enough to do that shit to yourself, you know, but to risk someone else, someone you really care about . . ." She wipes at one eye. "He was dying for over a year, did you know that? Each day he'd hurt a little more. You could almost see it spreading through him, like some sort of . . . leaf, going brown. Or maybe that was the chemo. Never could decide which was worse." She shakes her head. "Heh. At least *that's* over now."

"Is that why you did it? To end his suffering?" Thomas doubts it. Mercy killers don't generally disembowel their beneficiaries. Still, he asks.

She answers. "Of course I fucked up, I only ended up making things worse." She clasps her hands in front of her. "I miss him already. Isn't that crazy? It only happened a few hours ago, and I know it's no big deal, but I still miss him. That head-heart thing again."

"You say you fucked up," Thomas says.

245

She takes a deep breath, nods. "Big time."

"Tell me about that."

"I don't know shit about debugging. I thought I did, but when you're dealing with organics . . . All I really did was go in and mess randomly with the code. You make a mess of everything, unless you know exactly what you're doing. That's what I'm working on now."

"Debugging?"

"That's what I call it. There's no real word for it yet."

Oh yes there is. Aloud: "Go on."

Jasmine Fitzgerald sighs, her eyes closed. "I don't expect you to believe this under the circumstances, but I really loved him. No: I *love* him." Her breath comes out in a soft snort, a whispered laugh. "There I go again. That bloody past tense."

"Tell me about debugging."

"I don't think you're up for it, Myles. I don't even think you're all that interested." Her eyes open, point directly at him. "But for the record, Stu was dying. I tried to save him. I failed. Next time I'll do better, and better still the time after that, and eventually I'll get it right."

"And what happens then?" Thomas says.

"Through your eyes or mine?"

"Yours."

"I repair the glitches in the string. Or if it's easier, I replicate an undamaged version of the subroutine and insert it back into the main loop. Same difference."

"Uh-huh. And what would I see?"

She shrugs. "Stu rising from the dead."

What's wrong with this picture?

Spread out across the table, the mind of Jasmine Fitzgerald winks back from pages of standardized questions. Somewhere in here, presumably, is a monster.

These are the tools used to dissect human psyches. The WAIS. The MMPI. The PDI. Hammers, all of them. Blunt chisels posing as microtomes. A copy of the DSM-IV sits off to one side, a fat paperback volume of symptoms and pathologies. A matrix of pigeonholes. Perhaps Fitzgerald fits into one of them. Intermittent Explosive, maybe? Battered Woman? Garden-Variety Sociopath?

The test results are inconclusive. It's as though she's laughing up from the page at him. *True or false: I sometimes hear voices that no one else hears.* False, she's checked. *I have been feeling unusually depressed lately.* False. *Sometimes I get so angry I feel like hitting something.* True, and a handwritten note in the margin: Hey, doesn't everyone?

There are snares sprinkled throughout these tests, linked questions designed to catch liars in subtle traps of self-contradiction. Jasmine Fitzgerald has avoided them all.

Is she unusually honest? Is she too smart for the tests? There doesn't seem to be anything here that—

Wait a second.

Who was Louis Pasteur? asks the WAIS, trying to get a handle on educational background.

A virus, Fitzgerald said.

Back up the list. Here's another one, on the previous page: *Who was Winston Churchill?* And again: a virus.

And fifteen questions before that: *Who was Florence Nightingale?*

A famous nurse, Fitzgerald responded to that one. And her responses to all previous questions on historical personalities are unremarkably correct. But everyone after Nightingale is a virus.

Killing a virus is no sin. You can do it with an utterly clear conscience. Maybe she's redefining the nature of her act. Maybe that's how she manages to live with herself these days.

Just as well. That raising-the-dead shtick didn't cut any ice at all.

She's slumped across the table when he enters, her head resting on folded arms. Thomas clears his throat. "Jasmine."

No response. He reaches out, touches her lightly on the shoulder. Her head comes up, a fluid motion containing no hint of grogginess. She settles back into her chair and smiles. "Welcome back. So, am I crazy or what?"

Thomas smiles back and sits down across from her. "We try to avoid prejudicial terms."

"Hey, I can take it. I'm not prone to tantrums."

A picture flashes across the front of his mind: beloved husband, entrails spread-eagled like butterfly wings against a linoleum grid. *Of course not. No tantrums for you. We need a whole new word to describe what it is* you *do.*

"Debugging," wasn't it?

"I was going over your test results," he begins.

"Did I pass?"

"It's not that kind of test. But I was intrigued by some of your answers."

She purses her lips. "Good."

"Tell me about viruses."

That sunny smile again. "Sure. Mutable information strings that can't replicate without hijacking external source code."

"Go on."

"Ever hear of Core Wars?"

"No."

"Back in the early eighties some guys got together and wrote a bunch of self-replicating computer programs. The idea was to put them into the same block of memory and have them compete for space. They all had their own little tricks for self-defense and reproduction and, of course, eating the competition."

"Oh, you mean *computer* viruses," Thomas says.

"Actually, before all that." Fitzgerald pauses a moment, cocks her head to one side. "You ever wonder what it might be like to *be* one of those little programs? Running around laying eggs and dropping logic bombs and interacting with other viruses?"

Thomas shrugs. "I never even knew about them until now. Why? Do you?"

"No," she says. "Not any more."

"Go on."

Her expression changes. "You know, talking to *you* is a bit like talking to a program. All you ever say is *go on* and *tell me more* and—I mean, Jesus, Myles, they wrote therapy programs back in the *sixties* that had more range than you do! In BASIC even! Register an *opinion*, for Chrissake!"

"It's just a technique, Jaz. I'm not here to get into a debate with you, as interesting as that might be. I'm trying to assess your fitness to stand trial. *My* opinions aren't really at issue."

She sighs, and sags. "I know. I'm sorry, I know you're not here to keep me entertained, but I'm *used* to being able to—"

"I mean, *Stuart* would always be so—"

"Oh, God. I miss him so *much*," she admits, her eyes shining and unhappy.

She's a killer, he tells himself. *Don't let her suck you in. Just assess her, that's all you have to do.*

Don't start liking *her, for Christ's sake.*

"That's . . . understandable," Thomas says.

She snorts. "Bullshit. You don't understand at all. You know what he did, the first time he went in for chemo? I was studying for my comps, and he stole my textbooks."

"Why would he do that?"

"Because he knew I wasn't studying at home. I was a complete wreck. And when I came to see him at the hospital he pulls these bloody books out from under his bed and starts quizzing me on Dirac and the Beckenstein Bound. He was *dying*, and all he wanted to do was help me prepare for some stupid test. I'd do anything for him."

Well, Thomas doesn't say, *you certainly did more than most.*

"I can't wait to see him again," she adds, almost as an afterthought.

"When will that be, Jaz?"

"When do you think?" She looks at him, and the sorrow and despair he thought he saw in those eyes are suddenly nowhere to be seen.

"Most people, if they said that, would be talking about the afterlife."

She favors him with a sad little smile. "This *is* the afterlife, Myles. This is heaven, and hell, and nirvana. Whatever we choose to make it. Right here."

"Yes," Thomas says after a moment. "Of course."

Her disappointment in him hangs there like an accusation.

"You don't believe in God, do you?" she asks at last.

"Do you?" he ricochets.

"Didn't used to. Turns out there's clues, though. Proof, even."

"Such as?"

"The mass of the top quark. The width of the Higgs boson. You can't read them any other way when you know what you're looking for. Know anything about quantum physics, Myles?"

He shakes his head. "Not really."

"Nothing really exists, not down at the subatomic level. It's all just probability waves. Until someone looks at it, that is. Then the wave collapses and you get what we call *reality*. But it can't happen without an observer to get things started."

Thomas squints, trying to squeeze some sort of insight into his brain. "So if we weren't here looking at this table, it wouldn't exist?"

Fitzgerald nods. "More or less." That smile peeks around the corner of her mouth for a second.

He tries to lure it back. "So God's the observer, is that what you're saying? God watches all the atoms so the universe can exist?"

"Huh. I never thought about it that way before." The smile morphs into a frown of concentration. "More metaphoric than mathematical, but it's a cool idea."

"Was God watching you yesterday?"

She looks up, distracted. "Huh?"

"Does He . . . does It communicate with you?"

Her face goes completely expressionless. "Does God tell me to do things, you mean. Did God tell me to carve Stu up like . . . like—" Her breath hisses out between her teeth. "No, Myles. I don't hear voices. Charlie Manson doesn't come to me in my dreams and whisper sweet nothings. I answered all those questions on your test already, so give me a fucking break, okay?"

He holds up his hands, placating. "That's not what I meant, Jasmine." *Liar.* "I'm sorry if that's how it sounded, it's just—you know, God, quantum mechanics—it's a lot to swallow at once, you know? It's . . . mind-blowing."

She watches him through guarded eyes. "Yeah. I guess it can be. I forget, sometimes." She relaxes a fraction. "But it's all true. The math is inevitable. You can change the nature of reality, just by *looking* at it. You're right. It's mind-blowing."

"But only at the subatomic level, right? You're not *really* saying we could make this table disappear just by ignoring it, are you?"

Her eye flickers to a spot just to the right and behind him, about where the door should be.

"Well, no," she says at last. "Not without a lot of practice."

What's wrong with this picture?

Besides the obvious, of course. Besides the vertical incision running from sternum to approximately two centimeters below the navel, penetrating the abdominal musculature and extending through into the visceral coelom. Beyond the serrations along its edge, suggesting the use of some sort of blade. Not, evidently, a very sharp one.

No. We're getting ahead of ourselves here. The coroner's art is nothing if not systematic. Very well, then: Caucasian male, mid-twenties. External morphometrics previously noted. Hair loss and bruising consistent with chemotherapeutic toxicity. Right index and ring fingernails missing, same notation. The deceased was one sick puppy at time of demise. Sickened by the disease, poisoned by the cure. And just when you thought things couldn't get any worse . . .

Down and in. The wound swallows the coroner's rubberized hands like some huge torn vagina, its labia clotted and crystallized. The usual viscera glisten inside, repackaged by medics at the site who had to reel in all loose ends for transport. Perhaps evidence was lost in the process. Perhaps the killer had arranged the entrails in some significant pattern, perhaps the arrangement of the GI tract spelled out some clue or unholy name. No matter. They took pictures of everything.

Mesentery stretches like thin latex, binding loops of intestine one to the other. A bit too tightly, in fact. There appear to be . . . fistulas of some sort, scattered along the lower ileum. Loops seem fused together at several spots. What could have caused that?

Nothing comes to mind.

Note it, record it, take a sample for detailed histological analysis. Move on. The scalpel passes through the tract as easily as through overcooked pasta. Stringy bile and pre-fecal lumps slump tiredly into a collecting dish. Something bulges behind them from the dorsal wall. Something shines white as bone where no bone should be. Slice, resect. There. A mass of some kind covering the right kidney, approximately fifteen centimeters by ten, extending down to the bladder. Quite heterogeneous, it's got some sort of *lumps* in it. A tumor? Is this what Stuart MacLennan's doctors were dueling with when they pumped him full of poison? It doesn't look like any tumor the coroner's seen.

For one thing—and this is really kind of strange—it's looking *back* at him.

His desk is absolutely Spartan. Not a shred of paper out of place. Not a shred of paper even in evidence, actually. The surface is as featureless as a Kubrick monolith, except for the Sun workstation positioned dead center and a rack of CDs angled off to the left.

"I *thought* she looked familiar," he says. "When I saw the papers. Didn't know quite where to place her, though."

Jasmine Fitzgerald's graduate supervisor.

"I guess you've got a lot of students," Thomas suggests.

"Yes." He leans forward, begins tapping at the workstation keyboard. "I've yet to meet all of them, actually. One or two in Europe I correspond with exclusively over the net. I hope to meet them this summer in Berne—ah, yes. Here she is; doesn't look anything like the media picture."

"She doesn't live in Europe, Dr. Russell."

"No, right here. Did her fieldwork at CERN, though. Damn hard getting anything done here since the supercollider fell through. Ah."

"What?"

"She's on leave. I remember her now. She put her thesis on hold about a year and a half ago. Illness in the family, as I recall." Russell stares at the monitor; something he sees there seems to sink in, all at once.

"She killed her husband? She *killed* him?"

Thomas nods.

"My God." Russell shakes his head. "She didn't seem the type. She always seemed so . . . well, so cheery."

"She still does, sometimes."

"My God," he repeats. "And how can I help you?"

"She's suffering from some very elaborate delusions. She couches them in a lot of technical terminology I don't understand. I mean, for all I know she could actually be making *sense*—no, no. Scratch that. She *can't* be, but I don't have the background to really understand her, well, *claims*."

"What sort of *claims*?"

"For one thing, she keeps talking about bringing her husband back from the dead."

"I see."

"You don't seem surprised."

"Should I be? You said she was delusional."

Thomas takes a deep breath. "Dr. Russell, I've been doing some reading the past couple of days. Popular cosmology, quantum mechanics for beginners, that sort of thing."

Russell smiles indulgently. "I suppose it's never too late to start."

"I get the impression that a lot of the stuff that happens down at the subatomic level almost has quasi-religious overtones. Spontaneous appearance of matter, simultaneous existence in different states. Almost spiritual."

"Yes, I suppose that's true. After a fashion."

"Are cosmologists a religious lot, by and large?"

"Not really." Russell drums fingers on his monolith. "The field's so strange that we don't really *need* religious experience on top of it. Some of the Eastern religions make claims that sound vaguely quantum-mechanical, but the similarities are pretty superficial."

"Nothing more, well, Christian? Nothing that would lead someone to believe in a single omniscient God who raises the dead?"

"God no. Oh, except for that Tipler fellow." Russell leans forward. "Why? Jasmine Fitzgerald hasn't become a Christian, has she?" Murder is one thing, his tone suggests, but *this* . . .

"I don't think so," Thomas reassures him. "Not unless Christianity's broadened its tenets to embrace human sacrifice."

"Yes. Quite." Russell leans back again, apparently satisfied.

"Who's Tipler?" Thomas asks.

"Mmmm?" Russell blinks, momentarily distracted. "Oh, yes. Frank Tipler. Cosmologist from Tulane, claimed to have a testable mathematical proof of the existence of God. And the afterlife too, if I recall. Raised a bit of a stir a few years back."

"I take it you weren't impressed."

"Actually, I didn't follow it very closely. Theology's not that interesting to me. I mean, if physics proves that there is or there isn't a god that's fine, but that's not really the point of the exercise, is it?"

"I couldn't say. Seems to me it'd be a hell of a spinoff, though."

Russell smiles.

"I don't suppose you've got the reference?" Thomas suggests.

"Of course. Just a moment." Russell feeds a CD to the workstation and massages the keyboard. The Sun purrs. "Yes, here it is: *The Physics of Immortality: Modern Cosmology, God and the Resurrection of the Dead*. 1994, Frank J. Tipler. I can print you out the complete citation if you want."

"Please. So what was his proof?"

The professor displays something akin to a very small smile.

"In thirty words or less," Thomas adds. "For idiots."

"Well," Russell says, "basically, he argued that some billions of years hence, life will incorporate itself into a massive quantum-effect computing device to avoid extinction when the universe collapses."

"I thought the universe wasn't *going* to collapse," Thomas interjects. "I thought they proved it was just going to keep expanding. . . ."

"That was last year," Russell says shortly. "May I continue?"

"Yes, of course."

"Thank you. As I was saying, Tipler claimed that billions of years hence, life will incorporate itself into a massive quantum-effect computing device to avoid extinction when the universe collapses. An integral part of this process involves the exact reproduction of everything that ever happened in the universe up to that point, right down to the quantum level, as well as all possible variations of those events."

Beside the desk, Russell's printer extrudes a paper tongue. He pulls it free and hands it over.

"So God's a supercomputer at the end of time? And we'll all be resurrected in the mother of all simulation models?"

"Well . . ." Russell wavers. The caricature seems to cause him physical pain. "I suppose so," he finishes, reluctantly. "In thirty words or less, as you say."

"Wow." Suddenly Fitzgerald's ravings sound downright pedestrian. "But if he's right—"

"The consensus is he's not," Russell interjects hastily.

"But *if*. If the model's an exact reproduction, how could you tell the difference between real life and afterlife? I mean, what would be the *point*?"

"Well, the point is avoiding ultimate extinction, supposedly. As to how you'd tell the difference . . ." Russell shakes his head. "Actually, I never finished the book. As I said, theology doesn't interest me all that much."

Thomas shakes his head. "I can't believe it."

"Not many could," Russell says. "Tipler's theoretical proofs were quite extensive, though, as I recall."

"I bet. Whatever happened to him?"

Russell shrugs. "What happens to anyone who's stupid enough to come up with a new way of looking at the world? They tore into him like sharks at a feeding frenzy. I don't know where he ended up."

What's wrong with this picture?

Nothing. Everything. Suddenly awake, Myles Thomas stares around a darkened studio and tries to convince himself that nothing has changed.

Nothing *has* changed. The faint noise of late-night traffic sounds the same as ever. Gray parallelograms stretch across wall and ceiling, a faint luminous shadow of his bedroom window cast by some distant streetlight. Natalie's still gone from the left side of his bed, her departure so far removed by now that he doesn't even have to remind himself of it.

He checks the LEDs on his bedside alarm: 2:35 a.m.

Something's different.

Nothing's changed.

Well, maybe one thing. Tipler's heresy sits on the nightstand, its plastic dustcover reflecting slashes of red light from the alarm clock. *The Physics of Immortality: Modern Cosmology, God and the Resurrection of the Dead*. It's too dark to read the lettering but you don't forget a title like that. Myles Thomas signed it out of the library this afternoon, opened it at random

$$\ldots \text{Lemma 1, and the fact that } f_{if} = \sum_{k=1}^{\infty} f_{if}^{(k)} \leq 1, \text{ we have}$$

$$\sum_{n=1}^{\infty} p_{if}^{(n)} = \sum_{n=1}^{\infty} \sum_{k=1}^{n} f_{if}^{(k)} p_{jj}^{(n-k)} = \sum_{k=1}^{\infty} f_{if}^{(k)} \sum_{n=0}^{\infty} p_{jj}^{(n)}$$

$$= f_{if} \sum_{n=0}^{\infty} p_{jj}^{(n)} \leq \sum_{n=0}^{\infty} p_{jj}^{(n)} < \infty$$

which is just (*E*.3), and (*E*.3) can hold only if . . .

and threw it into his briefcase, confused and disgusted. He doesn't even know why he went to the effort of getting the fucking thing. Jasmine Fitzgerald is delusional. It's that simple. For reasons that it is not Myles Thomas' job to understand, she vivisected her husband on the kitchen floor. Now she's inventing all sorts of ways to excuse herself, to undo the undoable, and the fact that she cloaks her delusions in cosmological gobbledegook does not make them any more credible. What does he expect to do, turn into a quantum mechanic overnight? Is he going to learn even a fraction of what he'd need to find the holes in her carefully constructed fantasy? Why did he even bother?

But he did. And now *Modern Cosmology, God and the Resurrection of the Dead* looms dimly in front of him at two-thirty in the fucking morning, and something's changed, he's almost sure of it, but try as he might he can't get a handle on what it is. He just *feels* different, somehow. He just feels . . .

Awake. That's what you feel. You couldn't get back to sleep now if your life depended on it.

Myles Thomas sighs and turns on the reading lamp. Squinting as his pupils shrink against the light, he reaches out and grabs the offending book.

Parts of it, astonishingly, almost make sense.

"She's not here," the orderly tells him. "Last night we had to move her next door."

Next door: the hospital. "Why? What's wrong?"

"Not a clue. Convulsions, cyanosis—we thought she was toast, actually. But by the time the doctor got to her she couldn't find anything wrong."

"That doesn't make any sense."

"Tell me about it. Nothing about that crazy b— . . . nothing about her makes sense." The orderly wanders off down the hall, frowning.

Jasmine Fitzgerald lies between sheets tucked tight as a straitjacket, stares unblinking at the ceiling. A nurse sits to one side, boredom and curiosity mixing in equal measures on his face.

"How is she?" Thomas asks.

"Don't really know," the nurse says. "She seems okay now."

"She doesn't look okay to me. She looks almost catatonic."

"She isn't. Are you, Jaz?"

"We're sorry," Fitzgerald says cheerfully. "The person you are trying to reach is temporarily unavailable. Please leave a message and we'll get back to you." Then: "Hi, Myles. Good to see you." Her eyes never waver from the acoustic tiles overhead.

"You better blink one of these days," Thomas remarks. "Your eyeballs are going to dry up."

"Nothing a little judicious editing won't fix," she tells him.

Thomas glances at the nurse. "Would you excuse us for a few minutes?"

"Sure. I'll be in the caf if you need me."

Thomas waits until the door swings shut. "So, Jaz. What's the mass of the Higgs boson?"

She blinks.

She smiles.

She turns to look at him.

"Two hundred twenty-eight GeV," she says. "All *right*. Someone actually *read* my thesis proposal."

"Not just your proposal. That's one of Tipler's testable predictions, isn't it?"

Her smile widens. "The critical one, actually. The others are pretty self-evident."

"And you tested it."

"Yup. Over at CERN. So how'd you find his book?"

"I only read parts of it," Thomas admits. "It was pretty tough slogging."

"Sorry. My fault," Fitzgerald says.

"How so?"

"I thought you could use some help, so I souped you up a bit. Increased your processing speed. Not enough, I guess."

Something shivers down his back. He ignores it.

"I'm not—" Thomas rubs his chin; he forgot to shave this morning "—exactly sure what you mean by that."

"Sure you do. You just don't believe it." Fitzgerald squirms up from between the sheets, props her back against a pillow. "It's just a semantic difference, Myles. You'd call it a *delusion*. Us physics geeks would call it a *hypothesis*."

Thomas nods uncertainly.

"Oh, just say it, Myles. I know you're dying to."

"Go on," he blurts out, strangely unable to stop himself.

Fitzgerald laughs. "If you insist, Doctor. I figured out what I was doing wrong. I thought I had to do everything myself, and I just can't. Too many variables, you see; even if you access them individually there's no way you can keep track of 'em all at once. When I tried, I got mixed up and everything . . ."

A sudden darkness in her face now. A memory, perhaps, pushing up through all those careful layers of contrivance.

"Everything went wrong," she finishes softly.

Thomas nods, keeps his voice low and gentle. "What are you remembering right now, Jaz?"

"You know damn well what I'm remembering," she whispers. "I . . . I cut him open. . . ."

"Yes."

"He was dying. He was *dying*. I tried to fix him, I tried to fix the code but something went wrong, and . . ."

He waits. The silence stretches.

". . . and I didn't know what. I couldn't fix it if I couldn't see what I'd done wrong. So I . . . I cut him open. . . ." Her brow furrows suddenly. Thomas can't tell with what: remembrance, remorse?

"I really overstepped myself," she says at last.

No. Concentration. She's rebuilding her defenses, she's pushing the tip of that bloody iceberg back below the surface. It can't be easy. Thomas can see it, ponderous and massively buoyant, pushing up from the depths while Jasmine Fitzgerald leans down and desperately pretends not to strain.

"I know it must be difficult to think about," Thomas says.

She shrugs. "Sometimes." *Going* . . . "When my head slips back into the old school. Old habits die hard." *Going* . . . "But I get over it."

The frown disappears.

Gone.

"You know when I told you about Core Wars?" she asks brightly.

After a moment, Thomas nods.

"All viruses replicate, but some of the better ones can write macros—*micros*, actually, would be a better name for them—to other addresses, little subroutines that autonomously perform simple tasks. And some of *those* can replicate too. Get my drift?"

"Not really," Thomas says quietly.

"I really should have souped you up a bit more. Anyway, those little routines, they can handle all the bookkeeping. Each one tracks a few variables, and each time they replicate that's a few more, and pretty soon there's no limit to the size of the problem you can handle. Hell, you could rewrite the whole damn operating system from the inside out and not have to worry about any of the details; all your little daemons are doing that for you."

"Are we all just viruses to you, Jaz?"

She laughs at that, not unkindly. "Ah, Myles. It's a technical term, not a moral judgement. Life's information, shaped by natural selection. That's all I mean."

"And you've learned to . . . rewrite the code," Thomas says.

She shakes her head. "Still learning. But I'm getting better at it all the time."

"I see." Thomas pretends to check his watch. He still doesn't know the jargon. He never will. But at least, at last, he knows where she's coming from.

Nothing left but the final platitudes.

"That's all I need right now, Jasmine. I want to thank you for being so cooperative. I know how tough this must be on you."

She cocks her head at him, smiling. "This is goodbye then, Myles? You haven't come *close* to curing me."

He smiles back. He can almost feel each muscle fiber contracting, the increased tension on facial tendons, soft tissue stretching over bone. The utter insincerity of a purely mechanical process. "That's not what I'm here for, Jaz."

"Right. You're assessing my fitness."

Thomas nods.

"Well?" she asks after a moment. "Am I fit?"

He takes a breath. "I think you have some problems you haven't faced. But you can understand counsel, and there's no doubt you could follow any proceedings the court is likely to throw at you. Legally, that means you can stand trial."

"Ah. So I'm not sane, but I'm not crazy enough to get off, eh?"

"I hope things work out for you." That much, at least, is sincere.

"Oh, they will," she says easily. "Never fear. How much longer do I stay here?"

"Maybe another three weeks. Thirty days is the usual period."

"But you've finished with me. Why so long?"

He shrugs. "Nowhere else to put you, for now."

"Oh." She considers. "Just as well, I guess. It'll give me more time to practice."

"Goodbye, Jasmine."

"Too bad you missed Stuart," she says behind him. "You'd have liked him. Maybe I'll bring him around to your place some-time."

The doorknob sticks. He tries again.

"Something wrong?" she asks.

"No," Thomas says, a bit too quickly. "It's just—"

"Oh, right. Hang on a sec." She rustles in her sheets.

He turns his head. Jasmine Fitzgerald lies flat on her back, unblinking, staring straight up. Her breath is fast and shallow.

The doorknob seems subtly warmer in his hand.

He releases it. "Are you okay?"

"Sure," she says to the ceiling. "Just tired. Takes a bit out of you, you know?"

Call the nurse, he thinks.

"Really, I just need some rest." She looks at him one last time, and giggles. "But Myles to go before I sleep . . ."

"Dr. Desjardins, please."

"Speaking."

"You performed the autopsy on Stuart MacLennan?"

A brief silence. Then: "Who is this?"

"My name's Myles Thomas. I'm a psychologist at FPSS. Jasmine Fitzgerald is . . . was a client of mine."

The phone sits there in his hand, silent.

"I was looking at the case report, writing up my assessment, and I just noticed something about your findings—"

"They're preliminary," Desjardins interrupts. "I'll have the full report, um, shortly."

"Yes, I understand that, Dr. Desjardins. But my understanding is that MacLennan was, well, mortally wounded."

"He was gutted like a fish."

"Right. But your r— . . . your *preliminary* report lists cause of death as 'undetermined.'"

"That's because I haven't determined the cause of death."

"Right. I guess I'm a bit confused about what else it could have been. You didn't find any toxins in the body, at least none that weren't involved in MacLennan's chemo, and no other injuries except for these fistulas and teratomas—"

The phone barks in Thomas' hand, a short ugly laugh. "Do you know what a teratoma *is*?" Desjardins asks.

"I assumed it was something to do with his cancer."

"Ever hear the term *primordial cyst*?"

"No."

"Hope you haven't eaten recently," Desjardins says. "Every now and then you get a clump of proliferating cells floating around in the coelomic cavity. Something happens to activate the dormant genes-—could be a lot of things, but the upshot is you sometimes get these growing blobs of tissue sprouting teeth and hair and bone. Sometimes they get as big as grapefruits."

"My God. MacLennan had one of those in him?"

"I thought, maybe. At first. Turned out to be a chunk of his kidney. Only there was an eye growing out of it. And most of his abdominal lymph nodes, too, the ducts were clogged with hair and something like fingernail. It was keratinized, anyway."

"That's horrible," Thomas whispers.

"No shit. Not to mention the perforated diaphragm, or the fact that half the loops of his small intestine were fused together."

"But I thought he had leukemia."

"He did. That wasn't what killed him."

"So you're saying these teratomas might have had some role in MacLennan's death?"

"I don't see how," Desjardins says.

"But—"

"Look, maybe I'm not making myself clear. I have my doubts that Stuart MacLennan died from his wife's carving skills because any *one* of the abnormalities I found should have killed him more or less instantly."

"But that's pretty much impossible, isn't it? I mean, what did the investigating officers say?"

"Quite frankly, I don't think they read my report," Desjardins grumbles. "Neither did you, apparently, or you would have called me before now."

"Well, it wasn't really central to my assessment, Dr. Desjardins. And besides, it seemed so obvious—"

"For sure. You see someone laid open from crotch to sternum, you don't need any report to know what killed him. Who cares about any of this congenital abnormality bullshit?"

Congen— "You're saying he was *born* that way?"

"Except he couldn't have been. He'd never have even made it to his first breath."

"So you're saying—"

"I'm saying Stuart MacLennan's wife couldn't have killed him, because physiologically there's no way in hell that he could have been alive to start with."

Thomas stares at the phone. It offers no retraction.

"But—he was twenty-eight years old! How could that be?"

"God only knows," Desjardins tells him. "You ask me, it's a fucking miracle."

What's wrong with this picture?

He isn't quite certain, because he doesn't quite know what he was expecting. No opened grave, no stone rolled dramatically away from the sepulcher. Of course not. Jasmine Fitzgerald would probably say that her powers are too subtle for such obvious theater. Why leave a pile of shoveled earth, an opened coffin, when you can just rewrite the code?

She sits cross-legged on her husband's undisturbed grave. Whatever powers she lays claim to, they don't shield her from the light rain falling on her head. She doesn't even have an umbrella.

"Myles," she says, not looking up. "I thought it might be you." Her sunny smile, that radiant expression of happy denial, is nowhere to be seen. Her face is as expressionless as her husband's must be, two meters down.

"Hello, Jaz," Thomas says.

"How did you find me?" she asks him.

"FPSS went ballistic when you disappeared. They're calling everyone who had any contact with you, trying to figure out how you got out. Where you might be."

Her fingers play in the fresh earth. "Did you tell them?"

"I didn't think of this place until after," he lies. Then, to atone: "And I don't *know* how you got out."

"Yes you do, Myles. You do it yourself all the time."

"Go on," he says, deliberately.

She smiles, but it doesn't last. "We got here the same way, Myles. We copied ourselves from one address to another. The only difference is, you still have to go from A to B to C. I just cut straight to Z."

"I can't accept that," Thomas says.

"Ever the doubter, aren't you? How can you enjoy heaven when you can't even recognize it?" Finally, she looks up at him. "*You should be told the difference between empiricism and stubbornness, doctor.* Know what that's from?"

He shakes his head.

"Oh well. It's not important." She looks back at the ground. Wet tendrils of hair hang across her face. "They wouldn't let me come to the funeral."

"You don't seem to need their permission."

"Not now. That was a few days ago. I still hadn't worked all the bugs out then." She plunges one hand into wet dirt. "You know what I did to him."

Before the knife, she means.

"I'm not . . . I don't really . . ."

"You know," she says again.

Finally he nods, although she isn't looking.

The rain falls harder. Thomas shivers under his windbreaker. Fitzgerald doesn't seem to notice.

"So what now?" he asks at last.

"I'm not sure. It seemed so straightforward at first, you know? I loved Stuart, completely, without reservation. I was going to bring him back as soon as I learned how. I was going to do it right this time. And I still love him, I really do, but damn it all I don't love *everything* about him, you know? He was a slob, sometimes. And I hated his taste in music. So now that I'm here, I figure, why stop at just bringing him back? Why not, well, fine-tune him a bit?"

"Is that what you're going to do?"

"I don't know. I'm going through all the things I'd change, and when it comes right down to it maybe it'd be better to just start again from scratch. Less . . . intensive. Computationally."

"I hope you *are* delusional." Not a wise thing to say, but suddenly he doesn't care. "Because if you're not, God's a really callous bastard."

"Is It?" she says, without much interest.

"Everything's just information. We're all just subroutines interacting in a model somewhere. Well, nothing's really all that important then, is it? You'll get around to debugging Stuart one of these days. No hurry. He can wait. It's just microcode, nothing's irrevocable. So nothing really *matters*, does it? How could God give a shit about anything in a universe like that?"

Jasmine Fitzgerald rises from the grave and wipes the dirt off her hands. "Watch it, Myles." There's a faint smile on her face. "You don't want to piss me off."

He meets her eyes. "I'm glad I still can."

"*Touché.*" There's still a twinkle there, behind her soaked lashes and the runnels of rainwater coursing down her face.

"So what are you going to do?" he asks again.

She looks around the soaking graveyard. "Everything. I'm going to clean the place up. I'm going to fill in the holes. I'm going to rewrite Planck's constant so it makes *sense*." She smiles at him. "Right now, though, I think I'm just going to go somewhere and think about things for a while."

She steps off the mound. "Thanks for not telling on me. It wouldn't have made any difference, but I appreciate the thought. I won't forget it." She begins to walk away in the rain.

"Jaz," Thomas calls after her.

She shakes her head, without looking back. "Forget it, Myles. Nobody handed *me* any miracles." She stops, then turns briefly. "Besides, you're not ready. You'd probably just think I hypnotized you or something."

I should stop her, Thomas tells himself. *She's dangerous. She's deluded. They could charge me with aiding and abetting. I should stop her.*

If I can.

She leaves him in the rain with the memory of that bright, guiltless smile. He's almost sure he doesn't feel anything pass through him then. But maybe he does. Maybe it feels like a ripple growing across some stagnant surface. A subtle reweaving of electrons. A small change in the way things are.

I'm going to clean the place up. I'm going to fill in the holes.

Myles Thomas doesn't know exactly what she meant by that. But he's afraid that soon—far too soon—there won't be anything wrong with this picture.

Peter Watts: You know what separates us empiricists from you religious nuts? We demand replicable evidence for our beliefs. No blind faith in the Pope or Jerry Falwell for us. No, siree. We want the numbers.

Well, Tipler gave us the numbers. His book is real. Whether it qualifies him for the Nobel or for residency in the Ponoka Home for the Bewildered, I can't judge. He says you need Ph.D's in three different physical sciences to understand his arguments. Me, I study whales and seals. Whatever I decide about Tipler, it's going to come down to faith.

Maybe I'm not a real scientist. Maybe all those consonants after my name don't mean squat (a valid point if you've ever tried to get a job in the physiological ecology of marine animals). Or maybe scientists are creatures of faith after all, except we put our faith in other empiricists. I'd say it still gives us an edge.

I hope so. The only alternative is going back to grad school for twenty years. And we empiricists tend to be a lot lazier than we let on.

CONTRIBUTORS

VEN BEGAMUDRÉ was born in South India and moved to Canada when he was six. He studied public administration in Ottawa and Paris. His books include the novel *Van de Graaff Days* and the short story collections *Laterna Magika* and *A Planet of Eccentrics*. "In the Beginning, There Was Memory" is from *Laterna Magika* and was used by permission of Oolichan Books. *Laterna Magika* was a finalist in the Canada-Caribbean region for the 1998 Commonwealth Writers Prize, in the best book category. His next novel will appear in 2000 from Coteau Books.

BRENT BUCKNER is an empiricist living in Toronto, Ontario, where he performs quantitative investment analysis at ADA Investments Inc. "Flesh and Blood" is his sole published story; it first appeared in *ON SPEC* magazine.

DONNA FARLEY's fiction has appeared in Canadian venues *ON SPEC* and *Dreams and Visions*, as well as in SF anthologies *Catfantastic* and *Universe 2*. Mother of two and married to an Orthodox priest, Farley is also a columnist and was the poetry editor for the Orthodox women's journal *The Handmaiden*.

JASON KAPALKA is an expatriate Canuck currently slaving for the computer game industry in Silicon Valley. He dreams of one day becoming an underemployed slacker with spare time a-plenty.

ALLAN LOWSON—Scottish by birth. Pagan by heritage, anarchist by conviction, social worker by profession. Comics by collection, classic motorcycles by construction, sci-fi and fantasy by imagination. Happily married, three grown-up sons, living in "Lotus Land" twenty-five years and counting.

SUSAN MACGREGOR is an editor with three-time Aurora Award-winner *ON SPEC* magazine, Canada's premier magazine for speculative fiction. An SF writer in her own right, her work has appeared in *ON SPEC* and other venues. One of her works won an honorable mention in Ellen Datlow's 1995 *The Year's Best Fantasy and Horror*. Currently, she is compiling research and working on a non-fiction book on empirical spirituality, as well as considering work for a *Divine Realms II*. She lives with her family in Edmonton and works full-time at the University of Alberta.

LOUISE MARLEY is the author of a science fantasy trilogy about singers who inhabit an ice planet. *Sing the Light*, *Sing the Warmth*, and *Receive the Gift* are published by Ace Science Fiction. A new novel, *The Terrorists of Irustan*, will be out from Ace in 1999. Marley is also a classical concert and opera singer, a mezzo-soprano whose performances have taken her across the United States and to Italy and Russia. She lives in the Seattle area with her husband and son.

URSULA PFLUG is an award-winning Canadian writer who publishes short literary speculative fiction often in three countries. She has also had SF narratives produced for stage and independent film and video, including a television sale. An ex-Torontonian, she now lives in an Ontario village with her family. Currently, a pair of Canada geese are nesting beside her backyard river, the Ouse. Virginia Woolf fans, please raise your hands in recognition of this reference.

CLAUDE-MICHEL PRÉVOST has written and published many stories in French in Canadian SF magazines (*Solaris*, *Imagine*) and SF anthologies (*Tesseracts³*, *Northern Stars*). This is his first direct hit at writing in English.

KATE RIEDEL was born and raised in Minnesota and is now a card-carrying Canadian who lives in Toronto. She has published short fiction in *ON SPEC*, *Not One of Us*, *White Wall Review*, and *Highlights for Children*, and has the usual novel in her desk drawer.

KEITH SCOTT lives in retirement in Toronto. This is his fifth appearance in a short-story anthology, along with ten published stories in Canadian and U.S. small-press science fiction magazines.

JENA SNYDER has been production editor at *ON SPEC* since the magazine's debut in the spring of 1989. Her short fiction and poetry have appeared in *ON SPEC*, *Prairie Fire*, and *Underpass*. "Prescribed Burn," published in the SF anthology *Tesseracts⁶*, was nominated for an Aurora Award for Best Short-Form Work in English (1997). Currently working on a crime/SF novel, *Sister Morphine*, set in Edmonton, Jena takes her crime research seriously: she has completed classes in crime scene investigation (Edmonton Police Services), sudden death investigation (Alberta Medical Examiner's office) and fundamentals of investigative technique (Grant MacEwan Community College). She and husband Colin are partners in a forestry consulting and publishing business, Clear Lake Ltd., in Edmonton.

Erik Jon Spigel has an M.A. in Japanese literature from the University of Toronto, and has lived in Japan. He has also studied mathematics, physics, linguistics, and philosophy. In the eighties, he was a wildly unsuccessful poet and songwriter. He never intended to be starving. He has published a number of short stories, but still thinks the big money's in verse, the poor fool. He currently lives in Bloomington, Indiana, working towards yet another advanced degree in Japanese.

Steve Stanton's short stories and articles have been published in Canada, the USA, England, and Australia. Stanton is the founder of Skysong Press in Orillia, Ontario. From 1988 to 1993, he edited *Christian Vision*, a quarterly market newsletter for Christians in the arts. From 1989 to the present time, he has edited the literary journal *Dreams and Visions: New Frontiers in Christian Fiction*. His first novel, *In the Den of the Dragon*, was released in 1996. Visit the Skysong Press website for updates.

Diane L. Walton has been writing at least since she was twelve years old. She discovered SF at the age of thirteen when she picked up her first Andre Norton book, *The Stars Are Ours!* in the public library. She was briefly a junior high school drama teacher and then joined the Alberta public service in the mid-seventies. After eighteen years as a staff trainer and systems analyst, she left to explore the next phase of her life, and hopes to get more writing done. Publishing credits include: "Don't Know Much About Art," *CBC Alberta Anthology*; "Night Rider," *CBC Alberta Anthology*; "Best Damn Cheesecake in the Universe," *ON SPEC*; "Objects in the Mirror," *Northern Frights 2*; and "Bury Me Not on the Lone Prairie," *ON SPEC*. She also works as an editor with *ON SPEC*, is married, has one kid, two cats, two goldfish.

PETER WATTS has spent decades deciding whether to be a biologist or a writer; he's spent decades doing a really half-assed job at both. He won some sort of award for his first story and it's basically been downhill from there. Ditto for his marine mammal research. He has recently sold a novel to Tor Books, an inspiring tale of feminist empowerment and microbiology about a bunch of misandrogist cyborg chicks on a hydrothermal rift vent. Watts is pathologically fond of domestic shorthair cats and the music of Jethro Tull, although in terms of ancestry he probably has more in common with Alice Cooper; both are the sons of Baptist ministers.

He is not to be confused with the bald guy on *Millennium*.

MARY WOODBURY lives in Edmonton and has been active in the Alberta writing community for nearly twenty years. Her first children's novel, *Where in the World Is Jenny Parker?* was published by Groundwood in 1989. *Letting Go* was published by Scholastic in early 1992. *The Midwife's Tale*, a collection of her adult short fiction turned into readers' theatre, was released by Woodlake Books in 1990. Her children's mystery *The Invisible Polly McDoodle* was published by Coteau Books in 1994, and *A Gift for Johnny Know-It-All* in 1996. *Jess and the Runaway Grandpa* was released by Coteau in the spring of 1997, and *Brad's Universe*, a young-adult novel, by Orca in 1998. *The Intrepid Polly McDoodle*, second in the McDoodle mysteries, was released in the fall of 1998 by Coteau. Her adult poetry and short fiction have been published in various magazines and journals and performed at the Fringe, the Stroll of Poets, and over CBC. *Fruitbodies*, a collection of her poetry for grown-ups, was published by River Books of Edmonton in 1996. Currently, she is working on a new young adult novel, leading workshops and speaking to both adults and children, and teaching creative writing.